I

Wanted

to

Press

One

for

More

Options

A Novel by Michael Larrain

"Yesterday comes so easy."

Buck O'Neil, *I Was Right on Time.*

"Well, the doctor told me, son you don't need no pills.
Just a handful o' nickels in a jukebox'll cure your ills."

Ricky Nelson, "Boppin' the Blues"

For Wilder Kathleen the Rage of Paris Larrain

Chapter One

"I lost your watch. I'm sorry."

She looked at the ground, as though the missing watch might be found at her feet. She was a seven-year-old rookie named Izzy. Izzy was a good name for her because she always looked kind of dizzy and kind of fizzy at the same time. Her wavy red hair sprang out of her skull as though her brain had come up with an idea so crazy it turned her head into a tiki torch. She had told me she wanted to use the watch to see if it could win in a race between itself and a sundial out in a meadow about a mile away from our cottage. When I tried to explain to her why the race didn't make any sense, I got sort of dizzy myself and just let her take the watch. Now I felt like I had let my Poppy down. It was a gold pocket watch he had given me on my fourth birthday, inscribed on the inside with the words, "For My Little Coconut." I never used it to tell the time, but I liked the clicking sound it made when I opened and closed it and I liked winding it and holding it in my hand or keeping it under my pillow at night.

"Well, we better go find it."

My name is Wilder. Wilder Kathleen High. Someday I will be the queen of *Quietude*, this country where I live. Right now, I am only nine and not ready to be the queen of anything, except for maybe my own thoughts. My dad, Ace High, who is the king, says there are very few queens left out in what he calls the "great world," (I think he's being sarcastic when he says this because sometimes he adds, "or the not so great world.") and that I could be the last queen in all the world and a new kind of queen, too. I don't know what the old kind were like. I bet they had fancier clothes than me. My Mumza, who is a teacher, says I should keep reading history books so I can be guided by what went wrong with the other queens and kings and not become *corrupt*. I should probably start by learning what the word *corrupt* means. I would rather read books about horses or baseball. Plenty of books come here from the great world and sometimes they bring people with them. People from all over the world come here and they almost never leave. Izzy's dad thought he was bringing her here on a *vacation*, whatever that might be, after her mom had died but they never did go back. Maybe it would have made them too sad to be where they had lived with her mom, but I'm glad they stayed because I needed a shortstop and Izzy, even though she is always losing something or getting lost herself, can field a hard grounder and get it over to first most of the time.

"C'mon, Izz. Batting practice is at four. If we're going to take our licks, we need to get on the case. Let's roll."

Chapter Two

"I'm not an actor. I'm a movie star!" insisted the almost unendurably mellifluous tenor of Peter O'Toole, formerly known as the Greatest Living Irishman, but no longer able to lay claim to that title, since he had been laid to rest in 2013. I wasn't certain of the current date, but hadn't something like a decade gone by since his passing?

"When I was a windy boy and a bit/and the black spit of the chapel fold/(sighed the old ram rod, dying of women)/I tiptoed shy in the gooseberry wood/The rude owl cried like a tell-tale tit/I skipped in a blush as the big girls rolled/Nine-pin down on the donkey's common/And on seesaw Sunday nights I wooed/whoever I would with my wicked eyes/The whole of the moon I could love and leave/All the green leaved little weddings' wives/In the coal black bush and let them grieve." Bless me if that booming bass-baritone didn't belong to the most sonorous son of Swansea, Dylan Thomas himself, reciting a passage from his poem "Lament," though he too no longer walked and drank and talked and sank among us, having perished at the tender age of 39, in what year? 1953?

"It took more than one man to change my name to Shanghai Lily," murmured the sultriest of all contraltos, that of Marlene Dietrich, she of the feathers and boas, borrowing the line from her film, *Shanghai Express*. The movie had been made in 1932 and she unmade about sixty years later. I have a good ear for voices and knew perfectly well whose these either were or were meant to be, but could make no sense of their projectors standing at the foot of the rope ladder below the entrance to my tree fort. I was trying to clean the peanut butter out of my Swiss Army knife while waiting for the coffee to finish dripping, but had lost the little toothpick that comes with the knife. It's the ideal tool for cleaning peanut butter out of the knife, if only you can find it. As the king, you'd think I would have good silverware for eating peanut butter out of the jar, maybe even a special peanut butter utensil, and I may, but Bonny, my daughter's mother and my fiancée-for-life, had reorganized the drawers and cupboards of the kitchen in the palace and now the only things I could lay hands on were martini glasses, which did me precious little good since she had rid my crib of strong drink before taking her leave, almost as if she didn't trust me.

It was shortly after dawn and I could hear, along with my trio of visitors taking a bow from the beyond, the welcome sound of my coffee maker beginning to hiss and snuffle, announcing that its work was nearly done. The pot was close to full, so I slipped on a caftan, poured some French roast into a Los Angeles Dodgers mug and took a few sips. The Swiss Army knife was one of my two most treasured possessions, the other being my Rawlings baseball glove. I found myself wondering if anyone has ever known how, why or where their own nature is leading them. We are propelled by tremendous whispers toward an end we cannot guess much less prepare for. Well, if you don't like surprises, I suppose you have no business being alive. I had become a father for the only time at 59, a rather grandfatherly age, so that the first nine years of my daughter Wilder's life have been a sort of second childhood for me, one that arrived, as they often do, when dotage was closing in. Watching her play, I sometimes feel as though I am lying on the bottom of a creek looking up through cool water at a clear midnight sky, a croupier of celestial roulette. Wilder had borrowed the glove and never gotten around to returning it after forming a baseball team called the River Otters. At first, there was to be a girls' team and a boys' team, but after thinking it over, she decided the teams should be coed. When I asked her why, she said that if all the boys were on the other team, you couldn't pat the butts of the boys with the cutest butts after they did something to help the team win a game. This struck me as rather advanced thinking for a nine-year-old girl and I wondered whether I should take it up with her mother, who was, at the moment, off in Mozambique heading up a conference on an international educational initiative she was promoting.

Bonny was the founder of a remarkable, on-the-fly organization called "White Ops," which sent cadres of teachers and workers to trouble spots where, for a range of horrifying reasons—earthquake, hurricane, tsunami, uprising, revolution, civil war, famine-drought-plague—rudimentary education was being denied to children. She was supposedly semi-retired and had reduced her workload, but either necessity or simply the urge to get out and about often had her leaving our island nation to help disentangle logistical jam-ups confounding her junior colleagues. When she was here with us, she headed up our own young school system, a great relief from administrative duties and one that allowed her to log time in the classroom. She had come up as a grammar school teacher and loved helping her young charges to understand the world. When I was in her good graces, she occasionally permitted me to sit in and when I left the class, I found the world a bit kinder and more comprehensible myself.

When a modicum of consciousness had accompanied the coffee, I developed a suspicion that the three personages hailing me from below were actually only two, neither of them spectral, but both decidedly corporeal and familiar to me as well. I decided to test them.

"George, Marion, is that you down there? Materialize, damn you!" I poked my head out through the beaded curtain that serves as the door to my royal residence, but since the bedroom is on the third floor and there was little light to see by, my visitors might as well have been invisible. It seemed unlikely, however, that hallucinations, apparitions or dream figures, should I still be asleep, would honor requests. But I knew that my old friend, Jake Buchanan, actor-director-investigative-reporter and master impressionist, did a fine Cary Grant. And I suspected that his longtime heart's companion, my secretary, Creole, who had so winningly duplicated Dietrich, could do an acceptable impersonation of Constance Bennet (How hard could it be, after all, since no one in our day has the slightest recollection of what Miss Bennet sounded like?), so that passing themselves off as the (posthumously) fun-loving Kirbys from *Topper* (1937) would be an irresistible challenge.

"Maybe the poor man's tired," said the woman's voice, brightly.

"I don't know why he should be tired," said Cary. "We did all the singing." And they broke into a spirited chorus of "Old Man Moon." Jake would know that I would remember both the dialogue and the song, and that I had recited Dylan Thomas's "Lament" at my father's funeral. But why would my old friend and my secretary be performing for my amusement at an hour more conducive to snuggling? Jake usually let me know of his approach via the satellite

9

radio on my old friend Sporting Chance's Cherubini 44 ketch, moored most of the year in our harbor. Not so this time. And the early hour suggested matters demanding immediate attention.

"Request permission to come aboard!" called out Jake as Cary as the dashing Mister Kirby.

"Oh, George, don't be silly. You don't need to ask for permission. I'm your *wife*." declared Creole as Constance as Marion. On *Quietude*, a surefire way to win an audience with the sovereign is to hand him his first laugh of the day.

"Come on up, Brat. And bring your fancy man."

Chapter Three

"Watch out. You almost stepped on my foot." I was wearing my new grass sandals for the first time. I made them myself just like the Polynesians who lived here in the olden days. They were plenty comfy and kind of pretty, but not much protection against a clomping short-stop in hard rubber cleats. Izz wore her cleats everywhere. She said she even wore them to bed. Maybe she turned double-plays in her dreams.

"Sorry, Cap, I *was* watching out. But I was watching out for your watch. Did you remember to wind it? Maybe if we get close to it, we can hear it ticking, like the crocodile."

We were standing beside the sundial, but I couldn't see my present from my Poppy anywhere. Izz was looking intently at the dial.

"What's this stick thingie called?" she said, referring to the part in the middle that casts the shadow on the dial.

"It called a *gnomon*, I think. From the Greek, meaning *to know*."

"How do you know stuff like that, Cap?"

"I learned to read when I was really little." My Poppy says I collect old words like kids out in the great world pick up bottle caps, whatever they might be. We have bottles here on *Quietude*, and we have caps, mostly baseball caps, but the bottles don't wear baseball caps. The bottles mostly live at the Lost Doubloon Saloon, where my Poppy goes to relax and issue *decrees* sometimes when my Mumza is away. I think he misses her. A decree is a big new idea the king wants everybody to know about. I can never remember any of them.

"How do you wind the sundial?"

"You don't have to wind it, Izz. The earth winds it by moving around the sun."

"If you say so."

"Where did you go from here before you realized you didn't have the watch anymore?"

"I went to look for that other kind of watch."

"Which kind of watch?"

"The kind you press to find out how fast a batter gets to first? What's it called?"

"A stopwatch."

"Right. So I started to go to our dugout. I figured the stopwatch might be there on the bench and if I brought it back here, I could click it and make the race happen."

"So should we be looking for my watch in the dugout?"

"No. I couldn't find the ball field. So I decided I needed a compass. You told me the ball field is north of the Palace, and I could see the Palace because it sticks up in the air but I didn't know which way was north." I was getting hopelessly lost trying to follow Izzy's thought processes. Soon, I would need a compass myself.

"So you came to find me at the cottage?"

"Yeah. I was going to ask if I could borrow your compass to find the stopwatch to start the race between the sundial and your pocket watch but when I got there—your cottage is the only place I know how to find on the whole island because it's right by the waterfall at the foot of the mountain and you told me how in the afternoon the sun always shines off the water and I should look for the shining water and your cottage would be right next to it...what was I saying?" She was winded from the exertion of her explanation, so I let her take a few deep breaths.

"When you got there...?"

"When I got there, I started to look in my pocket for your watch but then I remembered that I didn't have a pocket and that's when I noticed that the watch was gone."

"Do you remember anything about where you went when you were trying to find the ball field?" She closed her eyes and concentrated.

"I remember there was a lake, a little tiny lake, like a baby lake. Only it wasn't round. It was like a square that's trying to stretch a single into a double. What's that called?"

"A rectangle?"

"Yeah, one of those. And it had a little wall around it."

"That wasn't a lake, Izz. It was a watering trough. Did you see any horses nearby?"

"Yeah. A lot of them. Fearsome brutes they were. They were fenced in, but I was still kind of scared. What if they got out and *stampeded?* I thought. They could run right over me and then I couldn't be on the River Otters anymore. I ran away before they could trample me into the ground and I followed the shining water right to your cottage."

"Those are Captain Primo's horses, his *remuda*, as they say in Spanish."

"What's a *remuda?*"

"A bunch of horses. That must be where you dropped the watch." Our cottage was on the way so I could make a quick stop there and fill my pack. "The sundial will say it's almost time for BP."

I will be throwing batting practice. I'm the River Otters' starting pitcher, though I get to hit, too. In our games, everybody hits. My Poppy has been teaching me to switch-hit—that means you can hit right-handed and left-handed—and his old friend, Cassidy McKeever, who lives here on *Quietude* in a big cave he calls the *Hibernaculum*, is my personal pitching coach. He doesn't come out of his cave very often, but when he does, he's showing me how to throw a curveball. Mister McKeever is a southpaw and I'm a righty, but the grip is the same. He told me to practice whenever I can, so I've been practicing throwing my curveball at the trunk of the tree in whose branches my Poppy's palace can be found. Sometimes when I'm practicing, I hear him talking to people but I'm pretty sure there aren't any people with him. I asked him if he talks to himself and he said no, he talks to people I can't see. He has lost an awful lot of friends. Maybe he's talking to them. The full name of our team is the Elsewhereville River Otters because the village where the Palace is located is called Elsewhereville. I asked my Poppy why it's called that and he said before there was the country of *Quietude*, people used to ask him where he'd like to be instead of wherever he was and he would say *elsewhere*. I can never tell when he's kidding but he says the same thing about me.

When we got to the village called Plunderland where Captain Primo's crew of retired pirates live on what's called a *mock-up* of his old submarine, the *Naughtylass*, there was no one around but the horses in their corral. Pirates like to sleep late. I'd brought over a backpack full

13

of apples and fed one to each horse. It was the Captain himself who gave me my Arabian stallion Holy Toledo! and then off he went to be the bartender at a nightclub on a ship off the coast of southern California. My horse doesn't live with the pirates, he lives in a small paddock next to the cottage where I stay with my Mumza when she is here.

I had known all the horses ever since I was about three. We are old friends and I know all their names. Most of them I have ridden and groomed and they seemed very happy to see me, though maybe it was mainly the apples. The watering trough was off in the shade at the edge of a grove of mango trees. It was made of the only cement on *Quietude*. The water was fed into it from a cistern built in the hills by an inventor named Elmer Wheeler. Elmer, my Poppy says, was one of the founding fathers of *Quietude*. He died when I was only three months old, so I didn't get to know him. I wish I had, I would love to invent stuff. I think of really cool inventions all the time, but I don't know how to make them be real.

While I'd been feeding the horses, Izz had walked over to the trough and was standing over it looking at the water. When I walked over, she didn't even look at me, just kept staring down. The trough was about two feet deep, the water was clear and on the bottom I could see a scattering of tadpoles. Izzy was studying them like she was waiting for them to turn into frogs and jump out and scare her half to death. Something had caught her attention. My pocket watch wasn't in the trough and a good thing too. It couldn't survive a long bath. The only other thing on the bottom was a dark branch about a foot and a half long. It must have fallen from the trees overhead, which seemed odd since there were no trees overhead. It could have blown there during one of our blustery afternoon storms but it wasn't a mango branch. Could it be some sort of water filter?

"What do you think that thing is, Izz?"

"I don't know. A flute? It looks like bamboo. Can we take it out, Cap"

"If it isn't attached to the bottom of the trough, I don't see why not." As team captain, I was in charge. I reached into the water and closed my hands around the branch, giving it a little tug. There was nothing holding it in place, it had just sunk to the bottom. I drew it carefully out of the water. It was black bamboo, you could tell by the

14

two joints, and did look a little like a flute, perfectly round and about the right length, but there the resemblance ended. It had no mouthpiece (in French, an *embouchure* hole. When I was a little kid, my Mumza thought I might be what's called a *prodigy,* a young musical genius, I have no idea why, and she brought all kinds of music instructors here and they tried to teach me how to play the violin, the piano, and, of course, the flute. I flunked the flute and all the rest but I learned a lot of swell words and I'm still friends with all of the instructors, none of whom could bear to leave *Quietude*) and no holes for your fingers. It was just smooth black bamboo. There are lots of little stands of bamboo in different parts of our island, but this was the first black bamboo I had ever seen. I handed it to Izz.

"What do you suppose this piece of bamboo is doing in the horses' watering trough, Izz?" She held it on her palm for a second.

"You got me, Cap," she said, "but it seems kind of heavy for bamboo." She gave it back to me. She was right. Bamboo is hollow, but this piece had been heavy enough to sink to the bottom of the trough when it should have been bobbing on the surface. "Maybe it's a magic wand. You'd probably need to know a magic word, though, to make it come to life. That's how it works with magic wands, I think."

I tried whispering *embouchure* to the bamboo, but nothing happened. It just sat in my hand. I decided I should show it to my Poppy, but right now it was time to let my teammates step into the batter's box and try to take an easy pitch right up the middle. I stuck the not-a-flute into my back-pack.

"C'mon, Izz. Let's go whack that old apple around the yard."

Chapter Four

"Hiya, Boss," said Creole, giving me the benefit of a perfumed embrace. She wasn't really my secretary anymore, far from it. By this time, referring to her as such was nothing more than a long-running gag. For many years, both while we were at sea aboard a full-rigged frigate named *Heather & Yawn* searching for the origins of language, and afterwards when our caravan of old friends and assorted fellow travelers had morphed into a rather unconventional detective agency working a strictly tropical beat—Hawaii, Tahiti, The Bahamas, the Mexican Caribbean—she had owned that title proudly, though it hardly did her justice. But since we had inherited a lush (and uninhabited) South Pacific island and decided *What the hell? Why not start our own country?* her eminence far exceeded that of Wilder's dad. Early on, because the United Nations charter stipulates having a government of some sort as a requirement for membership, we instituted what it pleased us to call a "revolving monarchy."

Anyone, man, woman or child over the age of twelve, could become the sovereign for a one-year term if their name was drawn from those written on slips of paper tossed into a hat. In truth, there weren't many takers. Most people reckoned the job might turn into real work and we are a rather laid back lot. Our first king, chosen from a slate of about five candidates, was a pale, studious sixteen-year-old boy named Walter who told me, in confidence, that he only entered the fray because he'd always had trouble talking to girls and thought being the king might ease the way to, if not outright romance, perhaps just friendly chats with the complementary gender. During his reign, the bespectacled lad remained so studious—he could usually be found on his makeshift throne bent over a schoolbook—that he was commonly referred to as "Walter the Studious." And he did get a handle on talking with girls, a breakthrough made possible by young ladies-in-waiting wannabes shyly approaching his throne (It sat outside, under a magnificent poinciana tree) and asking how they might serve His Majesty. He invariably answered that he wanted for nothing but would like to know more about *them*, their families, where they were from, how and why they had migrated to *Quietude*. Once they began to share their stories, all that was required of him was to slip in a question now and then and before you could say Walter the Studious, he had attained a reputation as a charming and sympathetic conversationalist, not what you would call a smooth talker, but a young gentleman who really listened and chose his words with care. I believe he is currently going steady with a girl from Duluth and awaiting one of those fateful envelopes in response to his early application to Yale.

The following year, Creole—the only woman in the country who boasted what could accurately be described as a "wardrobe," all other female citizens having converted to the ancient Polynesian manner of going topless in acknowledgement of the weather being the real ruler of *Quietude*, what with the heat and humidity making one's clothing stick so remorselessly, whereas a cooling breeze off the Pacific landing on bare skin rendered the most torrid of days tolerable—got it into her head that becoming the queen would give her a chance to dress up every day, draw crowds of admirers and get hauled all over the island in a sedan chair by rotating quartets of hunky young men who glistened in the sun. When her year of rule was done, my own name had been placed in nomination by my daughter (at the time, I wondered why she had insisted on picking out a fedora of mine to be used in the monarchical lottery), and then selected (I think she rigged it so she could be a princess), I, at first, took the mostly honorary position as a joke but after a time decided to treat it seriously. Walking out every day to speak with my neighbors and learn a little about nation building became a pleasure, one which grew into a responsibility. I had retired as a writer and my old gig as a private eye wasn't called for in a land without laws, money or private property and therefore no crime. As the largely uneventful year was winding down, a mysterious suicide and an even more mysterious homicide occurred among us. Thanks to a relentless rumor mill and a tirelessly chattering coconut telegraph, my minor role in the solution of these mysteries had elevated my stature to the point that I was, by acclamation, declared King for Life.

Of course, neither my secretary or my old friend, Jake, took my royal standing seriously. Even Wilder, who had initiated it, would wave a dismissive hand and call it "that whole king thing" when her Poppy was mistaken for a figure of consequence. It's pretty easy to stay humble when your nearest and dearest treat you like an old stumblebum.

"Ace, sorry to barge in on you at first light, and for not letting you know I was headed your way," said Jake, "but I believe there are people behind me, people with a definite purpose, and it's one I think you'll want to know about."

"Are these people following you?"

"I don't think so. Rather the reverse. I was, if I'm not mistaken, following them from in front."

"What do they want, these people unaware of your head start?"

"Well, I believe I've bought us enough time for me tell you the rather long story. Do you have a moment?"

"I have nothing but moments. Pull up a hammock. I'm afraid I can offer only coffee by way of refreshment. My beloved Bonny has taken flight and left me with nothing but a huge variety of food and fond memories." Jake grinned a grin I knew well and slid a silver flask out his inside jacket pocket, waggling it waggishly.

"Lest we grow immoderate in moderation and intemperate in temperance," he said. Creole handed round big mugs of vroom-juice and her sweetie doctored them with liberal doses of what my friend Cassidy McKeever calls "Irish non-dairy creamer." She sat on the lap of the man she called her "flyboy" and I waved a regal hand.

"Speak the speech, I pray you, young Buchanan, omitting no detail, however slight. Let us see if you can get a rise out of the king."

18

Chapter Five

"Lay it in here, Cap. I'll clobber one halfway to Sumatra." Izzy tapped the end of her bat on the plate. She was a determined hitter and always swung for the fences. Well, we didn't have any fences, but she swung real hard. If she ever made contact, the ball might sail over the royal palm tree way out in deepest dead center. I offered up a toss so soft it was just begging to be creamed from here to Christmas. She took a furious cut, spun around, let go of her bat and fell down. I was not going to give up until she had put the bat on the ball, if only once, just to know how good it felt. I trotted into foul territory to pick up her lumber and hand it back while she dusted herself off.

"Try choking up on the bat, Izz, like this." I wrapped my hands around it a few inches up from the knob to give her the idea. "Then you don't need to take a full swing. Just poke at it, see, like it's pestering you. Just give it a little tap to make it go away." Halfway back to the mound, I stopped so I could make it even easier for her. The fielders were more tired than if something had actually been happening. They had stopped chattering heybatterheybatterheybatter*swing*batter and were just standing around, throwing their gloves up in the air and catching them, turning cartwheels in the outfield. Walter, my oldest player and the used-to-be king, was standing out in center with his glove on his head, studying a physics textbook and taking notes in the margins. I lofted in an underhand cream-puff, and my shortstop flicked her bat at it and sent it back to me on four little hops. She clapped her hand over her mouth and raced out to me to celebrate her first mighty clout. It was a start. "OK, River Otters, bring it in. Time to hit the waterfall."

After I started the River Otters, we needed another team so we could play real games instead of just playing pepper and three flies up and pretend games with two half-teams. At first there was only one other team, not even a real team because the players were always changing and we played what are called "pick-up" games. Then I asked my Poppy if he'd like to coach us and he said no, he'd rather just watch us play, but he worked out a way for there to be two leagues worth of teams so all the kids on the island would have a chance to shine on the diamond. His system was based on the old National and American Leagues in what he calls the *bigs* back in the States when he was a boy. The Windward League and the Leeward League each have eight teams. At the end of our 50-game season, the champions of the leagues will play each other for The Crown of *Quietude* and he will present the winners with a big trophy and give all the players their own lobster to cook for dinner at a bonfire on the beach.

If you live on the windward side of the island, the leeward side seems like a whole different world, farther away than Australia, where Izzy's dad had brought her from. I can't even remember any of the names of the teams in the Leeward League. But on our side, eight proud villages have teams to call their own. The Windward League teams are: 1. The Elsewhereville River Otters. 2. The Her Majesty's Grace Goofballs (Her Majesty's Grace is named in honor of my Poppy's used-to-be secretary, Creole, who is also the used-to-be queen, which is why my name for her has always been Queenie). 3. The Child's Play Peanut Butter Cups: 4. The Heavenly Peace Parrot Fish: 5. The Cowabunga Junction Javelinas. (Cowabunga Junction is the village where my fellow surfers hang. Coolest dudes on *Quietude*. Javelinas are wild pigs, sort of like the fierce and fearless boars we have here, whose tusks are half as long as those of my elephant, Tickety-Boo). 6. The Come What May Coyotes (in honor of the small colony of coyotes my Poppy brought here from the Florida Keys. At night sometimes they come very close to our cottage and the howling makes me shiver with fear but at the same time it makes me wish I was a coyote, too.) 7. The Shake It Up, Baby, Tiger Sharks (Shake It Up, Baby is the village where the most musicians live. Sometimes the conga drumming goes on there all night. I love to sneak out and dance to it under the moon). 8. The Everywhen Once Upon a Timers. (Everywhen is the village where the used-to-be movie star, my pal Poppy Tobago lives. She left Hollywood at the height of her fame to come here and study coral reefs and undersea life). The pirates over in Plunderland are all old bachelors or have ex-wives and kids they left behind out in the great world, so they couldn't field a team, but they give us gumdrops when we win. I have no idea where the gumdrops come from but they're real big and they're always black. It must be a pirate thing. We play on Buck O'Neil Field, named after a Negro League immortal my Poppy says was an even cooler dude than my fellow surfers.

In the bigs, my Poppy says, they have clubhouses with buffet tables to feed the players and big tiled showers so they can get cleaned up after their games. On *Quietude*, we are even luckier. We shower under a waterfall not far from Buck O'Neil Feld. The boys and girls all stand under the water together and razz one another the way ballplayers always do. Sometimes the boys leave their shorts on, boys being kind of shy. Walter, who is the tallest, makes some of the girls wish they knew how to talk to him about something other than baseball. As his team captain, I think they're kind of silly. What could be more important than baseball? Well, there was one thing. I didn't know if it was important, but it was definitely bugging me. It was that not-a-flute in my backpack. It seemed what you might call *alien*. The weight of the thing meant there was something inside the bamboo that wasn't made out of bamboo. It didn't think it came from *Quietude*, yet here it was.

If it belonged to the pirates (some kind of secret weapon for repelling invaders?), they lived on the full-sized mock-up of their old submarine not fifty feet from the watering trough where I'd found it, so why wouldn't they just keep it on the sub where they could protect it from their enemies? They were so used to living on the real sub that they still called other people who lived here *landlubbers*. If the not-a-flute was some sort of pirate ray-gun or mini-torpedo or what Izzy had said, a magic wand, a watering trough wasn't a very clever hiding place. I had found it while I was looking for my watch.

I told Izz that I had accidentally left my glove in the dugout and had to go back for it. Really, I wanted to have some time alone with the not-a-flute. I got there and had the field to myself. No other teams would be playing or practicing until tomorrow. I pulled out the mystery object and *beheld* it, as they say in the old stories. I had wanted to get away from the other River Otters because I thought *What if it's a bomb?* I could blow up my whole team and there would go our chance at the championship. What if it was a *time-bomb*, set to

21

go off who knows when? It wouldn't even help to have my watch without knowing how long away the ka-boom would be. I could cast it into the sea like one of those notes-in-a-bottle in the old stories by guys like Robert Louis Stevenson and Daniel Defoe, but then I would never find out what it was.

I tried shaking it gently. It didn't make any sounds like a maraca, say, or a rain-stick. It did have two joints, but they were no different from any other bamboo. Maybe there was a combination? But a combination has numbers and there were no numbers anywhere on the not-a-flute. Could Izz be right and it would come to life if you spoke the magic word? Because I have so many friends who have come to *Quietude* from all over the world, I know a lot of words: words in English, words in French, in Spanish, in Hawaiian, in Italian, in Fijian, in Gaelic, in Swahili (my close pal, Permanent Wave, who is sort of the Buck O'Neil of *Quietude*, is from the Kalahari desert and he has taught me how to make some of the clicking sounds that form the words of his people, the African Bushmen), but no matter how many words you know, how can you guess which one is the magic word? And maybe there was more than one word, a whole series of words that would combine into what they call a *password* out in the great world. If that were true, only the people who left it in the watering trough would know the right words. I better ask my Poppy. He used to be a poet. Sometimes he teaches me new words. Just the other day he taught me the word *disconsolate*, which means exactly how I felt just then.

Chapter Six

"I was, you'll be happy to know, sitting in The Salty Dame, that dive where you used to wile away the time with your copper friend, Irish Mike Hannigan, in Venice," said Jake, "listening to a Russian émigré who claimed to be both distantly related to the poet, Anna Akhmatova, and to have gained entrance to the innermost circle, the bullseye within the bullseye, as it were, of President Vladimir Putin. So far had he penetrated, so he said, that he'd overheard a tale to which—and I quote, 'no man on earth should ever have been made privy.'"

"Don't tell me. A love child tucked away in a deep forest dacha?"

"No. Something rather more in the opposite direction: Evidence purporting to demonstrate his, the President's, incapability, not only of fathering a child, but of performing the procreative act."

"I can see how that might be embarrassing to the man, bad day at the office for Vladimir, etc., but how on earth could such a claim be substantiated? It's the old problem of proving a negative."

"Interesting that you chose the word "negative." The nature of the supposed proof was photographic."

"What? A still with a limp dick Putin and a naked hooker? Even if he was seriously underhung, that wouldn't prove anything."

"Better. Much better. A feature film-length video of the President of Russia in a bedroom with a gorgeous unclothed escort who, no matter how diligently and ingeniously she strove to arouse him, was unable to help him to.... um, manifest desire for a full two hours. With *sound*. Putin, I was told, carries on at drunken top volume, cursing the escort, his damnable equipage and the western spies who must have dosed his vodka with some sort of anti-hard-on tonic, all of it captured on an iPhone 14. The émigré believed that the mere threat of the video being leaked on-line would embarrass the President so badly it would leverage him into withdrawing his military personnel and armaments from Ukraine. It was not a good look, in other words, for a leader who considers himself a strongman."

"And the man, the émigré, claimed to have the video?"

"Not only the video, but the escort herself, both of whom he had managed to smuggle out of mother Russia. For security reasons, he explained that he didn't have the goods on his person. And the escort, who feared for her life, he was moving every day from one secret location to the next, none of which he was at liberty to disclose."

"What did he want in return?"

"Oh, my. What didn't he want? Money, immunity, witness protection, an open tab at the bar. I explained that as a private citizen, I wasn't in a position to provide most of those things. But I did keep buying him drinks. Oh, here's a touch I think you'll like. He was ordering Grey Goose rather than Stoli, as an act, he said, of solidarity with the brave Ukrainian people. I told him that raising the money might be possible, but that I would have to make a few phone calls. As you know, they keep an old-fashioned pay phone on the wall in the corridor by the gents at The Salty Dame, a thing I've found useful over the years when I didn't want to pull out a cell and speak in front of whoever I happened to be with.

"Well, I called around and spoke to a couple of fellas I knew had been on the Russki beat this past year and they knew all about the émigré. He'd been trailing this tale all over town for weeks, with nobody buying. Apparently, he was a harmless lush with a lively imagination. Curiously enough, I think that he may really be related to the great Akhmatova."

"So you've not come to me with a tale of espionage and international intrigue?"

"I fear not. Sorry. But I may, thanks to the selfsame émigré, have brought you a story you'll not soon forget. And it is, or is about to be, set right here on this very island nation over which you rule so sleepily."

"A good start. You know how I hate leaving. You have my attention."

"And I think I can keep it. When I returned to the bar and told the émigré that I hadn't been able to interest my editors in his daring exposé—they had found it a trifle too salacious, and we were among the more respectable glossies—he remained undeterred. He waved a

24

blasé hand and launched into another fanciful tale, at least I thought he was just yarn spinning. At that point, I was no longer paying much attention, though I found the man entertaining. Then, with a single word from his lips, my newshound ears pricked up. I distinctly heard him speak the word *Quietude*."

"In itself, that seems innocent enough," I said, though I couldn't help remembering that it had been Jake himself who had once referred to my nation as "so far under the radar, it's actually under the sonar." "Surely, that reference alone could not have sent you on an eighteen-hour flight and a two-hour hop flight via seaplane on top of it."

"Well, despite the other persuasive reasons—" He smiled at Creole, who mussed his hair affectionately, "It would have taken a lot more. And a lot more is exactly what I got."

"Okay, young Buchanan, spill."

"It seems," Jake went on, "that the émigré had been lunching a few days earlier at the bar of Barney's Beanery when he fell into conversation with a young couple, young being a relative term—the émigré is in his mid-to-late-fifties, I would say—who had overheard him speaking ill of Putin's unconscionable war-mongering in Ukraine, one of his 'fund-raising efforts,' as he calls them. Having overheard them as they were overhearing him, he knew they were neither print journalists nor tabloid TV reporters, so he had no great interest in the pair. The woman, charmed by his accent, approached *him*, and tried to enlist his aid in an effort of her own. He thought he might have seen her before but could not for the life of him remember where. She was in complete agreement with his sentiments and felt they were natural allies. She needed a good man, she said, to pilot a boat with which she and the fellow meant to haul away a treasure from a remote south Pacific island whose name you know well, having coined it yourself, a treasure which, out in the world, could be translated into, I quote, 'unimaginable wealth.'"

"'Unimaginable wealth' is all well and good, I suppose, though personally I've always preferred 'riches beyond your wildest dreams of avarice' but do go on." I was beginning to think that Jake and Creole had concocted this nonsense out of whole cloth, that they might enjoy a long overdue episode of their ongoing "pre-marital honeymoon." while having a little sport with me.

"The couple would rendezvous with the man and his boat on the eastern end of this island at such and such a date and time, load the treasure and slip away. The boat pilot would receive a generous piece of the action and be promptly cut loose after they had arrived safely on Easter Island. She thought the émigré might be just the man for the job, since, she claimed, her sworn intention was to donate her own percentage of the spoils to the President of Ukraine to help to put Putin's forces there to rout. The couple began to squabble right in front of the émigré. He couldn't make out what their differences were, but when he asked the woman to elaborate, she went on to say only that the two of them were to travel by conventional means to the westward side of the island, there to employ some sort of location-finding device which would, so they said, guide them to the exact spot where this treasure was cached. Thereafter they would meet with their boatman, ready to make a clean getaway.

"The émigré, convinced he was being scammed, felt insulted. His professional pride was getting dinged up. Who did these two think they were, running such an obvious game on *him* of all people. At that point, feeling like he'd been pegged for a mark, he begged off. He assumed they were about to ask for some good faith money from him up front, which would of course be returned a hundredfold on the back end. He explained to the couple that he could not pilot so much as a bathtub duck and furthermore was prone to seasickness, and bowed rather abruptly out of the conversation."

"I can't say I blame him. Forgetting for the moment that the whole operation sounds composed of half-baloney and half-malarkey, I'm pretty sure we have nothing here that fits the description of 'unimaginable wealth.'"

"So far as you know. But according to the pair who were peddling this hokum, the treasure has been here for over 200 years. If it's really well hidden, there's no reason you would know of its existence." It was true that our nation was a young one, only three years older than my daughter. We had inherited the island from a Polynesian chieftain shortly before his passing. His ancestors, in turn, had inherited it from either the French or the British—he was unclear on that point—when his people had helped one to kick the other's ass off. The historical record was quite sketchy. We liked to think Captain Cook might have landed here in his hope of observing the Transit of

Venus or discovering the hypothetical continent of Terra Australis. HMS Bounty could have paused at our island in its crew's pursuit of breadfruit. Darwin and the *Beagle* were known to have put in at Matavai Bay in Tahiti in 1767, as, on the French side of the ledger, did Louis Antoine de Bougainville about a year later. Another French explorer, Jean-François de Galaup, comte de Lapérouse, was known to have dropped anchor in Samoa roughly two decades after that. No history book can tell us if any of these gents stopped here because our island remained uncharted until we set up shop. If they had visited, it hadn't gone into the record. So, if you wanted to deal in speculative fiction, you could theorize your brains out about who might have enjoyed a sleepover and/or buried a humongous hoard of swag here many years ago. But those expeditions were primarily scientific in nature.

"This 'device,' you mentioned. Will the treasure hunters be bringing it with them?"

"No. That's the other thing you need to know. The device, so they said, is already in place."

"Do they know where it is?"

"One of them does."

"Do you?"

"No."

"Do you know how to use it?"

"No. But one of them does."

"The same one who knows where it is?"

"No. The other. It's rather a delicate situation. It seems there is a map, and a *key* to the map. The key is hidden in this device. But you cannot understand how to use the key until you have seen the map."

"And without the key, the map will do you no good?"

"That's how matters stand. One has the map, the other knows how to find the key to the map."

"So the man and woman need each other. It's almost touching, practically romantic. How did the émigré put all this together?"

"Ah, part two." Creole made the rounds again. The coffee was starting to kick in and the additive to stir my imagination.

"He, the émigré, hadn't quit Barney's" Jake went on, "merely slid down the bar to confer with various other elbow-benders, still

27

working his own hustle. But he found himself brooding over the story he had been told by the couple, his grifter's instinct was telling him he might be onto something. And the woman, as I say, looked maddeningly familiar to him. There was an obvious current of tension between the two and he believed he could exploit it, if only to discover where he had met her previously. When the man repaired to the gents, he slid back to the woman's side, bought her a drink and asked her why, since her companion seemed so disagreeable, she didn't just mount her own expedition? That's when the émigré learned that she was keeping the map under wraps. She was tipsy enough to confess that she would like nothing better than to be rid of her partner, who was, she whispered, a self-serving malcontent who favored an uneven split, the majority share going to himself, the irreplaceable member of the team since he and he alone knew where the device could be found. Oh, he pretended to be in sympathy with the people of Ukraine, but that was just for show. Once the score had been made, he planned to donate his end to nothing and no one but his, and I quote, 'grand slam retirement program.' Back to the end of the bar went the émigré and returned to the tale of the escort and the iPhone. He decided, whether there was anything to the couple's story or not, he had no desire to get caught in the cross-fire of their bickering. On his way out, he wished them luck, apologized for having no nautical skills and bid the two adieu. He could find no angle of advantage to himself in the situation, though he was as opportunistic as the gent and as ferociously anti-Putinistic as the lady. So he tucked it away in the back of his mind should it come in handy down the road. As luck would have it, the road led him to me."

Chapter Seven

"*Stee-rike* three!" said the tree. It was a very old tree, a giant banyan my Poppy thought might be the oldest tree on the island. So I guess it could be plenty smart, in whatever way a tree can be. But even in *1001 Tales of the Arabian Nights*, which a beautiful lady named Laurelai, the official Reader Aloud to the Royal Family has been reading to us for over half of my life, there aren't any talking trees. And even if a very old tree *could* talk, why would it be calling balls and strikes?

I like practicing my pitching against the trunk of the tree because the trunk is really a cluster of smaller trunks so one can be the outside corner and one the inside and every pitch bounces off a little differently, *unpredictably* you might say, so I get to take fielding drills along with pitching. I retrieved the ball, scuffed and grass stained but still OK for batting practice and whumped it into the deep well pocket of my glove. It used to be my Poppy's glove. I hope he realizes that he gave it to me for good.

"Way to go, Little Coconut," said his voice from three stories above me. "This old tree never had a chance against that wicked hook of yours. Now that you've sent it back to the dugout, whatayasay I come down we can play a little catch oh that's right I can't because somebody's idea of a team captain made off with my glove."

"Can I come up, Poppy?"

"Not right now. I have company. Your old friends Mister Buchanan and Queenie are acquainting me with a story I'll tell you about later. Why don't I come down and give you a hug?"

"How about we meet in the middle, Poppy?" I loved to swing up from one *lateral* branch to another instead of using the rope ladder. Lateral means sideways, I think. The branches are big enough to sit on, though my father always acted like he was on a flying trapeze or something when we sat there and went over the events of the day.

29

"OK." He looked kind of doubtful, and it took him a really long time to climb down. By the time he made it to our branch, I had climbed up with my backpack and taken out all my notebooks. "You must have been playing a lot of road games, Wilder Kathleen. I haven't seen much of you recently." His knuckles were white from gripping the branch so hard, even though we were only about fifteen feet off the ground. He doesn't leave the palace much anymore. Inside my backpack was the not-a-flute. I didn't know if I should show it to him. Well, I knew that I *should*, I didn't know if I was *going* to. My Poppy used to be what's called a private eye, a detective who found things and people who were missing out in the great world. If I told him about the not-a-flute, he might figure out what it was and how to use it and I wanted to do it on my own and then surprise him with what a good detective *I'd* become. Besides, when he asked where the not-a-flute had come from, I would have to explain about losing my watch.

"Oh, Poppy, you know we don't have road games, not until the championship, anyway." All the Windward League teams played on Buck O'Neil Field. The Leeward League teams played on their own field called Paradisiac's Park. If we won the pennant of the Windward League, we would play some championship games at home and some at Paradisiac's Park. For those we would troop around the island on foot with me leading the way on my elephant, Tickety-Boo. I had already told my teammates that if we won, they would each have a chance to ride on Tickety-Boo as their reward for our coming in first. Some of them were very excited at the prospect and some of the littler ones were kind of scared but excited anyway. It's a long ways up to the back of an elephant.

"Oh, that's right. I clean forgot." He glanced at my notebooks. "You know, your Mumza will be home before too long. I think you know the first thing she's going to ask you."

"If you've been going down to the Doubloon with Mister McKeever much?" He smiled.

"No, that's the second thing she's going to ask you. The first is whether you've been getting your homework done." Oh, good. Now I had a reason that wasn't the not-a-flute for popping in on my Poppy.

"Sure, I know that. In fact, that's why I came to see you, to show you how much work I've finished." My Mumza had left me some study guides and some practice tests. "I finished all the chemistry, all the world history and all the calculus. She said you should check them and tell her how I did when she gets home. Here." I could tell by his face he didn't know where to put the papers to carry them back up.

"Could you just tuck these into the hollow of the trunk and I'll look at them later after I say goodbye to our friends?" he said. The hollow of the trunk was our trusty old hiding place. "Howze that sidekick of yours coming along?"

"Sidekick?"

"Your friend, the middle infielder with the carbonated name."

"Izzy?"

"That's the one."

"She can throw the leather, Poppy. But she still can't hit a lick."

"You taking good care of my glove, Little Coconut?"

"Sure, Poppy. I treat it everyday with that Neatsfoot oil you gave me and put the ball in the pocket at night and keep it under my mattress like you showed me." *Neat* is an Old English word for cattle. The oil is made from the shin bones and feet of cows. If you have to squeeze the feet of cows hard enough to make oil come out, I'm glad I don't have to make the stuff myself, but a team captain needs to set a good example. I slid the papers back into my pack and tossed it down to the ground. "Happy trails, Poppy. See you round the next bend in the river." I jumped down, landed and rolled and jumped back up again. *Ta-da!*

"Not bad for a princess," called out my Poppy, climbing ever so slowly back to his tree house.

In a village named Daffadowndilly about an hour's hike into the interior, live a dozen or so older Englishwomen who are my heroes. Well, they're some of my heroes, I have a LOT of heroes. The *good ladies of Daffadowndilly*, as my Poppy calls them, had gallantly volunteered to make uniforms for all us River Otters. That isn't the only reason they're my heroes. They have the loveliest manners and always sit me down to a fancy tea-party no matter when I show up. They serve all kinds of what they call *biscuits* which are what we would call *cookies*. I asked my Poppy what they call what we call biscuits and he said maybe they were called *crumpets*, which Izzy thinks is a good name for a baseball team. These rookies have some strange ideas, let me tell you.

I mainly wanted to see how our uniforms were coming along. They should be ready to make what's called their *debut* any time now. At the moment, we were all wearing shorts and t-shirts along with our cleats but some of the other teams already had their own uniforms. It's not so easy to slide in shorts or to headfirst slide with only a t-shirt. My Poppy says I look like a *strawberry field*, whatever that might be. A lot of us already have cleats but some still play in flip-flops which is most unfortunate. Trying to handle bad hops while wearing flip-flops leads to a lot of errors. Everyone has a glove. When old friends come to visit from the great world, they know to bring baseball gloves. And my Poppy and lots of the other dads and moms write to friends and family and they send gloves from the great world. Once every two weeks, we have a mail drop and that's how the gloves arrive. They fall out of the sky. You would need a pretty sturdy glove to catch a baseball glove falling out of an airplane. So we wait in the dugout while the mail plane swoops down over Buck O'Neil field and drops bundles of letters and sometimes baseball gloves. Most of our bats come here on ships, and some are made here by *master carvers*. The carvers make them on what are called *treadle* lathes that you have to push with your foot. It takes a long time to make a baseball bat this way, but on *Quietude*, we have plenty of time.

When we arrived, most of the ladies were tending their flower gardens with both their long hair and their long skirts pinned up and big hiking boots and wide-brimmed bonnets. My friend Bess waved to us from the door of her cottage to invite us in.

"C'mon, Izz."

"I think I'll just wait out here, Cap. I can look after the ball bag." Bess's cottage was much tidier than most of the huts and houses on *Quietude*. She had fancy chairs and fancy china and the last time we'd come, Izzy had put one of those lace dealies called *doilies* on her head and spilled her tea on the fancy carpet. I expect she was kind of nervous now.

"Okie dokie. You can do your stretching." I loved going into Bess's cottage. She has beautiful cut glass vases all over the place and the furniture shone with polish that smelled like lemons. Her teapots were very old and she always poured the tea very carefully.

"This kind of tea is called 'Darjeeling,' dear," she said, once we were seated at a lovely low table. "I hope you like it. How is your father, His Majesty the king?" I said what my Mumza has taught me to say.

"He is enjoying the most robust health, ma'am. The tea is very good. Thank you."

"Oh, Wilder dear, you needn't call me 'ma'am.' I'm not the queen. You know you may always call me Bess. Do have a biscuit." They came in fancy round tins all the way from England. There were shortbread biscuits and chocolate chip biscuits and a kind called 'Hobnobs.' The tins looked like you could keep your jewelry in it if you had any. I dunked the biscuit into the tea the way Bess had taught me until it was just a little soggy and took a bite. That was one *delicioso* biscuit. I wondered how I could take one out to Izzy without seeming greedy. While I was wondering, I looked around at the cottage. It looked so much like what are called *engravings* in old books and so different from all the other homes here, it made me wonder why.

"Did you and the other ladies of Daffadowndilly build your own houses, Bess?"

"Oh, goodness no, dear. We are gardeners, not builders. We till the soil in our modest fashion, but we didn't have so much as a single hammer between us. When we first came here, my friends and I, we lived in those little tents called pup tents, I think. It was rather inconvenient, what with the bugs and all. And ladies of our vintage don't much enjoy sleeping on the ground. We had traveled here together after losing our husbands. We wanted to be where the ocean was warm, you see. After a few weeks of living in this unaccustomed manner, a troupe of young men were passing through here one day and we offered them refreshment. They were, I believe, what used to be known as 'soldiers of fortune,' roaming around the world. They asked us how we were getting along and we confessed that the camping style of life was hard on some of us. They said they would be happy to build us cottages in exchange for room and board and regular meals. Well, that seemed like a splendid arrangement. A lot of the materials had to be shipped in from the UK and it took quite a while, but when they were finished, they had built us homes that looked just like the pictures we showed them of our places back in drizzly old England. They worked on our cottages for upwards of six months or so, and then moved on. I never thought they would stay. They were nomads, you might say. Slow nomads, but still. I often wonder what became of them. Well, I expect you'd like to see your uniforms, dear. Shall I show one to you? You could try it on."

"Oh, yes, ma'am. I mean, Bess. That would be just ducky." She told me to close my eyes while she went out of her parlor and into her sewing room (the ladies have sewn our uniforms on old sewing machines you worked with a foot pedal sort of like the baseball bat lathes only it's *pedal* instead of *treadle* and you feel like you are playing an organ in one of those big churches they have out in the great world) and came back and told me to open my eyes. When I did, there was Bess with a big smile in her eyes, holding up a shirt with the words River Otters stitched on the front along with a picture of an otter sliding up out of the water and on the back my number 18. I couldn't even speak I was so excited. Bess led me behind what she called a dressing screen though I think it should be called an *un*dressing screen but it didn't really make any difference because I didn't have a top on to take off so I just buttoned up my uniform shirt and looked at myself front and back in the full-length mirror. It was kind of a girly thing for a team captain to do, I guess, but I twirled around twice and jumped up and down I was so happy. I just love being a River Otter!

When I went back out to show Bess, she handed me a cloth napkin full of different sorts of biscuits. "I thought you might like to share these with your shy teammate," she said. "You can bring back the napkin when you come to pick up your uniform trousers." I thanked her and gave her a hug. "See you someday else," I said, which is something they tell me I have always said.

"The bamboozler looks funny" said Izzy. *Bamboozler* was her new word for the not-a-flute.

"What were you doing with my not-a-flute, Izz?"

"It was in the ball bag, Cap. I figured that since I was with you when we found it, it was *our* not-a-flute. I was using it to practice choking up the way you showed me. Then I learned you can bunt

34

rocks with it if you throw the rocks up in the air, though I don't guess that would get the runner over."

"How do you mean, funny?" z

"Well, I noticed that the bamboo was getting sorta scratched up from the rocks and I was trying to rub out the scratches with some of that needs-a-foot oil you gave me for my glove even though I don't know why my glove would need a foot but when I was rubbing it, I noticed that the ends of the not-a-flute were closed up. See?" She was right.

"Could it be dried mud, do you think, Izz?" But if it was mud, wouldn't it have loosened up and floated out in the trough?

"Maybe there's something inside the not-a-flute, aka the bamboozler," said Izzy, who loves aka's. She sounded doubtful. "Maybe it snaps open when you pull on it, like one of those Christmas crackers the ladies showed us. Though calling them crackers makes about as much sense as calling cookies biscuits." It wouldn't snap no matter how hard I tried. Our old friend who keeps his boat moored in our harbor has flares that you need to twist the top off. But it wouldn't twist any more than it would snap. Whatever the not-a-flute was, it was plenty solid.

"And nothing happened when you were bunting the rocks?"

"Well, I fouled off a lot of rocks. And one hit me in the head on its way back down. But you know me, Cap, always ready to take one for the team." I hoisted the ball bag, now filled with our new uniforms, and sent Izzy off to Buck O'Neil Field to get ready for our game while I hurried to the *Naughtylass* to take care of the horses.

Chapter Eight

"And why would you choose to believe a word of this utter codswallop? I begin to suspect that Wilder put you up to this." My daughter dearly loves to prank the king. It gives her monster bragging rights among her teammates. "You couldn't sell it as a movie based on a video game based on a terrible movie. I like the anti-Putin angle, but so far the only Russian in the story you've already outed as a fabricator and prodigious guzzler of strong waters."

"Granted, he's a bit of a con artist, a known elbow-bender and not averse to prevaricating his way through the day, but it turns out the émigré is also a man of parts and considerable experience, one with quite the checkered past: money-lender, brothel-keeper, flagman on the Trans Siberian Railroad, defrocked priest (unfrocked rather, since he had never been frocked in the first place, something to do with icons and orphans and the widows of slain mobsters), theater owner and part-time actor, dissident. But the very nature of the con he first tried to run on me speaks to his deepest, most passionate motive— his hatred of Vladimir Putin. He didn't know that *Quietude* constitutes half of my dual citizenship. It was really the mention of your land that put the story over the top for me.

"Before meeting the couple at Barney's, the émigré had never heard the word spoken. As far as I know, only two people on the North American continent, myself and Irish Mike, who now resides in Montreal, are aware of your fine country."

It's true, though unintentional, that we keep a low profile in the States. I'd been kicking around the idea of opening our first embassy in a lingerie boutique called We Stop at Nothing on Abbot Kinney in Venice, but nothing had come of it yet. I'd been thinking more seriously of brokering an inter-island trade agreement, our first, with Kauai, our sister paradise which was currently overrun with chickens thanks to a hurricane releasing an entire Philippine community's population of illegal fighting cocks and their hens. The birds had become first a nuisance and then a health hazard. On Kauai, they had no natural predators. On *Quietude*, if the chickens were to go rogue, our colony of coyotes would cull their numbers in a hurry.

The idea had come to me after Wilder and her friends had taken to petitioning me to preside over an island-wide Easter egg hunt. Her contemporaries born on different continents have told her about Easter eggs. But we had no chickens, and thus no eggs. It matters little which came first if you have none of either. Doubtless, the good people of Kauai would be glad to be rid of a portion of their chicken plague, but what could I offer them in return? A trade agreement requires a trade, after all. We have successfully transplanted some of the delicious northern California apples called Gravensteins. Maybe Hawaii could use some bushels of those? Apples for chickens felt about the right size for our initial foray into foreign affairs.

"OK. A man and a woman we have no way of recognizing may be headed this way with the intention of reconnoitering with a mysterious device with which to locate, dig up and abscond with a treasure so grand as to tax the imaginations of Rudyard Kipling and H. Rider Haggard were you able to put them together."

"Correct. Is there a question?"

"Only this: Let us suppose that I, from, oh, I don't know, a love of adventure or an excess of sleep deprivation, were to invest the slightest smidgen of belief in this charming fairy story, telling one and all to be on the lookout for a pair of sinister characters and to shadow any such to a burial ground for fabulous goodies and catch them in the act, fingers dripping with gems, shoulders bowed by the weight of bullion, etc., what, I ask you, would be the point of it?"

"Beg pardon?"

"I mean, why bother?"

Creole immediately gleaned where I was going. "I see what you're getting at, Boss," she said. "Since we don't use money on *Quietude*, and since finding a form of value other than money is practically our national raison d'être, why wouldn't we simply caution the couple to avoid overloading their canoes with loot and send them on their way?"

"Exactly. We have no need for whatever this supposed treasure trove might be. If it's gold, it would only weigh us down. If it's jewels, we are well supplied with homegrown lapidaries, male and female, who fashion earrings and bracelets and necklaces and such from shell and pearl—indigenous gems, as it were—to keep our womenfolk handsomely adorned. So there's no need for secrecy, and *if* there is a treasure, though I'd love to hear the story of how it came to be here, that's only because I love a good story. Otherwise, it don't make no nevermind to me." I sat back and sipped my coffee. When I shot Jake a look meant to be one of triumph, I realized he had, and not for the first time, end-arounded me. If a man could be said to have two lights in his eye at one time, master Buchanan was that man. I knew both lights of old. One signaled *It's the story of a lifetime and I mean to be the newshound who will hammer it out.* The other meant simply *There's more.* I should have known.

"We all have a ballgame to get to," I said. "Treasure of storied proportions is not be sneezed at, I agree. Even if it doesn't exist, I would love to learn why someone cooked up such a legend. But we're talking about the fate of the River Otters here. Let's reconvene once the deal has gone down at Buck O'Neil Field.

Chapter Nine

Captain Primos's Remuda:

1. Black Jack: an almost blue mustang from Texas.
2. Fast Buck: a pinto cow pony from Montana.
3. Blow the Man Down: an Appaloosa chestnut mare from Marin County in California.
4. Four Pounder: a dappled grey Andalusian from the Iberian Peninsula.
5. Devil May Care: a French Trotter from Normandy.
6. Freebooter: a bay Morgan from Massachusetts.
7. Privateer: a palomino Quarter Horse from Kentucky.
8. Fire in the Hole: a sorrel Basuto from Lesotho.
9. You Ain't Just a Whistling Doxy, a dun Mongolian wild horse of a breed called Przewalski. She is very rare and may be the only one outside of Mongolia the Captain told me. *Doxy* is a word that means a pirate's lady friend.

You would think that pirates who had been *the scourge of the seven seas* on a submarine would have little or nothing to do with horses, wouldn't you? And you'd be right, at least that's how it was when Captain Primo's crew of old sea dogs had first dispersed into what he called a pirate *diaspora*. They had shipped out to ports of call all over the world. But each had grown lonely and began to miss their old mates. When word reached them that the Captain had built a full-size replica of their old sub on the beach and began to live aboard it, all were eager to rejoin him. But when the Captain, who loves to ride horses and had one brought here on a sailing ship from California, issued an order that none of his old crew would be allowed to come here and live on the new *Naughtylass* unless he brought a horse, they had no choice but to comply. It was what he called the *price of admission*. He told me that every night during his years at and under

39

sea, he had dreamt of riding horses and captaining his own herd, or *remuda*. Now the pirates ride their horses on the beach and stage races and they invented a kind of pirate polo I don't understand. Sometimes you are allowed to hit the ball into the ocean and other times you got a penalty if you do. Their original submarine now lived, minus some of its outer plates, on the bottom of our harbor. Sometimes my Mumza and I and Poppy Tobago dive down to it and swim in and out of it and get friendly with thousands of little fishes. It's what my other Poppy, my dad, would call a *blast*.

The Captain had asked me to look after his remuda while he was off bartending in the great world. He knew I was good at taking care of horses because he watched me take care of Holy Toledo!, the Arabian stallion he gave me before he left. He'd confided to me that his aging crew had been known to hole up on the pretend *Naughtylass* for days at a time doing stuff he didn't want to tell me about and forget to feed and groom their mounts. That's why it's important to keep the watering trough full. Horses need plenty of water. I helped to plant a kind of grass from the Marquesas, in a high meadow that gets lots of direct sunlight. When it has grown long, we cut and carry it on sleds into a barn—well, it's not a real barn with a hayloft and everything, it's just a peaked roof with some shelves under it held up on long bamboo poles. But it's enough protection to keep the grass dry until it matures into hay without getting soaked which makes it useless. The sled rides are the most fun. I pile on the grass, hold it down with a bungee cord, push the sled to the edge of a pretty steep hill, sit on it and push with my foot until I am sliding like a *Quietude* tobogganer over slick short grass, picking up speed and hollering yahoo. The horses love the fruit I bring them every day but they need grasses too or their digestion gets wonky. I love that word, *wonky*. I give each horse a chance to graze as often as I can, so they can eat fresh grass, but I can't graze all nine at once because I'm only one *paniola* (Hawaiian for cowboy) and I have the River Otters and my homework and looking after my Poppy and my own horse and my elephant and these good-for-nothing pirates only ride the horses in races and their crazy polo matches and Izzy is afraid of horses, so it's a good idea to keep a supply of hay in the not-quite-a-barn. Izzy says I should set them all free to roam, just let them out of their corral one night while the pirates are snoring and doing what's called *sleeping it off,* whatever that might be. But my Poppy says they would probably turn into wild horses and we would be letting the Captain down. I know that when you give your word, you have to keep it, but I do think living on an island where you might see a wild horse at any time would be plenty cool.

I had finished feeding and watering all the horses, taken the Captain's mare for a ride, returned her to the corral, walked up to the pasture, cut down a bunch of long grass with a scythe, piled it on a sled and slid it down to the not-a-barn to dry. If I do this every day, we will have a nice stockpile of hay. Captain Primo is due home soon from the great world and I want him to be proud of the way I have taken care of his remuda. Finally, I had a chance to get down to Buck O'Neil Field and take a bullpen session (well, I call it that, but since we don't have a bullpen any more than we have a bull, I threw the ball thirty times from the mound on the field) before our game against the Javelinas.

My Poppy is having real baseball caps made for us on the mainland. When I get mine, I'll be able to tug on the bill and glare ferociously at batters just before I buckle their knees with my twelve-to-sixer. A twelve-to-sixer is a kind of curveball that starts out at a batter's chest and drops all the way to his knees. Mister McKeever says it's all I'll need in the way of breaking stuff except maybe for a screwball, aka (as Izzy would say) a *scroojie,* or, in the old days, a *fadeaway,* which is also fun to say. Sometimes, I would like to just fade away myself until everyone wondered where I went and then I would magically reappear in the midst of my family and say, "What's shakin', chilluns?" or "What's the rumpus?" which is something my Poppy told me all private eyes know to say. A fadeaway machine would be a good invention.

We were in the midst of what is called a "tense pitcher's duel," The score was tied at eleven. Both me and the opposing pitcher, a twelve year old surfer dude from Kauai named Dalton who calls himself "Mogu Mogu," though I have no idea why, had each, for once, struck out almost as many hitters as we had walked. My control was improving under Mister McKeever's tutelage and I had fanned seven, hit only two batters, thrown only one wild pitch and issued a mere five bases on balls!

It was the bottom of the seventh (the last inning in our games, unless we go to extras) and we had Mogu Mogu on the ropes. He was beginning to tire and taking his time between pitches. I was at the plate, with the bases loaded, hoping to bring the girl in from third and get the whole thing over with so I could go home to Holy Toledo!. The runners were dancing off the bases and I could hear my Poppy shouting "C'mon, Little Coconut!" from the sidelines, which always embarrasses me but he does it anyway. Everyone can hear him because being the king he had some young dudes rig up a beach chair on a rope and pulley and they haul him way up on the trunk of a palm tree behind the plate. Then they tie off the rope so he doesn't slide back down. He likes to sit up there watching me pitch and sipping mango nectar from a thermos. I tried it one time when he wasn't looking and I thought the mangoes might have gone bad. Coming to the games is about the only times he comes out of the palace anymore, so I guess I should give him a free pass on the embarrassment business. Izzy was shouting encouragement from the dugout and PW offering advice from the third base coaching box. He is the only grown-up coach in the league but nobody on the other teams seems to mind, probably because no one understands anything he says anyway. The few bits of English he knows are surfer and baseball expressions, but he gets them mixed up. Just then, he hollered, "Goofy-footers rule!," (a *goofy-footer* is a southpaw surfer dude) which I thought nicely put, since he was standing in the coaching box with his right foot forward, just the way he does on his board, and I was hitting left against Mogu Mogu who is a righty.

He had me in an 0-2 hole and I was fouling off pitch after pitch just trying to stay alive. He wound up and came in with a heater right at my head. I jumped out of the way just in time, then stepped out of the box to take a deep breath. I didn't think he was trying to hit me, just to get in my kitchen and the ball got away from him. But Izzy was having none of it.

She charged out of the dugout, shouting, "Mogu, you pitch like you surf! You're all over the place on the water *and* on the mound! You're a disgrace!" I think she had a crush on the cute Hawaiian boy. But what she had yelled in anger was really true. He was a total hot dog when the big sets were rolling in, but whenever he'd tried dropping in on me over a wave I knew was mine, I burned him harder than his heater had come at my coconut. Now I put my mind inside his and knew he thought I would try to drill the next strike he laid in right through the box to get back at him. I took a quick look down at PW, who had taken the not-a-flute out of the ball bag and had been using it all game like a baton to wave runners around third. It gave me an idea.

I laid off a couple of outside pitches he knew I couldn't do anything with: Full count. He had to either come in or slink back to Kauai after walking in the winning run. Pitching from the stretch, he lobbed up a slow curve, maybe thinking I would come out of my cleats trying to cream it and swing and miss instead. What I did was to borrow Izzy's program, laying down a picture perfect bunt along the first base line. Nobody moved but the runner on third, who crossed the plate with her arms reaching for the sky. Final score: 12-11 River Otters.

"Way to go, Cap. Now we're only a game out of first."

"Thanks, Izz. It was you who gave me idea to drop one down, when you were using the not-a-flute—"

"Aka the Bamboozler," she said.

"That's right. The bamboozler, to practice your bunting up in Daffadowndilly the other day."

"Glad I could help, Cap. By golly, you bamboozled 'em good and proper. I can almost taste that lobster right now."

Chapter Ten

"OK. Jake. Let me have it."

"Your maj?"

"The part you were saving for last. The wow finish." It was among his gifts as a reporter, to make the reader (or, in this case, the listener) believe he had been told all, and then pull the tablecloth out from under the good silver. He grinned, looking simultaneously sheepish and wolfish.

"Ordinarily," said Jake "I would agree with you. It's a given: In *Quietude* terms, all jewelry is paste, all gold fool's gold. But I know you well enough to know that your own sentiments would line up with the woman's. If, however—" He tilted my secretary's chin and gave her a kiss on the lips, "if we beat them to it, we can rightfully claim her partner's share, and use it just as she would like. Treasure hunting is a first come, first serve deal. I ask you, what better use could there be for that which on *Quietude* you have no use, than to fence it ourselves and get the proceeds, *all* the proceeds, to the people of Ukraine?"

"You make a compelling case, young Buchanan," I said. "But I am kind of busy just now. There is Wilder's baseball team, who are vying for the championship of their young league. And the first law of parenting is You Damned Well Better Show Up. Also, I'm trying to hammer out a trade agreement with Hawaii—" If you could mangle the word "trying," into meaning you've begun to toy with an idea.

"What's that all about?" asked the ever inquisitive investigative reporter. I explained the basic notion. "What a great way to arrive at an egg hunt," he said. "But you've not set this deal in motion yet, is that right?"

"Yeah," I admitted. "I'm just kicking it around in my head."

"Well, chew on this," said Jake. "While we're waiting both for your trade agreement to come together and for the disputatious couple to arrive, you can issue an island-wide decree inviting all the children of

Quietude to take part in *your first treasure hunt*. It'll be even better than an Easter egg hunt. And we would have our own battalion of scouts with endless amounts of energy to offset our ignorance and thereby level the playing field. Why, it would be nothing less than child abuse to do otherwise. If word got out, you be denounced all over the civilized world as nothing less than an, oh, I don't know, a monarchy in restraint of fun." His enthusiasm, though contagious, also struck me as somewhat pre-cooked.

"You already have a book deal in place, don't you?" I said. "You've talked some rag into paying you for an article, which will be stretched into a best-seller, resulting in mammoth up-front money, foreign markets, ancillary rights, etc. It's all pre-sold, isn't it?" He had a habit of coming up with ingenious ways of visiting my secretary while adding to his worldly estate.

"Well, I needed per diem, now, didn't I?" he said.

"Suppose it's all flummery?" I said. "And it turns out there never was a treasure?"

"In that case," he replied, "I will travel to Kauai as your special envoy to facilitate the trade agreement, and I will personally provide all the egg dye for the hunt." It would be a week or so before Wilder's mother returned from her travels. And days off had been scheduled between all the ballgames, days on which the kids could occupy themselves looking for the stuff of legend. Stringing along with Jake's foolhardy exploits would certainly help to pass the time. And, I had to admit, I found the prospect of buggering the Kremlin irresistible.

"I wish I'd had a chance to interview this émigré of yours myself," I said to Jake. "If he has really set eyes on this couple, he's the only one who could identify them."

"Well, since you've already climbed into your kingly raiment," he replied, "it should be an easy matter to slide into those 'kamaboku slippahs' I see over there and follow us back down the way we came."

"Why would I do that?" I had grown so used to people coming to me, their sovereign, hunkering down had begun to agree with me. As a result, I was finding it hard to quit the palace.

"To meet the émigré," said Jake. "I brought him with me. At this very moment, he's soaking up local culture down at the Doubloon."

"I'll get my hat."

45

Chapter Eleven

Today was my day with my best girl. Holy Toledo! is my very best boy and a pretty big one at that. But my best girl, Tickety-Boo, is even bigger and I don't have to keep her in a stall or a corral. An elephant can go anywhere she likes. Neither the coyotes nor even the savage wild boars—those pirates of the undergrowth—would dare to mess with her. The best part is that she always comes back to me. Captain Primo's horses might turn wild if set free, but Tickety-Boo is so devoted to her mistress that she returns to the cottage every night. I think she thinks I am part of her herd, a little herd made of just the two of us. She was given to me by the Maharajah of Ranchipur because my Poppy is the king and Maharajahs and kings like to give each other things.

She's not at all fussy about her diet. She'll eat pretty much anything within reach and she can reach pretty much anything on *Quietude* except for young coconuts. It would be pretty funny to see an elephant try to shinny up a palm tree. But it would be what my Mumza told me was *beneath her dignity*. So what she does is just bump against the trunk of the tree until a couple of coconuts fall down. Or sometimes she'll go trunk-on-trunk, wrapping her trunk around the trunk of the tree and shake shake shaking until she has won a coconut. At night, she stays beside the water tank my Uncle John made for her. She can just reach over the side of the tank with her trunk whenever she wants a drink. Elephants drink even more water than horses, about 75 gallons a day, sometimes 100. It's a good thing we get big afternoon showers every day. Before nightfall, she roams around the island, eating and drinking water from ponds and rivers and thinking the long thoughts of elephants. I don't know if she misses other elephants, but maybe she does and maybe that's why she stays so close to me and has made friends with Holy Toledo!.

When I ride her, we go bareback except on what are called *ceremonial* occasions when I'm supposed to act like a princess and then we put on her howdah. It takes two people to put it on and I like riding her bareback better anyway because I can feel what she's doing

46

with her muscles under my heels. I call her with a special way of whistling through my teeth that I pretend she is the only one who can hear. Probably other people can hear it too because it's very loud—very *piercing*, my Poppy says—and she can hear it from pretty far off. When she comes to me, I clap my hands twice which is our signal for her to reach out her trunk, let me climb on and then lift it until I'm level with her head. From there, I can scramble onto the top of her head and then onto her back. My Poppy saw us doing this one time and said I was a very weird princess. I try to ride Holy Toledo! every day and Tickety-Boo at least once a week so she doesn't get lonely. My Mumza thinks I don't take enough baths but she doesn't know about all the showers I get from Tickety-Boo when I ride her to the beach or the river and she stands in the water, sucks up about half a lagoon's worth and sprays me with it, which always makes me laugh. People think elephants are kinda sorrowful creatures but when I laugh, Tickety-Boo waves her trunk up and down and makes a little trumpety sound, which is her way of laughing along with me. I think she's pretty happy to be with me here on *Quietude*, even without any other elephants.

When I whistled her up, it was so we could go find PW. After Izzy and I had finished celebrating our victory over the Javelinas, he was gone and I realized he still had the not-a-flute. I couldn't stop thinking about it. Maybe he had already figured out what it was for. I sure couldn't.

We romped and stomped from the cottage to my best surfing beach. We call it No Hodaddies Allowed Beach. PW and I have been catching waves there since I was a tiny toddler. Tickety-Boo is a bit too hefty to shred but she loves walking out into the waves and cooling her heels. My Mumza does the same when she's here. One of the advantages to riding on an elephant is that from so high up you can see for a long way. I could tell right away that PW wasn't here. Sometimes he fishes in the ocean using just his hands—he's very quick—and sometimes he fishes in our rivers with a bow and arrow. He taught me how to make my own bow and he makes arrows for me and now sometimes we fish together in the Long Engagement River or the one called the Neverland Express and have fish fries at night on the beach. I waited for a little while, hoping he would bob up and see us, but we had the beach to ourselves. Then I saw my

47

Poppy's motorcar, Brigitte, go by in a flash of red and white down by the water. Two people were hanging off the running boards. It must have been Queenie and Mister Buchanan because they were both dressed up.

I thought maybe they were going to the Doubloon for a decree or to talk with Mister McKeever. My Mumza says I'm not supposed to go into the Doubloon but they always let me in anyway and give me maraschino cherries from behind the bar. If my Poppy isn't there, he can't *rat me out*, and if he is, we can't rat each other out, now can we? If I'd been riding Holy Toledo! I could have gone over there and tied him up at the hitching post in front, but Mister McKeever and some other dudes put up a sign that says No Pachyderms Allowed. *Pachyderm* means elephant. Since Tickety-Boo is the only elephant this side of India, wherever that might be, they must be talking about her. I think they're worried about her getting all rampageous and running through the Doubloon and knocking over all the tables and their drinks. They don't know her very well.

Taking care of Captain Primo's remuda isn't the only way I'm making ready to welcome him home. I've been teaching Tickety Boo to do a trick where she walks into the ocean until she's completely underwater, all except for the very tip of her trunk. Then she marches back and forth on the bottom of the sea breathing through her trunk as calm as you please just like people using a snorkel. It's like the only time I ever saw the Captain's real submarine submerged with its periscope poking up to take a look around. When he sees her spying on him from the water, he will know he is home.

I thought this was a good time to practice the trick, since I couldn't find PW and the Captain would be home in a week or so. I rode her out until we were past the breakers and she would be almost invisible from the shore. Then I slid off, which is the sign that she is to go one step farther so her back and head will be beneath the waves and to lift her trunk to breathe. Now that she knows to do it when I slide off, the next part will be for her to learn it by handclaps, so I can stand on the beach next to the Captain and see his face when Tickety-Boo goes all submersible. We worked on it until it was time for me to go back to the cottage to grab the ball bag full of uniforms for my fellow River Otters. We were about to play the Goofballs from Her Majesty's Grace and I wanted us to look our best.

48

Chapter Twelve

The folks who started this funky little country and the people who have moved here since have in common the desire to get away from money economies. They want to be able to think straight. That's really all there is to it. It's difficult to describe to someone who has lived on the mainland—any mainland, take your pick—his whole life what it's like to call a place such as *Quietude* home, to lay your head down at night and awaken in the morning in a land where, for instance, you will (almost) never hear the sound of an internal combustion engine turning over. You need to have escaped that ubiquitous annoyance for a while before you can measure the difference. Imagine: No revving autos, no rumbling trucks, no snarling exhausts, no squad cars blasting by or crowding your ass with lights a'flash, no flatulating motorcycles blaspheming against peace and quiet, no turbocharged anything. No rush hour freeways. No eighteen wheelers grinding up slow grades. No parking lots! No tailgating! No sirens! No diesels! No leaf-blowers! Instead of getting flipped off by irate motorists, you receive a cordial greeting from one of god's creatures. Instead of traffic, we have the lulling comfort of surf landing upon our shore. Oh, the sweet relief. For a time, while you're getting used to it, silence seems like some kind of bizarre sound effect. But gradually, with no anxiety about making the rent/mortgage/utility bills/mounting debt preying upon your mind, that mind begins to relax and you find that you can follow one thought with another. You may still be doomed but at least it's not on the installment plan.

I say *almost* because there is one (and only one) motor vehicle on *Quietude*: Brigitte, my 1932 Rolls Royce Phantom II woody. I hadn't taken her out for a spin in quite a while and there had been no medical emergencies calling for her services, so it occurred to me that her battery might be ebbing and in need of a charge. Jake and Creole accepted my offer to ferry them to our saloon in my luxury jalopy, though rather than sitting inside with the king, each chose to ride a running board on opposite sides of Brigitte, from which vantages they waved to one another and traded mildly lewd banter over the gentle breeze caused by my cruising along the shoreline at about ten miles per hour.

On the rare occasions that I take Brigitte out anymore, I like to follow the waterline (we have no roads, properly speaking, only paths and trails), letting the sea foam edge up to her white sidewalls. It's a perfect marriage and seems to satisfy something in me, though I could not say what. Small diversions come in handy, though, when my Bonny is away. Now I had what was beginning to feel like a very large diversion on my hands. And the timing was good. Since she was off at a conference, I wasn't burdened by the worries that beset me when her "guerrilla education" adventures lead her into possible cross-fires or cartel pistoleros. I found myself looking forward to meeting this outré Russian émigré and glad I had slid out of my caftan and into an old aloha shirt and jeans topped by a beautiful fur felt fedora, far more fitting for a man on a case. A caftan was all very well for lounging around the palace, but now I felt more like an old gumshoe than a king in his redoubt.

Just before we got to the Doubloon, I could swear I saw Wilder and her pet elephant, Tickety-Boo, strolling down toward the beach in my rearview mirror. I have only the one daughter and there's only one elephant in the country, so I'm pretty sure it was them, but they were too far away to hear a shout-out, so I contented myself with pulling up in front of our tiki-bar-style saloon and letting my passengers jump off. Creole, our national fashion plate, was wearing white cambric 1800s-style pantalettes and a lipstick red baby-doll that billowed most becomingly in the offshore breeze. It must have been the ensemble she had greeted her inamorata in before a brief and doubtless rambunctious reunion. Jake, a very spiffy fellow who, on his visits to *Quietude,* never lets our rather casual (i.e., slovenly) style of dress interfere with his own dandified sense of apparel, was a good match for her in white duck trousers, a clean, pressed French-cuffed shirt of Irish linen, a new Panama and tan woven Italian loafers. They were a smashing couple.

In most any afternoon or evening, my secretary's entrance would have caused a sensation among the lads, who rarely saw a fully dressed woman and found the sight curiously stimulating. But at the moment, the room was nearly unoccupied. One old gent, who looked like a prospector washed up from a gold rush at sea, was crashed out in a hammock, snoozing by way of postponing his hangover. The only person standing was a man of medium height in a shiny relic of a black three-piece suit and black shoes of shoddy manufacture with a well-trimmed Van Dyke beard and long silver hair combed straight back. He was standing at the bar, engrossed in conversation with a young lady lying thereupon. She was propped on one elbow, in cut-offs, topless and laughing at something he had just said. I thought she was one of our barmaids but it's hard for me to tell them apart. They are all very young, semi-nude and range from powerfully cute to excruciatingly beautiful. But since they don't wear tops that can accommodate name tags, I can never remember what to call them. This one had long blonde surfer girl hair and a beguiling laugh.

Rather than swinging her legs around and hopping down off the bar, she jumped up and bowed to me from above, a pretty sight. Most of the women and girls here bow to me when we meet. It may be sincere or may be ironical, I can't tell. But it always embarrasses me and then embarrasses me further when it occurs to me that a king ought not to blush. Jake, the investigative reporter, remembered her from his last visit. "Good morning, Marlowe," he said. Marlowe. Of course. As a once and future private dick, you'd think I would remember that one. "I've brought your ruler, such as he is."

"Your majesty," she said, and hopped down. "You do us honor, daddy-o." All the barmaids had taken to calling me daddy-o when they were feeling informal and not a one of them had ever felt the least bit formal so far.

"Good morning, Marlowe. You can't be on-shift, surely."

"No, not exactly. I slept over. I was out night surfing and then came over to help clean up and close the joint. I guess I fell asleep on the bar. Then this dude—" She pointed to the fellow in the shabby suit, "came in and I decided it must be happy hour at dawn's early light." He turned to me.

"Konstantin Smirnoff," he said. "At your service." He too bowed, but then stuck out a hand to shake, proving himself both a

51

monarchist and a democrat. In other words, a man prepared either to zig or to zag, depending on how he sized up the situation. I shook his hand and studied his face, cratered with pock marks ranging in size from a nickel to a quarter. Rather than making him ugly, though, they made him appear more worldly, as though through disfiguring experience, he'd seen and done things others had only read about. He had conniving eyes, conniving but sympathetic. Eyes that could see right through you but had decided to stop halfway, as though what they'd seen had given them pause. Then he met your eye and took an interest. It was like a carny trick you couldn't help falling for.

"Mister Smirnoff. Happy to make your acquaintance. Please call me Ace. Jake here has been telling me about you. Are you really related to the great Akhmatova?"

"Well, is not so much a blood relation as a, how would you say, *kinship of the spirit*." he smiled, pulling me into a small conspiracy. His voice was deep and theatrical, the Russian accent slathered on like so much caviar.

"And with the Smirnoff family? The distilling branch, perhaps?"

"With that family I once maintained a kinship of the *spirits*," he said. "But no longer. I am perhaps some sort of distant cousin, so whenever it was not inconvenient, I used to sample some of the product so as not to dishonor the family name. But during the reign of the pretender, Putin, I disdain to swallow any and all Russian beverages." He had a half-filled glass at his elbow, the liquid in it clear.

"Marlowe, would you be kind enough to refresh this gentleman's breakfast and set the rest of us up with coffee?"

"Sweetener?" She meant the Irish non-dairy creamer.

"Sure." She dumped a goodly amount of Grey Goose into Smirnoff's glass along with a couple of ice cubes, a dash of tonic and a big wedge of lime on the rim, then supplied the rest of us with French roast and Jameson's.

"Did you improvise that story about Putin and the escort with an iPhone? Just go with it off the top of your head?" He nodded, modestly.

"First time, yes. It jumped out of my mouth before I could stop to think. Thinking, I find, sometimes gets in the way, no? Thinking and the imagination, do they work together or try to work around each other? Hard to say. Is good story, yes? And might be true, too, if world was different, you know?"

"Different in what way?" He frowned into his glass.

"Different so as to be assembled more in accordance with our wishes—no, not wishes, *desires,* I think is the word in English—and not so much our what is the other word, *apprehensions?* These desires that the world has put into our heads but then same world denies," he said, contemplatively. "Perhaps these desires that have been denied are making ready another world, no?" He raised his glass, looked at me and seemed on the verge of proposing a toast but hesitated and asked, "May I run what you call a 'tab'?"

"Well, I suppose you could," I said, "but there's no way you could pay it."

"No?" I shook my head. "Well, is true I am a bit short of funds at the moment. We left Los Angeles in such a rush, I had no time to get to my bank, but..."

"You misunderstand, good sir. We have no use for money here. We don't accept the stuff."

"In that case, Nostrovia! He downed his second or third or fourth round of breakfast with dispatch and sighed happily. "Your associate, Mister Buchanan, told me that your island nation is, and I quote, 'a sort of half-assed paradise.' Now that I have been here for a while, I begin to see what he meant, only I think is more fully assed than he said."

"Well, thank you, I think."

"I am here to help your majesty in any way I can," said Smirnoff. "Please tell me how I might be of assistance."

"Well, Mister Smirnoff, it might help me to get your take on the two my friend Jake thinks are headed this way. Do you believe they were merely trying to take advantage of your credulity or is there really a treasure and are they hurrying here to lay claim to it?"

"They may be here already," he said. "As to their sincerity, it can be measured, I think, by the woman's sympathy for the people of Ukraine. She has a sort of rapacity for justice, I believe, and is, like myself, a sworn enemy of the pretender Putin. This I saw in her eyes, and it made her a countrywoman of my heart. Every day more Russians turn against this blustering fool, not wishing to watch their country turn into monstrosity factory. I would say treasure is actual, or at least that man and woman are convinced is so."

"And you think she can be trusted?"

"Like us all, she can be trusted to remain true to her nature. And this nature is, I should say, a passionate one. She wishes to, what is the word, *transmute* her indignation into useful action. And she will remain true to her *dis*trust of her traveling companion. She told me in confidence that he cares only for the money." He paused, reflectively. "I am also thinking I have seen this woman before. Or not same woman, but girl who looked like woman. Young daughter, perhaps. But I cannot say when, or where. Is getting closer, the memory," he said. "Is like goldfish swimming around in bowl. Every time it goes by, I can almost catch it, and the time between its passings is growing shorter and shorter. Soon circularity of goldfish will end in my hand.""

"You must be tired after the long journey out, Mister Smirnoff. Let me show you to your quarters."

Chapter Thirteen

I can sort of remember when I was seven, or five or even four. Maybe three, but maybe not. But before that there was a tiny toddler and before her a little baby who was me and I feel like I never even met her! That would be a good invention, I thought, a machine that shows you what you thought when you were a tiny baby. Do babies even think, I wonder, or do they just poop and gurgle and want to be fed and then go to sleep? My Mumza and my Poppy always tell me I was such a happy baby but maybe they're making it up so I won't feel bad about being a cranky baby who cried all the time. They tell me I was born at sea, but basically I'm a child of *Quietude*, I've lived here my whole life so why wouldn't I be happy? Not many girls out in the great world have their own horse much less an elephant or a baseball team. Before I had all these horses to take care of, I went on lots of trips with my Mumza when she was being the leader of White Ops and as far as I can tell the great world is mostly about telephones and automobiles. People yelling into the phones and pounding their fists on the steering wheels of the automobiles. It's very noisy. I don't get it. It felt like people were charging at me all the time, the way ballplayers do when they are having what's called a *rhubarb* and the rhubarb turns into what is called a *donnybrook* with all the players on both teams clearing the benches and rushing out to the mound to take big swings at each other and fall down. I do like riding in airplanes and looking down at the clouds. That's about it for me.

When my Mumza is off traveling without me, I'm supposed to stay at the palace with my Poppy, but I need to go to the cottage early to feed and water Holy Toledo!. So I went up into his majesty's bedroom, aka the King's Chamber, on the top floor and gave him a little kiss to say goodbye. Half asleep, he mumbled and grumbled in his persnickety way and I let him smell my hair which he always says smells like "a little bit of heaven right here on earth," whatever that might mean. Then I jumped off the observation platform where he keeps his telescope and into the lagoon, my favorite way of waking up. I made a zip line with nylon rope that runs from the platform down to our cottage, but since I was already in the lagoon and didn't want to climb back up, I ran all the way down the hill to dry my hair and say good morning to my horse.

My Mumza and I planted lavender all around the cottage and the paddock after she read about how the smell of it helps to calm horses. I know it's true because I can tell by the slower way Holy Todedo! is breathing when I put my hands on his neck and he sort of nuzzles me back. By now, I don't even need to keep him on a tether or in the paddock. He will walk out and all around the cottage where he can smell the lavender and wait for me. I guess for him the lavender is *a little bit of heaven right here on earth.*

My special treat, saved for my best boy, is when friends in the US of A send tall round boxes of Quaker Oats, which I feed to him in secret. Not even Izzy or my Mumza know about this. We don't grow oats on *Quietude* and there are never enough sent to share them with the Captain's remuda. I give them hay and mangoes and apples and bananas and breadfruit and papaya and passion fruit and kiwis and soursop and even the black sapote that tastes like chocolate pudding. But no Quaker Oats. Those are only for the big fella with the thundering hooves. Someday I guess I'm supposed to love a man with my whole heart but really I could only love him with *most* of my heart because my whole heart can only belong to an Arabian stallion. I'm not sure why they have to be a secret. I guess I don't want the other horses to feel bad about not getting any Quaker Oats. Once when I was sneaking a handful to Holy Toledo! Tickety-Boo wandered up to catch da haps and I gave her a little so she wouldn't feel left out. She made a low rumbling sound after eating the oats that felt like a big version of the purring a cat made when I petted it one time on a visit to Rome with my Mumza. We don't have any cats here on *Quietude*, or any dogs either unless you count coyotes and you better not try to pet them. Right now I needed to hike back up to Daffadowndilly and pick up those uniform trousers.

"I hope I got the sizes right," said Bess, holding her hands to her face as though she were distressed.

"Mine fit just fine," I said. "So I guess the others will too." My

Poppy and Mister McKeever had designed the pants to look like the ones old-timey ballplayers like Babe Ruth and Satchel Paige wore in the bigs. Instead of going all the way down to the tops of our cleats, they were what's called *bloused* at the knees to show off our long sox. A blouse is a kind of top that women out in the great world wear to stay warm, I guess. In other countries it's not so hot as here. I don't know how a woman's top could be confused with a ballplayer's trousers but I do know we're going to look plenty sharp with our cleats and caps and new uniforms.

"Oh, Wilder dear," said Bess, as we sat down to tea. "Since you asked about the gentlemen who built our cottages, the ones I call the 'slow nomads,' I thought you'd like to know that one of them has returned."

"Only one?" I asked. "Didn't you say there were six?"

"Yes, I did. And so there were. But the one who has returned tells me that the others have scattered to the four winds. That would make it zero point eighty winds apiece, unless my skills at mathematics have deserted me. They lost touch, I believe, just like we cannot seem to get back in touch with the vicar." I had heard Bess speak on this subject before. The vicar was the ladies of Daffadowndilly's old *minister* back in England. A minister, my Poppy explained to me, is a person who tells you what god wants you to do. How the minister knows this in the first place is a mystery to my Poppy. Anyway, the ladies had been inviting and expecting the vicar for many years now, but he seems to be taking his own sweet time. I think Bess may have a crush on the vicar, like Izzy does on Mogu Mogu, but it's not the kind of thing it's polite to ask about.

"What kind of tea is this, Bess? It's very good."

"It's called Lapsang souchong, Wilder dear. It's from China. Lapsang souchong means—" Bess hesitated and then in the voice people use when they are reciting from memory, said, 'standing mountain small strain,' though I don't have the faintest idea what that refers to. Straining the tea, perhaps? It's very strong, don't you find?"

"Yes, it is, but not so strong as the coffee my Poppy makes. I took a sip of that stuff one time and I buzzed around like I was stealing bases all day." Bess gave me a worried look.

"Oh, I'm sure you would never steal anything, Wilder dear. Besides, here on *Quietude*, I don't think it's possible to steal anything.

Though, come to think of it, I cannot seem to find my favorite pair of shears. But I don't think anyone took them. Apart from my neighbor ladies, the only people who have been here are you and the soldier of fortune and his female companion. And I don't believe either baseball players or soldiers of fortune are much given to gardening. I fear I am growing a bit absent-minded. Maybe that's what has been happening to our dear vicar, and he just forgets to visit." She sighed. "More tea, dear?"

"No thank you, ma'am, I mean Bess," I said. "I should be getting back. We have a game this afternoon against the Goofballs. They're the team in first place and we're in second only one game behind them. If we win this afternoon, we'll be tied for first."

"Well, being tied sounds nice," said Bess. I believe she was still thinking of the vicar.

Chapter Fourteen

Here on *Quietude*, our young women are almost as beautiful as our old women. Our young men are as beautiful as our young women. Our old men are just old men, they undergo no magical transformations, though they don't piss and moan and bellyache so much as old men everywhere else. They still have all the usual regrets, but they stretch them out in the telling, they stretch them out and study them, as you would with hands on the map of a new world. They study them and then stop and shake their heads as if to say, These are good regrets. They took a lifetime to collect. If I didn't have them, I couldn't remember them. And then they amble off down the beach. I should know. I'm one of them.

Old poets are a little like old gun-fighters. There aren't many around. Wild-catting for words, it's a strange business. You recognize the material as it arrives, you recognize it as something that belongs to you, temporarily, anyhow. That's all you can do. You don't know where it came from. You don't know where it's going after it's done with you, only that it's stopping in your head for a moment and that you damn well better get it down. Otherwise, you cannot sleep. And if you cannot sleep, you cannot dream. And if you cannot dream, why would the material ever come to you?

I couldn't remember if I'd stopped writing about the time I stopped sleeping. Recently, I've begun to write again for the first time in years. Not what they call "journaling," or keeping a record of the growth of our fledgling country, I'll leave that for younger hands. And no fully formed poems, only here and there in a notebook the first lines of poems I never finish. What I do write now (and no one ever reads) are letters to my family. It's a habit I picked up when I was away from them for a few weeks in southern California a couple of years ago. I missed them so fiercely I could barely concentrate on the case I was trying to solve, something to do with abduction and bloody murder. Actually, there were two cases and I couldn't concentrate on either. I sat up all night in the room above a tiki bar where I was living and wrote these desperate letters. The content of the letters wasn't desperate, only their author. I was desperate to reestablish my connection to my daughter and my fiancée-for-life. I wrote chatty nonsense about old friends with whom I was reunited and happy reminiscences about Wilder's early years. I knew when I posted the letters the next morning I might beat them home. That became my strongest motivation to solve the case. Getting mail to *Quietude* is a slow process and I thought if I got back there first, I could tear them up and keep from embarrassing myself. Luckily, they were delivered to the palace while Bonny and Wilder were bunking at the cottage, so I found them myself and destroyed the evidence of how pathetically lonely I had been. Now I was doing it again, pouring my heart out to the people I loved best. Maybe I would put them in a cedar chest for my family to find after I was long gone.

Bonny seemed to be amused at the way this dissolute old scribbler and part-time private eye had landed on his feet as the king of a newly minted south Pacific island nation. I could no longer be destitute since *Quietude* goes about its business without the encumbrance of an economy. But I was still not what you'd call "handy around the house." I could neither cook nor make the simplest of repairs. A good thing I was the king. I did make good coffee, but my daughter, at nine, knew her way around the kitchen better than her doddering dad. I had spent too many years concentrating on the poetic line as though trying to start a fire with moonlight and a magnifying glass.

I've never been one for meditation unless you can count the state of mind I enter when I lean against the mighty Wurlitzer jukebox that sits under a palm tree right outside of the palace. It was left to me, inadvertently, by my old friend, Elmer Wheeler, upon his passing. I found it under a ratty tarp in his cluttered compound when I was searching for a murder weapon. The Wurlitzer turned out to be the opposite of a murder weapon: It fires life into me on sleepless nights when Bonny is away. On sleepless nights when she is beside me at our cottage at the foot of the Grieving Widow, I have her permission to draw the comforter down off her and contemplate until the comfort is all mine.

But when she is gone and I must admit that no dreams await me, I put on a robe and climb down to the Wurlitzer. In the pocket of the robe is a highly specialized lock-pick made from a muselet (the wire cage that fits over a champagne cork) that Cassidy McKeever designed to hot-wire (as it were) the Wurlitzer. You can get three songs for a quarter but I can never keep track of coins. Since we don't use money, the only use for quarters is to activate the jukebox. I pick the lock and release the quarters and select three songs that suit my mood.

Now here is an odd thing: Elmer and I, so far as I can recall, never discussed music, never championed this band or that singer or player or went into nostalgic reveries about which numbers had ushered us into first love. He was a political firebrand and lifelong rabble rouser and I wouldn't have taken him for a man impassioned about song. But once I had cleaned off the Wurlitzer and plugged it into a generator, I realized, to my growing astonishment, that our musical tastes were as one. I felt like I had programmed the box myself. And the songs were all on 45 rpm records! Just like when I'd first discovered Elvis and Chuck Berry and Bo Diddley and Buddy Holly and they led the way to Dylan and the Beatles and the Stones and all the world-shaking commotion that followed.

When the Wurlitzer's mechanism lifts the platter into place, the needle meets it and it begins to spin, I am fourteen again, not quite kissless yet uninitiated still into the mysteries of what was then called "heavy petting." As long as the songs continue, I am that age, waiting, like my daughter, with elation bordering on ecstasy, waiting with fear aligned to an almost unholy glee, to see what happens next.

My three choices were Leonard Cohen's "The Stranger Song," "When I Get to Heaven," by John Prine and Mark Knopfler and Emmylou Harris doing "If This Is Goodbye," from *All the Roadrunning*. I wanted Mister Smirnoff to get enough bed rest to recover from the long trip out, but I knew that time was, as they say, of the essence and we needed to make something happen. The "device" seemed to be the essential ingredient to a successful search and seizure. If we could get to it first, we would own the high ground. Of course, having no idea what form it took or where it might be found, much less how to operate it were not working in our favor. Jake knew the island pretty well, but he spent little time here and most of it with his lady fair in her tower known as the "Idyll Dipper." And I still hadn't crossed paths with PW. He knew the island in a way we could not. For the rest of us, our home turf was beautiful unto breathtaking and helped us to be carefree. For him, a landscape was something you read for your life. He paid it the closest attention. Again, I wondered what he was up to. Before I could decide on my next three songs, Creole and Jake showed up, with Mister Smirnoff, looking a bit bleary, in tow. I had prepared a thermos of sweetened coffee to buck up our guest, who looked quite grateful when I offered him a cup of high octane go-power.

"Did you bring your steno pad, Brat?" It was our old game. For many a year, whether we were on a case or just kicking around together, she would whip out pad and pen and pretend to take notes. I never saw any notes, you understand. After a minute, she would set the pad aside and take out an emery board, using it to file and shape her nails. I never could figure out where upon her person she concealed the emery boards.

"Yowza, Boss" she said, " employing a word she only brought out when we were on a case.

"Let us suppose, young Buchanan, that you are basically right in these outlandish assumptions. If there is treasure to be found on *Quietude*, how it came to be here and how the hunters got wind of it are questions we can, for the time being, consider deep background for the article and book you've already contracted to write. I would love to know, but we don't need to know right now. Brat, you know our island better than I, being an ardent hiker. Wilder knows it extraordinarily well, having learned it on foot, on horse and on elephant back as well. But she will be preparing for her next game. I will try to convince her third base coach, the only real tracker among us, to sign on with the hunt, or at least to take part in it on his own." Even more than the rest of us Quietudians? (Quietudinarians? Thus far, there is no agreement on this important question. Wilder prefers the term *Quietude* Dudes), he would not regard treasure as being of value, but he would know it for something foreign to our soil. "When next I see the Otter's captain, I'll ask her to bring him round." Meanwhile, let's do the island version of getting out and knocking on doors."

Chapter Fifteen

Buck O'Neil Field, bottom of the seventh, River Otters 9, Goofballs 8.

"Heybatterheybatterheybatter*swing*batter!" All the River Otters chattered together, myself included. This time I was standing at short where Izzy usually stands and rooting her on as she pitched for the first time. She took over after five innings when my arm started to feel like it was about to fall off. In a fifty-game season, you really need more than one pitcher, but we had gotten into the habit of me starting every game and then picking out a teammate to *mop up* for me. None of the others had turned out to be real *flame-throwers* or born *closers*, which are things you call a relief pitcher that no hitters can catch up to. In fact, we should have played the last two innings with three of four catchers instead of just one. Well, none of my fellow Otters have been coached by Mister McKeever, so it isn't surprising that they are a little wild or bounce everything in front of the plate or hit more batters than the batters have a chance to hit balls. I do like filling in at the different positions because it makes me what's called *versatile*.

I glanced into the tree behind home and noticed that my Poppy still wasn't up there in his beach chair sipping from his thermos and Queenie still wasn't on the sideline in her old sedan chair with four young gentlemen holding it up for her and two surfer dudes holding big palm leaves over her for shade. When we play the Goofballs, it is necessary for her to stay what is called *neutral*, since they are from her own village of Her Majesty's Grace, but I, team captain of the River Otters, am her goddaughter. But today neither of them were even here. My Poppy has never missed one of our games before, not ever, and Queenie is usually turns up to cheer for both teams at the same time. I know that her beau, Mister Buchanan, is here for a visit, so maybe that's why she is missing, but what about my Poppy? This is game number fifty, the last day of the season, unless we win and there is a playoff. I couldn't worry about it right now, though, because I needed to calm Izzy down. I strolled over to the mound.

"Hey, Izz, you're doing great," I said. "That last pitch made it all the way to the backstop. That means you're bringing some serious heat." She didn't look pleased by my attempts at encouragement. Her right arm gets the job done at short, but it's different throwing off a mound. It's downhill instead of level and you have to worry about beaning the batter instead of just beating a runner. "You don't have to throw quite so hard, Izz. Half as much giddy-up is enough to blow it by these guys. If they're lucky enough to get some wood on it, we're right here with you. Trust your fielders." My Poppy has taught me that for every situation in baseball, there is a *cliché* you can fall back on. A cliché is a word or a phrase that's kind of tired out but in baseball all of them are true anyway. I thought of another one. "Throw strikes but don't give 'em anything good to hit." I patted her on the butt and jogged back to short.

There were runners at the corners and only one out. If both of the runners score, our dreams of glory are done for. With a measly one run lead, we needed a double play in the worst way. Izzy checked the runners. I had taught her how to pitch from the stretch, but I saw she had forgotten and gone into a full wind-up. The runner on first decided to try to steal second, getting a great jump and making it easily, rounding the bag just as the runner on third decided that Izzy pitching from a wind-up gave him just the advantage he needed to try to swipe home, making it a double-steal and sealing the deal. He lit out like he'd just gulped some of my Poppy's coffee as soon as she reached her arms over her head, getting ready to rear back and put everything she had into her next delivery. It gave him an extra instant to reach home before the ball and our catcher's tag. But the batter wasn't paying attention to the runner. He only had eyes for the ball headed his way. Izzy managed to groove one, right down the pipe, and he *lambasted* it. But since she had followed my advice and taken a little off the pitch, he was out in front of it and lashed a wicked liner right at his teammate who was streaking toward home plate with the tying run. Well, he didn't streak for long. Not after being sucker punched in the *bread basket* (what us ballplayers call your stomach) by a line drive from about twenty feet away.

64

"Oof," he said, and went down hard, curled around the ball, which meant he was out. It also meant the ball was dead. So there were two outs but they had a runner on third, since the dude who had stolen second had gone ahead and taken third as well. He looked quite pleased to be there all by himself. But I had seen him rounding the second base bag when he'd stolen it. I had looked at him and looked at the umpire to see where he was looking. These two things happened about a half a second apart, a bang-bang play only without there really being a play. I walked over to the mound, took the ball from Izzy and strolled easy as a cool breeze toward second. Once the fallen runner was carried into the dugout, the ump, a big mellow Samoan dude named Iakopo, called out "Play ball!" That was my cue. I tagged the bag with my toe and the ump jerked his thumb into the air to declare the runner on third out for never touching second base on his way by. Talk about a double play in the worst way! But it counted. We were tied for first.

Even so, Izzy couldn't stop crying. I think she thought the line drive dude was dead. She may have talked a lot of trash, but she was really a tender-hearted girl. "Izz, *you* didn't hit the ball that struck that baserunner."

"I know," she said, sniffling. "But I *threw* the ball that the other dude hit that hit the poor baserunner dude and knocked him down to the ground. I don't think I like pitching. Can I just play short from now on, Cap?"

"Sure. Look, he's sitting up. He's all right."

"Okay," she said. Maybe I should take him some breadfruit pudding or something."

'That would be a very *magnanimous* gesture," I said, glad of the chance to use that fine word for the first time. But what I was thinking was that I needed to feed my horse and find my Poppy and Queenie and where on earth was PW? We played the whole game without a third base coach. As soon as I thought of him, I wondered if he had taken the not-a-flute with him. Were they still together? More than anything, I wish my Mumza was here. We could pile up all my favorite blankets and pillows on the big bed in the cottage and she could tell me about her travels in the great world. In a way, it was even better than when I got to go with her, because she told the stories so well and always brought me the softest new blankets from

65

all the different countries. Being a team captain in the Windward League is very tiring. I sure could use a good long snuggle with my Mumza. Still, the River Otters deserve a celebration.

"Let's not keep the waterfall waiting, Mizz Izz."

Chapter Sixteen

The given name of the man I had mentioned could only be pronounced in the clicking tongue of the San people of the Kalahari Desert in southern Africa, known popularly as African Bushmen. Many years ago, while searching for the origins of language, we had accidentally lured him into our orbit when a small party of us were foolishly exploring in his homeland and become stranded. Seemingly out of nowhere, this small handsome person had appeared and led us to safety. As a token of gratitude, I had given him a picture postcard of the Pacific Ocean off the coast of California that turned up in my satchel. Neither he nor any of his people had ever set eyes on the sea, but he lit up instantly. A decision was made deep in his being. After trading a few words with a small band of his compatriots, he hoisted his bow, a duiker skin quiver of arrows, an ostrich egg of drinking water and made it clear to me that he wished to join our expedition. My attempts to ascertain why he wanted to decamp and tramp off into the unknown with a group of strangers were met only with his repeatedly pointing at the postcard. It quickly became evident that he wanted to meet the sea. It must have been a nearly otherworldly moment for him, looking at this representation of a body of water equal in breadth to the desert vastness of his homeland, where surface moisture was virtually unknown. Only the occasional subsurface "sip wells," from whence water could be drawn up through long tubes by one strong of lung allowed his people to traverse this all but trackless waste.

After a long ocean voyage, which he spent mostly at the rail, staring out to sea, utterly enraptured, we ended up on the island of Maui. One morning, standing on a north shore beach, he found an untended surfboard stuck in the sand. He looked at the board, looked out to sea, picked up the board, marched out into the waves, pushed past the breakers and began to use the board for its intended purpose. He had never seen a single living soul surfing. But once he saw the board, the rest followed naturally.

He took up baseball in the same way. As soon as any man (or a rough and tumble tomboy) closes his or her fingers around a baseball, that person knows what it is for: to be thrown with optimum velocity and accuracy to a designated destination. When PW (after he had initiated himself into the surfing life, we had tagged him with the nickname of Permanent Wave, eventually abbreviated to its initials) wandered onto the ball field where Cassidy McKeever and I were playing for a minor league team that year, he picked up a ball rolling toward him, looked at it as though it might have been the selfsame ostrich egg of years gone by, saw me waving to him from first base and winged it to me straight and true as though he had woken up and taken infield drill every day of his life.

At the plate, with a bat in his hand, he remained a hunter-gatherer at heart, his swings as selective as the firing of arrows he had once used to feed his people. Sometimes, he would watch serenely as three consecutive pitches rode through the heart of the strike zone and never take the bat off his shoulder. But when the game was on the line and runners in scoring position—and despite our never explaining the rules and objectives of the game to him—he would invariably pick out a pitch to his liking and slap it through the infield. In either case, he remained unfailingly merry and bright. He had become one of Wilder's closest friends and earliest surfing mentors, carrying her, at age three, on his shoulders as he carved waves and shot curls with one hand on her ankle. She was now one of the finest shredders on the island and PW one of the best in all the world. Tubular characters from all nations came here just to see the man dance with the elements. When they left, it was never for long. *Quietude* often has that effect on people.

We were working our way east, stopping to talk with various of our neighbors and keeping our eyes peeled for anyone out of the ordinary or anything that might be described as a "device," when Creole, a far more vigorous walker than I, brought her flyboy to a halt in the middle of a sunlit meadow. I recognized the spot. The trail we were using had been formed, I thought, by my daughter's feet. It was where she scythed tall grass to be carried down to Plunderland for Captain Primo's remuda. We had come upon a bare patch which

Wilder's own hand had denuded of greenery that it might one day become hay. My secretary hadn't stopped because, like her king and Mister Smirnoff, she needed a breather. She and Jake, I soon learned, had come up short in order to inspect a body lying at their feet. A few steps later, it became clear to me that the body's owner hadn't decided to take a late morning nap or passed out from following Mister Smirnoff's liquid breakfast regimen. A more likely explanation for the fellow's stubborn recumbency was the large pair of scissors that had been plunged into his chest.

Chapter Seventeen

Usually, the waterfall washes all my troubles away. But right now, even while it was washing I was wishing I had learned more of the clicking language of PW's people in southern Africa. If I get really good at it, maybe I can click him into telling me if he had cracked the code of the not-a-flute. Of course, I will see him at the next game. At least I'm pretty sure he'll show up and bring the good old thing. The Otters have begun to believe it brings us luck.

As long as it's helping us to win, I figure I can wait to show it to my Poppy. If I don't grow up to be a ballplayer in the bigs, maybe I can be a private eye, and making sense of the bamboozler could be the way I prove myself worthy. Or maybe I'll be a marine biologist like Poppy Tobago, or a teacher like my Mumza, or a movie director like Mister Buchanan. Or a queen, of course, but I think you can be the queen of *Quietude* and still do other stuff too. But as the Otters' captain, my responsibility now is to my team. If the series goes to three games, all we have to do is win the ones we play at home and the first Crown of *Quietude* will be ours. Years from now, when I am older, little kids with their first baseball gloves will talk about us like I talk about Satchel Paige and Fernando Valenzuela and other legends that my Poppy has acquainted me with. Dudes I have never seen but feel like I watched them play.

Right then I remembered that I'd been promising Izzy a ride on Holy Toledo!. I had said that it would be a fun way to celebrate winning the Crown, but if I took her for a ride today, I could give her one on Tickety-Boo if we emerge victorious from the Championship Series. It would be like what my Mumza calls *getting bumped up to first class* when we go flying off on White Ops missions, Tickety-Boo not being better, you understand, only bigger. So she could hear me over the waterfall, I yelled right into Izzy's ear, telling her to meet me in Daffadowndilly and she'd get a big surprise. I said it with a lot of exclamation marks in my voice because little kids love exclamation marks. "I'll meet you at Bess's cottage, Mizz Izz!!!" She's a very slow

70

walker. She stops a lot to throw rocks or mangoes or papayas or guavas into the air and catch them in her glove. But she's a very fast runner and I knew the promise of a surprise would make her motor like never before. There was something I needed to talk to Bess about but it should be just her and me. I had been putting it off but I didn't want it in my head when I was supposed to be concentrating on our next game. If I rode over and Izzy ran after me, I could buy just enough time to meet up with her after I had *unburdened* myself to Bess. I thought Izzy's first horseback ride would make up for me abandoning my good old shortstop without explaining why.

Izzy is my sidekick, Queenie is my godmother, Laurelai is my soul-sister, my Mumza has raised me to persist in the face of hardship and to always choose kindness, and my Poppy has taught me to fear nothing (except for maybe the tiny spiders that crawl onto my Poppy's Wurlitzer), but I couldn't talk to any of them about this, especially my dad. Bess, bless her, is my god-grandmother, and I thought she would know what I should do.

I put Holy Toledo! into a full gallop.

"Wilder, dear, what a pleasant surprise! If I had known you were coming, I would have made a fresh pot of tea. I do, however, have a pitcher of lemonade in my ice-box. Would you care for a glass? And I expect I can scare up a biscuit."

"Yes, ma'am, I mean Bess. That sounds mighty fine."

"And can I get your horse anything?" We both looked out the window and saw Holy Toledo! browsing nose to the ground among some fallen apples beside a bright orange plot of daffodils.

"I think he's decided to help himself," I said. "Such is the way with Arabian stallions." Bess probably knew I had something on my mind because I couldn't stop fidgeting. I took a sip of lemonade, set the glass down, started to speak, picked up the glass again, took another sip, and finally said, "This is good. Thank you, ma'am, I mean Bess." She smiled her sweet smile. I still couldn't figure out how to start. She pretended not to notice how nervous I was.

"So what brings you all the way out here, Wilder dear?" she said. "Surely you're not riding to hounds, for we have no foxes, nor any hounds either." She smiled her gentle smile. "Barbaric practice that. One of the things I do not miss about my mother country."

"No, ma'am, I mean Bess. I should think you wouldn't." She smiled again.

"One day I shall be calling you 'ma'am,'" she said. "For you will be my queen. Though, to be proper, one says 'Majesty' first and 'ma'am' afterwards. That is the protocol, I think."

"But Bess, I like it so when you call me *Wilder, dear.* Couldn't we just keep doing it that way when I, well, you know, what you said. It could be our secret."

"If you wish, Wilder dear. I've never shared a secret with a queen." This was my chance.

"That's kind of what I've been wanting to talk to you about, Bess. The whole queen thing." I took a deep breath. "I don't think I'm ready. For one thing, I'm not tall enough."

"Well, dear, you are only nine years of age at the present time. I foresee growth spurts on the horizon. Both your mother and father are fairly tall, are they not?"

"Yes. My Mumza is one of the tallest of all the ladies on *Quietude.* My dad calls her his soft giraffe. And he sometimes calls himself *a towering figure.* Though he's usually lying down when he says that."

"Well, there you have it, dear. Before too long, your subjects will be looking up at you."

"That *before too long* part is just what I'm worried about, Bess. My poppy keeps talking about how old he is."

"Oh, Wilder, dear child, your father is younger than I. And you don't think I'm about to leave you any time soon, do you?" I shook my head. "Probably he's just tired at the end of the day. It's true that the years do begin to weigh on one. Here's what you do. The next time you see his majesty, give him a big hug and tell him what a good father he is and I expect he will feel like his younger self again in no time."

"Okay, I can do that. But there's more. I asked my friend, Creole, my dad's used-to-be secretary who is also the used-to-be queen, which is why I call her Queenie, how you're supposed to do it, be the queen I mean, and she said she only was one for a year and mostly just goofed off. She treated it like one of those things that are sort of a joke and sort of a bird."

"A lark?"

"Yeah, one of those. So what I really need is for someone to give

72

me queen lessons. I know where you came from there was a woman who was the queen for a really long time. If you got to see her doing her stuff, I was thinking maybe you could give me some pointers and I could practice. Like when Mister McKeever showed me how to grip my curveball and my scroojie." Bess smiled her biggest smile yet.

"I would be honored, Wilder dear, to tutor you in the ways of royalty. We have made a good start with the Queen's manner of waving to her subjects. At our next meeting, we shall work on carriage and demeanor. Oh, I think your friend is here. She looks quite out of breath."

"So what's the big surprise, Cap?" Izzy was still flushed from running all the way from the waterfall to Daffadowndilly, a distance of about two miles. She was still kind of shy about coming into the cottage, so Bess sent me out with a glass of lemonade for my shortstop. She gulped it greedily and I made the double-clicking sound with my tongue against the roof of my mouth that calls Holy Toledo!. He walked right over to me. Usually, riders make that sound when they give a light touch with their heels to their horse's ribs to make the animal go. But HT and I are so closely connected that he knows to come when I do it. I wish I could nicker like him so we could talk together like two horses, but I don't think even PW, who can imitate almost any living creature can do that. One time when he was with me, I made the double-clicking sound to call HT and PW answered me in Bushman! I don't know if that counted as a conversation or not.

"It's time to go for your first horseback ride, Izz. We'll start at a walk, proceed to a canter, and when we hit the beach, we can let Holy Toledo! all the way out and it will be about the finest feeling you've ever had." I was very relieved after my talk with Bess, and I knew that charging down the beach on my best boy, the receding surf lapping around his ankles, would blow any other worries I had clean out of my head. Izzy looked up at the saddle with her head cocked to one side.

"How do I get up there, Cap? And where do I sit? On your shoulders?"

"No, Izz. That would be pretty awkward. You'll sit in front of me on the saddle." I wanted to be able to hold on to her.

73

"Can I help you steer?" She's from Australia, and so is used to the language of automobile drivers.

"Yes, my dear shortstop, I will let you handle the reins after we get going." I didn't think she could lift her foot into the stirrup. "Let me give you a leg up." After we'd settled into the saddle, we started slow but I could tell right away that Izzy was born to go horseback. Holy Toledo! likes cutting loose and running for all he's worth better than anything. After he had galloped hard down our longest beach, me holding tight to Izzy while she gave my boy free rein, we rode back over to what my teammates and I call the *Otterfall* and the three of us let the tumbling water wash off the dust and sweat of the trail. To go with Izzy's first ride, it was HT's first time under the falls. A good thing he's so sure-footed. I could tell by the way he lifted his head to be splashed that he liked it plenty.

"There's just no aka for that," said Izzy. "It was like nothing else on earth."

Chapter Eighteen

"They're not scissors. They're gardening shears," said Creole, who should know. She keeps a rooftop garden at the top of her tower, along with several beehives. Mostly, she grows vegetables but also experiments with herbs and flowers new to this part of the world, cross-pollinating to keep them pest resistant.

"I'll take your word for it, not being a man of the soil," I said. "But of more immediate importance, I think you'll agree, is the state of the guy's health." Mister Smirnoff walked up and peered down at the one on the ground, kneeling and checking for vital signs.

"I'm afraid this man is what you might call *futureless*," he said.

"Dead, to us laymen," said Jake. "Though, even without a pulse or breath in his body, I think we can consider him our first lead." Lead to what? I wondered.

"Do any of you recognize him?" I said. We all knew that, though we should have been mourning the loss of the stranger, Jake and I were really hoping to peg him as one of the two treasure-hunters, reducing their number to one. It would make our job easier, after all, if we needed to keep track of a lone suspect rather than a pair of suspicious characters.

"I wouldn't know him from Yogi Berra," said Jake.

"How about you, Brat?"

"Fraid not, Boss."

"What about the shears?"

"They're not mine. That's really all I can tell you about them, other than the fact that they look very old."

"I most certainly have seen this man," said Mister Smirnoff. "Is one from Beanery of Barney. A drinker of light beer," he rolled his eyes quite eloquently, "meaning of course no disrespect to the recently departed." Despite myself, I was beginning to enjoy the way the émigré expressed himself.

"Well, that would make him one of the treasure hunters," I said, "and suggest that his partner, now former partner, might be nearby."

"If so, she would stand out," said Creole. "I know everyone who lives here." It was true. I knew my family and my old friends and had met many of my subjects, some of whom I remembered when we met a second time. But sometimes, reintroductions were called for. My secretary had a way with both names and faces and never forgot a living soul.

The man in question wasn't bad looking, apart from being dead. He was deeply tanned, somewhere in his mid-forties, with long dark hair I suspected of being styled and three of four days' worth of beard, trimmed to the exacting standards of the film industry. It's hard to judge a man's height when he's lying down, but he looked pretty *long*, at any rate. Nothing about him rang any bells, however, and a quick check of his pockets turned up no papers of identification. I closed his eyes.

"We need to get him in the ground," said my secretary, who can be practical when it's called for. "There are scavengers in these parts."

"Right you are," said Jake. "But we have no shovels and your king has a bad back. "What say we cover the late Mister Anonymous here with brush and send some of those big young Samoans back as a burial detail. Let's get a read on the longitude and latitude, shall we?" Creole always carried a compass and chronometer on her walks. It occurred to me that Wilder might swing through on one of her hay-gathering missions, which meant we had no time to lose. I didn't want her to stumble over a butchered stranger in the early stages of decomposition. As soon as I thought of her, I realized I was supposed to be attending her ballgame at Buck O'Neil Field.

"I have to go."

Her mother would never forgive me and I would never forgive myself. As for Wilder, she would wave off my dereliction with a blasé hand but the pain of my failure would follow her for life. It would be imprinted. Because I didn't *show* up, she would *grow* up to marry some inconsiderate bastard who couldn't keep his word but could be counted on to let her down. And it wasn't as if I could claim to be working a homicide. I hadn't known about the slain gentleman when we'd set out. I'd allowed myself to be swayed by a fairy story about some fabulous treasure and abandoned my girl. My memory of the River Otters' record was returning. Today's game was the last of the season, unless they won and forced a one-game playoff. But wait. Maybe the game was still going! If I arrived late it would still be all right so long as I was there when the Otters carried the day. And if victory was not claimed, I could invite all her teammates up to the palace for a movie showing. I wondered if the ancient Polynesians had a god of extra innings to whom I could apply for an extension.

But when I arrived at the field, the crowd had melted away, leaving only a young Samoan whose name, I remembered, was Iakopo. He was one of the brave souls who had volunteered to umpire games for the Windward League. As such, he was a more imposing authority figure than my daughter's father, the king. He was packing away the bases and still had his chest protector on over his bare chest. I must have just missed the last out.

"Iakopo, good day to you."

"Good afternoon, your majesty," he said, bowing. "I'm afraid the game is over, but you would have liked the ending."

"That right? How'd we do?" He told me the score and I let out a breath I didn't know I'd been holding in.

"Your girl is one heads up no foolin' ballplayer child," he said. "She turned da far outest double-play I ever did see and dat was all she wrote." As he explained the particulars of the unusual twin-killing, I stopped thinking for a moment of the other killing—ruling out suicide was an easy call—and found myself dreaming up ways to make up for missing out on today's game. I would not only attend the playoff game, I would do it in style, bringing out the palace guard to perform some of their swordsmanship routines as a warm-up festivity. Flower wreaths could be presented to the players. Conga drummers atop the dugouts, native dancers, coconut vendors, roving bartenders. Most of the games attracted small, attentive crowds, but this one, for the pennant, would warrant a big-time turnout. People would come from all over. Even our ever-growing population of hermits, most of whom lived in the interior, might venture out into the sunshine with the season on the line.

On impulse, I asked Iakopo if he had seen Permanent Wave around. I knew my old friend was the River Otter's regular third base coach and that the young Samoan would be familiar with the old

77

Bushman. Everyone on *Quietude* knew and loved our resident hunter-gatherer. No one could understand a word (or click) that he spoke, but PW seemed always to comprehend whatever was said to him in any language whatsoever. He had a wife and child. She, Okalani, was the sister of my former barber, Laurelai. Their little one, a girl of five, went by the name of Kalahari. But Okalani also didn't know where he'd gotten off to when I fell by their little thatched hut to ask after his whereabouts. She wasn't worried. He often went off hunting or surfing or just walking around. Bushmen cannot abide being confined, so his cutting loose to sleep under the stars had become a regular feature of their family life. She told me she would send him round the palace when he got back home.

Iakopo told me that the Otters had had to make do without a third base coach that day, the first game PW had missed. It probably didn't make much baseball difference in any case. The kids seemed to regard the base coaches socially more than strategically. When they were obliged to stop at first or third, they would invariably turn to whoever was there and begin working on the rhyming cheers and complicated hand-shakes that the modern day ballplayer cannot do without. I had no idea why he had gone on walkabout. Maybe Wilder did. But I didn't want to intrude on her team's celebration. So I asked Iakopo to round up a couple of his brethren and lay the stranger up in the meadow to rest. Later, we could erect a small marker on the spot, though I didn't know what it should say. Tomb of the Unknown Fortune Hunter seemed a bit frivolous. Fortune hunting had seemed sort of playful when the case had been proposed to me, an escapade that might prove world-shaking. Now a life had been taken. We didn't know who had taken it or even whose life it had been. But there was, in a rather Biblical development, a snake in the garden. And there was somebody's blood on the gardening shears.

"*Manuia le aso*," (have a good day) said Iakopo, bowing again. Most Pacific islanders are not only fluent in their mother tongues but conversant with English. On *Quietude*, we are beginning to develop our own pidgin, a lively mixture of American English seasoned with surfer lingo, Hawaiian slang, Tahitian slang, Fijian slang, Samoan slang, baseball parlance, aging American hipster argot and musician's jive. I felt we needed some of the salt and savor that Yiddish would provide, but you can't force these things. Perhaps the émigré will

78

leave us a memorable and confusing phrase or two. But the former fortune hunter, if such he had been, had left us with nothing but another couple of question: Who was pruning the human population and wherefrom had come the old shears?

Chapter Nineteen

It's movie night at the palace! I think my Poppy feels bad about
missing our thrilling victory over the Goofballs (even though we
pretty much won by accident). Usually, it would be another two
weeks until the next movie night. He's been showing us different
baseball movies to help create what's called *camaraderie* among the
River Otters. That's what he says, anyway. I think he just likes
watching old movies and doesn't like to be alone when my Mumza's
gone. When I was real small, he stretched a sail from his old ship
between two palm trees and the three of us would lie back on a
blanket at night and watch old movies under the stars. I didn't know
they were old. I didn't even know what movies were. I guess I
thought they came from outer space or someplace like that. Until I
was six, I thought that was how everyone watched movies, on a
rippling old sail under the stars. But then a friend of my Poppy's
from out in the great world built what's called a *projection room* on the
third story of his tree house palace. It has just enough seats for the
River Otters and my Poppy and my Mumza and me if she sits on his
lap or I sit on hers only now I'm getting kinda big for that but we still
do it anyway.

He served us hot dogs with mustard and ketchup and popcorn
with butter. The hot dogs are what's called *imported*, which means they
came from someplace else. The butter is from here. We have dairy
cows and Queenie has a churn that my Uncle John made for her. She
uses it to make butter which is really good and melty on popcorn and
on biscuits with mango marmalade. The movie is called *The Pride of
the Yankees* and by the end all the girls and one of the boys began to
cry even though in the last movie we saw the manager of the team in
the movie said there was no crying in baseball. Izzy was sitting next
to me, sobbing over the loss of the tall handsome first baseman in
the movie. It was a black and white movie, like they used to make all
the time. When I was little, My Poppy once told me as a joke that

they were made that way because a long time ago, the whole world was in black and white. When I asked him where all of our colors came from, he said they came into the world with me when I was born. I thought that was true for a long time, too. It's crazy what a little kid will believe.

"It's OK, Izz. It's all pretend, anyway," I said, though I knew that was kind of a fib. I knew the actor in the movie was pretending but the person he was pretending to be was a real person who had died of a horrible disease. I understand because I was in a movie one time only the person I was pretending to be was a made up person. I didn't think I should tell Izzy about the real guy, she would only start crying again. She's only seven, after all.

I didn't have to worry about her for long. Before we could climb down the ladder or slide down the pole to go downstairs and build a fire on the beach to make s'mores for dessert, a couple of the boys started throwing their popcorn at the boy who cried at the end of the movie and pretty soon the projection room was like a little battlefield full of buttery ballplayers crawling under the seats to grab the ankles of other ballplayers whose ankles got all buttery and everybody was all slippery and squirming around like a nest of sea snakes that Poppy Tobago and I saw one time when we were diving the reef.

"Butter up!" yelled Izzy, who wasn't sad anymore and some of the boys tried to grab her and throw her out the window into the lagoon. All the River Otters were sliding around like, well, like a bunch of river otters covered in butter. It was what you might call *pandemonium*.

One of the boys got ahold of the plastic bottles of mustard and ketchup and started stalking after the girls, holding up the bottles like red and yellow squirt guns. The girls pretended to be terrified. It took me a minute to realize that this cheeky boy was none other than the used-to-be king, my center fielder, Walter the Studious! I had seen him looking down at a schoolbook in his lap during the movie. He even reads books in the dugout during games. And here he was getting all goofy and two-fisted with condiments. This camaraderie stuff was working out pretty good.

But when I saw our catcher, a big ten-year-old boy named Zachariah from Puerto Rico, jumping up and down on one of the seats, I thought the team captain should try to restore order. My Poppy isn't the strictest of fathers, but I didn't think he'd be too

81

happy about our busting up his projection room. We might not get invited back for another movie night. Luckily, he had gone up to his library in the middle of the movie and not yet returned. But I knew he'd be coming back down soon to say goodbye to the Otters. The projector is kept in a sort of cupboard or I guess you would call it a *cabinet,* with doors that close in front of it and behind it is a ladder that starts at the floor and leads up to the library. But between the ceiling and the top of the cabinet for the projector is a little space that I used to slip into when I wanted to hide for some reason or just to be alone with my thoughts. I looked there now expecting to see my Poppy climbing down the ladder any minute but instead I saw two gleaming eyes.

My Poppy couldn't possibly fit into that space, I knew. If I tried it now, I'd probably get stuck. Izzy maybe but it would be a squeeze. And anyway, I could see her doing a handstand on the shoulders of our second baseman, a girl named Jubilee. Izzy calls her Jubilee from Tennessee. I don't know if Jubilee really is from Tennessee or if Izzy just likes calling her that. She also calls her Jujubee sometimes. Jujubees are this kind of hard chewy candy my Poppy got for us one time on movie night. They were imported, like the hot dogs. Izzy is very proud of her handstands and having nicknames for everybody. It's another way of aka-ing, I guess you could say.

The eyes were looking right at me. There was something about them that was like looking up at the Southern Cross at night. They were what you might call *quietly dazzling.* There's only one pair of eyes like that on all of *Quietude.* As soon as I locked onto them there in the dark of the projection room, I knew that my good old third base coach was back.

PW led the charge down to the beach, dancing around under the moon. All the River Otters followed him out of the palace and into the surf. He grabbed me up and pulled me onto his longboard and we rode a couple of waves together the way we like to do sometimes. *Tandem,* it's called. I've been surfing by myself since I was about five, but before that, I always used to ride with PW, who shreds the way I horseback. The sea is sort of his Holy Toledo!. Whether it's cantering or galloping, he feels it all the way from his fingers to his heels.

When we came out, the bonfire was already blazing up. PW stood half in shadow at the edge of it, looking up at the moon. Some of the boys began playing a kind of pretend baseball they call firelight ball. I think they like it because it's easier to slide in the sand. They set out big shells for bases and use sticks of firewood for bats. There's no ball, they just act like they've hit one and begin to run. PW, as usual, was the third base coach. He knew it was pretend, but he liked it just as much as the regular kind.

Then Jubilee, who is eleven, the oldest girl on the River Otters, started pointing at PW and giggling like she was about five. Specifically, she was pointing at his *loin-cloth*. and giggling. *Loin-cloth* always reminds me of that word *doily,* but really they are very different things. We're all used to seeing our third base coach in his loin-cloth, since it's pretty much the only thing he ever wears except for sometimes a top hat, so why was Jubilee having such a fit of giggles? When I looked more closely at PW, I noticed that the part she was pointing at seemed bigger than usual, longer like. But when a pretend runner rounded pretend third, PW pulled out the part that Jubilee had been pointing at and started waving the runners toward a make believe home. No wonder it had seemed longer than the other thing. It was really my good old not-a-flute, aka—as Izzy would say—the bamboozler. We had found it. Maybe I was turning into a detective after all.

Chapter Twenty

"Is sleep a net we cast for mystery?" some degenerate poet or other once wrote. I was trying to recall the author's name after waiting up and waiting up and finally deciding I needed sleep more than a goodnight kiss but then failed to find it, despite being wiped out.

As a possible soporific, I took to counting the women I had known before I met Wilder's mother, a dangerous practice, since I was obliged to stop at each and wonder why she had found me wanting. Most of them had either loved and left me or took a shortcut and just left. Some of those women were truly beautiful, a few genuinely striking. But, at some point in our acquaintance, they had all taken to scowling. People scowl when they're angry, and you cannot be angry and happy at the same time. So it follows that they scowled because they were unhappy. But as soon as a woman scowls, she desecrates her own beauty as surely as a knife-wielding maniac slashing a canvas destroys a work of art. After the first scowl, I lived in fear of another and never thereafter found the women beautiful. I suppose I thought I had made them unhappy. That the real knife-wielding maniac had been myself.

All the women I had ever seen on *Quietude* owned a measure of radiance that made them lovely to look upon. Not a one could even be called plain. The reason I had come to believe there were no plain women in my adopted country wasn't so much that only great beauties gravitated to our shores, but because, in the final analysis, there may well be no such a thing as a plain woman. There are women, there is worry, there is stress, there is a world of anxiety, and if you combine these elements (and add the ever-present threat of unflattering light), you sometimes arrive at a careworn face. And careworn is another word for plain. To put it another way: All women have moments of luminosity. Or, to put it more actively, moments when they are free to *luminesce*. At such a moment, she might be plain, but plain only in the sense of plain-spoken, i.e., direct and unadorned. But a woman then is neither dowdy nor homely. Such words have lost all meaning. If you don't believe me, take a moment of your own to watch a woman when she is watching her child sleeping. During that moment, worry, stress, aggravation, anxiety, fear, despondency and despair take leave of her and she grows as beautiful as the one she is watching.

On the mainland, such moments are rare, each regarded in retrospect as a brief golden age. Here, the reverse is the commonplace. It helps, of course, that—most especially in the early mornings and early evenings—we have very flattering light.

Obviously, I was missing Bonny. I had taken to wandering around the palace making up decrees which I later forgot to issue and a good thing too. As previously mentioned, I don't sleep much when my lady is away. But when I do, I probably qualify as one of the world's great dreamers, though, come to think of it, what would be the basis of comparison with other dreamers? How does one gain entrance into the Dreamers Hall of Fame? Who are the judges and how do they judge? I could issue a decree announcing public dream reenactments, which could replace our bygone river baptisms. Those occasions had been our most boisterous gatherings. But by now we have named all seven of our rivers. Then it occurred to me that dreams are only interesting to those who dreamed them, so dream reenactments would not be joining our brief history of weird theatricals, which ranged from Samurai puppet shows to ramshackle Shakespeare (We'd once mounted a production of Hamlet with a driftwood Ophelia). But maybe now that we'd finished with the rivers, we could start giving names to our creeks, one per year. That would last a while. Not surprisingly, given how many rushing rivers roar across *Quietude*, our island is prolifically braided with creeks, purling her wild hair into plaits, as do our girls. Missing Bonny was easy. Even daydreaming about waterways led back to her. I yawned, even as I yearned for my daughter's Mumza.

My dreams are usually about getting lost and being unable to find my way back to where I started, with occasional side trips into carnal desire coming almost true. But on this night, I dreamed I was following Permanent Wave all over *Quietude*. There are many parts of the island where the king has never set foot. In the dream, PW didn't seem to know I was following him, he didn't turn and acknowledge me anyway. But he led me to places I recognized and many I didn't. I had no way of knowing whether the places that were strange to me were real places or dream locations cobbled together from memory and fantasy. In the dream, I walked better than I do in life these days, took long easy strides and stood beside pools and in groves and even hiked to the summit of our dormant volcano, Mt. Elmer. We were coming up to the cottage at the foot of the Grieving Widow where Bonny's Falls can be found. At the top of the mountain is a geo-thermal spring, which sends an everlasting supply of hot water downhill into larger and smaller falls. My lady's favorite among them for lounging and decompressing was the principal reason for the placement of our cottage, and had therefore been named after her.

I was about to call out to her when a small voice said, "Poppy, tell me a story about when I was little and we went to the movie premiere in Hollywood." I awakened to find that Wilder had straggled up to my room to say goodnight after dancing and playing around the fire until the wee smalls and found me nodded off. Now she was crashed at the end of my bed in the half-asleep state that gladdens the hearts of all parents. It means that the sweetest peace is nigh. I knew which story she wanted to hear and I knew how many times she had heard it before and that she knew it by heart but that I was supposed to pretend it would be brand new to her ears.

"OK." I paused, as if trying to choose between a wealth of such stories. "Your Mumza and you and I were staying in a room in a very fancy hotel in southern California. So fancy that they would bring you whatever you asked for. They would bring you a hot fudge sundae with whipped cream and cherries in the middle of the night."

"How did you ask for whatever you wanted?"

"You called them on the telephone."

"Whatever that might be." We had no phones on *Quietude*, cellular or otherwise, but Wilder, who often served as a sort of apprentice gallivantrix on her mother's travels, knew more about phones than I hope ever to learn. When they were away, her mother supplied her with a cell phone in case she got lost in airports. But Wilder's counterfeit bafflement was part of our storytelling tradition. I explained as best I could how phones worked.

"So you called the hotel people and before the ice-cream even

86

began to melt, a gentleman in a smart uniform showed up at your door with your heart's delight."

"OK. But when do I come into the story?"

"Hold your horses, Little Coconut, we're getting to that part. But there are more telephones involved. Two telephones, to be exact."

"Why two telephones?"

"Well, my friend Jake, the gentleman you called Mister Buchanan when he was your director on the movie, he gave your Mumza and I each a cell phone so he could keep track of us. He called your mother to tell her we needed to get to the theater so the photographers on the red carpet could take our picture." My old fear of having my picture taken came over me just from relating the story.

"Where were you, Poppy?"

"I was in the bathroom, trying to figure out how to tie my necktie." As it happens, I never had figured it out. "After your mother got off the phone with Jake, she handed the phone to you and told you to push the numbers that would make my phone ring in the bathroom so she could tell me to hurry up. You pushed the right numbers, but my phone didn't ring in the bathroom because it was turned off or I didn't know how to turn it on. Anyway, you were sent to what's called *voicemail* and instead of hearing your father's voice, you heard a pre-recorded message. Your mother, meanwhile, was growing antsy and demanded that you give her back the phone."

"What happened then? Tell me. Tell me." This was her favorite part of the story.

"When your mother insisted you give the phone back to her, you looked up at her with huge imploring eyes and said, sadly, 'But mom, I wanted to press one for more options.'" Wilder clapped her hands and laughed and laughed. Her laughter was like antlers of sunlight dowsing for seawater. It sustained me, especially when Bonny was away. Wilder could hold down her delight no longer. She jumped up and began to dance around on the bed, improvising a crazy song whose lyrics—never to be repeated or recalled—were all about room service. She twirled around and fell down, panting and laughing.

The telling of the story was ever thus, an unvarying routine. I loved it as much as she, but for different reasons. For Wilder, now a big girl of nine, it was such a blast to kick over the traces of her younger days. For her father, it was a reminder of how hungry she

87

had been to find out What Happens Next. So hungry but still young enough to be unaware of how much of it could bury you alive in the blues.

"I'm sorry I missed game number fifty, Little Coconut," I said. I guessed this was as good a time as any to get into it, though I had to tread cautiously. "I got caught up in something—" I stopped when I realized that I had no idea how to finish the sentence. There's a not so subtle difference between treading cautiously and just, you know, *drying up*. Apart from her first three months and some trips with her mother, Wilder had spent her whole life on *Quietude* and was its most impassioned patriot. The only homicide in our history had occurred when she was an infant and so had no place in her memory banks. Her mother and I—and in truth the entire population—had agreed not to mention it in her presence until she reached her majority. She hadn't known the stranger, and his sudden demise would probably not haunt or traumatize her. Still, I was hesitant to speak of it until it was well in the past.

"King biz?" Wilder offered, to fill in the silence.

"Kind of," I said, then went sideways as a stall. "Did all you Otters have a good time on the beach?"

"A rollicking old good time, gov," she said, dropping into a cockney accent she picked up from some London-born friends. "And—crikey!—you'll never guess who showed up. PW!"

"Oh, good," I said. "I've been trying to find him, though I guess I haven't been trying very hard. I heard he missed the game too."

"Yeah. I don't know where he went. But last night, at the end of the movie, he turned up in that little space above the projector. He seems to like watching movies, but I can't tell. What do you think?"

"Yes, I think he does. His people are great storytellers. I bet it's fun for him to follow the stories without understanding what the characters are saying." I pointed to her ball bag, which she hauls along behind her everywhere. "Is my glove in there?"

"Somewhere. Why?"

"I'm not going to take it away from you, Wilder Kathleen. I'd just like to put it on my hand for a minute, if you don't mind. I'll give it back." The feel of the old Rawlings glove on my hand is a quick and easy method of binding all my days together, even as the mighty Wurlitzer.

88

"OK, Poppy." She dumped the contents of the big canvas duffel on the bed, separating out scuffed baseballs, lip gloss, liniment, bandaids and an ace bandage, a hair brush, a water bottle, an apple, homemade sunblock, a couple of bats, bobby pins, a resin bag, and a long dark stick, highly polished but nicked up. Then, from the very bottom of the bag, my old glove. I slipped it onto my hand and immediately felt more comfortable. I pointed at the stick.

"What's that?"

"I wish I knew" she said. "I call it a not-a-flute because, well, because we thought, Izzy and I, when we found it, that it might be a flute, but it isn't and Izzy calls it a bamboozler, because it looks like bamboo but it's black and we don't have black bamboo here that I know of, so it seems to be trying to trick us. PW, before he disappeared for a while, was using it like an orchestra conductor's baton only instead of conducting music like your friend Mister Alderman, he conducts runners around third base, he waves them on." She stood up on the bed and demonstrated, pin-wheeling her arm with the stick in hand.

"Where did you find it?"

"In the pirate's watering trough when I went to feed the Captain's remuda." She grabbed up one of the baseballs. "Wanna see my screwball grip?"

"What father would not?" She wrapped her fingers around the ball and made a throwing motion that included a sharp twist of the wrist. "Doesn't that hurt?"

"No, not really. Though Mister McKeever told me I shouldn't use it too often until I'm older. I haven't used it at all in a game yet. I'm saving it for the playoff. It'll be my secret weapon."

"It's you who will be the bamboozler then, Little Coconut."

"I sure hope so. Can I sleep here, Poppy? I'm awfully tired." She was fading fast, and now I didn't need to worry about whether I could sleep or not. The only thing more nourishing to my spirits than sleep was watching my daughter sleep.

"Why, sure, Little Coconut. You know what your Mumza and I always say, 'When in doubt, conk out.'"

My daughter's beating heart was at the foot of my bed. No man could ask for more.

Chapter Twenty-One

"When I went up to say goodnight to my Poppy," I said to Izzy, "he asked to see his glove, and I had that stupid ball bag with me so what was I supposed to do? I was going through the bag and out fell the not-a-flute. Now my Poppy has it and I so wanted to be the one to solve the mystery."

"That's OK, Cap, we need to concentrate on the game, anyway. Did your dad the king know what the bamboozler is? Maybe it's a king thing."

"No, he called it a *stick*. If it was a king thing, I think it would be called a *staff*, or maybe a *scepter*."

"I've heard of a pitching staff, but I don't think there's any such thing as a pitching scepter," said Izzy, trying to keep our minds on baseball.

"Anyway, he still has it. I think he slept with it under his pillow. He asked where I'd found it and I told him it was in the trough but not that we were looking for my pocket watch, only that I'd gone there to feed the horses. So now I've fibbed to my Poppy and I don't have the not-a-flute and I still have no idea where my pocket watch is. Guess I wouldn't have made such a much of a detective, after all."

"Well, who cares? You are a striking example of a starting pitcher, Cap. Now go out there and mow down those Goofballs."

It was kind of like that movie premiere back in Hollywood, except I wasn't wearing a diamond tiara like that time. Well, they weren't real diamonds but they sparkled like the stars over *Quietude*. For our first playoff game ever, my Poppy had pulled out all the stops. We have bigger bleachers to contain the crowd, food vendors galore, three pretty ladies called Butter Rum Than Never playing ukuleles and singing on top of one dugout and three hula dancers called The Swivel Servants—whatever that might mean—on the other, little boys running around flying dragon kites, a line of five-year-old girls giving out with a cheer that Izzy and I and Jubilee had made up. It goes: "Come one, come all. Welcome to the River Otter's Ball. Bring your sons, bring your daughters. All will love to see the slaughter, when the team from Elsewhereville, drives those Goofballs over the hill." Permanent Wave was back, and he had worn his old top hat.

Even Mister McKeever has come out of the big cave where he, as my Poppy says, *parks his ass* most of the time. The only other game he came to was the time I told him I was ready to start using my twelve-to-sixer. Afterwards, he said I did all right and we talked about the grip and what were the best counts to throw it and then I thought he left. What he really did was to go behind the bleachers and give a lot of the pearls from our lagoon to the boys who rig up my Poppy's beach chair to the palm tree—the boys give the pearls to girls they like—in exchange for them going straight home and forgetting to bring the king down after the game. And they did it! They left him up there all night! Mister McKeever brought him down in the morning and they had a big laugh, my Poppy said. He also said that his thermos had come in handy even after he ran out of mango nectar. I don't know what he meant by that.

I felt like my people were all around me, all except my Mumza, but her work is very important, not just to her but to the whole world.

My Poppy doesn't need to be neutral like Queenie. He's the king and can do whatever he wants. And what he wants to do the most of all is root root root for the River Otters. Izzy calls him our *loyal royal*. This time he was up in the palm tree behind home plate again in his ritzy beach chair sipping from his thermos of mango nectar and cheering like a madman. But so far we weren't giving him much to cheer about.

For the first time, all the River Otters were wearing our full uniforms: Caps, cleats, shirts and trousers (*bloused* at the knees, natch) along with our dark blue sox. At first I thought they were bringing us luck but then it seemed to be the wrong kind of luck. We'd been holding on to a slender lead until everything started to fall apart. This time it was Izzy coming to the mound to calm *me* down. She looked deep into my eyes.

"Do you think Mogu Mogu likes me?" she said.

"I'm sure he does, Izz," I said. "But this might not be the best

91

time to talk about it. Maybe you can come over and help me feed the Captain's horses later and we can discuss your love life. Right now, we need to keep our heads in the game."

"Right. I just thought I could take your mind off our troubles." She was right about the troubles. There were troubles aplenty.

"We're getting trounced," I said.

"Aka *drubbed*," said Izzy, "aka *creamed*, aka *walloped*, aka *pounded*, aka *mauled*, aka *stomped*, aka *hosed*, aka *shellacked*—" She went on for a while, getting more and more excited by the terms describing how brutally we were being humiliated. Once Mizz Izz starts aka-ing, there's no stopping her. You might as well just tie yourself to the nearest palm tree and ride it out. She got to her favorite and practically screamed, "aka *beaten to a bloody pulp!*" Then she grinned her goofy redhead's grin and turned serious. "But don't worry, Cap," she said, "It's early yet," and walked back to her position at short, slamming her fist into her glove.

It was true, the game was only three innings old. And yet, we were down 7 to 1, with the pennant on the line. It wasn't so much that I was getting lit up, but everything they hit was falling in: bleeders, bloops and cue shots off the ends of their bats, dribblers, dinks and dying quail. A swinging bunt had driven in two with the help of an overthrow. My curve was breaking so well that our catcher couldn't catch it and I had to run in to cover the plate so many times I was getting winded.

I took one more look at the palm tree behind home plate. My Poppy had stopped hollering and was now holding out his right arm and making a quick throwing motion, twisting his wrist and looking right into my eyes. I tugged on the bill of my cap to tell him I knew what he meant and waved Zachariah out to the mound. Our signs are very simple: he puts down one finger for the fastball, two for the twelve-to-sixer. I haven't learned yet how to throw a slider or a change-up. Mister McKeever is concerned about not placing too much of a strain on my arm. We don't have a sign for the scroojie. I'd only ever thrown it at the trunk of the banyan tree, never to a living person.

"Hey, Cap. Whass da haps?"

"Zach, I'm going to try something new. When we get to two strikes, hold down one finger and I'll shake you off. Then hold down two. I'll nod yes. They'll be looking for the curve, but I'm going to throw a screwball. But only when we get to two strikes, OK?" He looked confused.

"A screwball? Is that like a Goofball?"

"No. It's a breaking ball that will break *into* a right-hander and *away* from a left-hander. So you won't have to worry about my curve going into the dirt and getting past you. But remember, only when we get to two strikes. Before that, we'll stick with number one, OK?"

"Totally copacetic, Cap." He trotted back and went into his crouch. I had decided to stay with my heater until I got two strikes on a hitter and then *banjax* them with the scroojie. If their lead got any bigger, we'd be watching the championship series from the bleachers. My heater is easier to control than the twelve-to-sixer. It doesn't have as much giddy-up as some others—Mogu Mogu's high hard one is plenty tuff to get around on, for instance—but I've gotten so I can hit the corners pretty often and even make it ride up and in now and then. Sometimes too far up, but Zachariah is tall and it's easier for him to spring out of his crouch to flag those down than to corral crazy bouncing curve balls in the dirt.

My plan depended partly on what's called the *element of surprise* and partly on how well I could control my fastball. Surprising them with the scroojie wouldn't make any difference unless I unleashed it when we got to two strikes and it tied them up. It needed to be what Mister McKeever calls my *out* pitch. And I needed to use it sparingly, only once per batter so none of the Goofballs would know it was coming. Maybe because it was a really hot day, my heater was rising as it neared the plate. So I threw it letter high and the hitters would start their swings but then it would sail up a little and they would swing under it and miss. By the time there were two strikes, they would know to lay off the fastball. But then the scroojie was upon them and they all took pathetic little hacks like they couldn't believe what was happening and then they went back to the dugout to sit down. Now the Goofballs were the disconsolate ones. They'd been what's called *sitting on* the curveball when we got to two strikes, thinking I'd try to get them to go fishing off the corner. When the scroojie appeared instead of the curve, they were utterly defeated. Thanks to Mister McKeever and that good old banyan tree, I struck out the side, stranding three.

93

"You used it!" cried Izzy, hurling herself into my arms in the dugout, "You used your secret weapon! I've never seen one before. But I knew right away what it was. And it worked! You made 'em *fade away*, Cap. Aka you *scroojied* them good and proper. Way to go."

Now we had to put some crooked numbers on the board. Maybe from the unveiling of my new pitch, the Otters got all fired up and began to pound that old pineapple. Walter got us started in the bottom of the inning, lacing a double into the left field corner. Our first baseman, Ella Rose (she calls herself a first base *babe*, which I think is kind of conceited but she does have great footwork around the bag and can dig out the low throw in the dirt with ease) timed a fastball and lined it up the middle, scoring Walter and making it to second when the center fielder bobbled the ball. It makes me happy to have about the same number of girls as boys on the River Otters. My Mumza says it's more *egalitarian* that way. I don't know what eggs have to do with baseball, but that's why it's a good idea to keep growing older. You get to learn more stuff. Next up was our third baseman, Jaxxx from Jamaica.

"Take your hacks, Cracker Jaxxx," called Izzy from the dugout. She calls him that after a kind of sticky sweet popcorn and peanut treat that my Queenie and my Mumza fixed up for us one time. It was good but I can't eat it during a game because my fingers get all icky you're not supposed to get what are called *foreign substances* on the ball when you pitch. Jaxxx has the longest dreads on *Quietude*. He's just a little older than me so he must have been growing them his whole life. We had to make a special cap for him with two extra openings for his dreads to come out. He hits righty and swings those dreads slowly back and forth when he stares out at the pitcher, like he's going to hypnotize the poor dude. He likes to draw bases on balls. He walks so often we calling him The Walking Dread. This time he walked on four straight. Now we had two on with one in and nobody out, still down by five.

The Goofballs' pitcher had more trouble finding the strike zone and walked Zachariah after walking Jaxxx, loading the bases. But he found his groove and struck out both Tobias and Alakai who play left and right field for the River Otters, bringing yours truly to the plate. This could be our best chance for a comeback. I checked the outfielders and noticed that the littlest was out in right, playing kind of shallow. So I decided to hit lefty, hoping to pull one in the air deep to right. The first pitch was in my wheelhouse and I swung with all my might. But I got under it and popped it up foul straight back. I heard the crowd roaring and turned to see my Poppy in his palm tree trying to catch the pop-up but since I had his glove, he not only muffed it but dropped his thermos besides. The thermos fell on a tall weird person in some kind of animal costume. I couldn't tell what kind of animal it was supposed to be. Luckily, it hit the big weirdo in the shoulder instead of the head but the crowd ooh-ed and ah-ed anyway.

I kept fouling off strikes and taking outside pitches until the count was full. I had the pitcher in the same position as Mogu Mogu in our last game against the Javelinas. He had to come in. Well, he didn't *have* to, they had a five-run lead, but no pitcher *worth his weight in warm spit*, as Mister McKeever says, wants to walk in a run. The next pitch was over and on the inner half, just as I had hoped. I kept my head down and drove it over the head of the little right fielder. It rolled and rolled and I ran like Holy Toledo! going after a train robber until I touched home plate. Goofballs 7, River Otters 6.

The score was the same when we came up in the bottom of the seventh. Both of the pitchers had settled down and done our jobs. Once I established the scroojie, they didn't know whether to look for it or for the twelve-to-sixer, which made it easier for me to tease them with heaters just off the plate. Now that the scroojie had gotten into their heads, I mixed in some curves to keep them guessing. If we kept records in the Windward League for most strikeouts, I might have set one but we don't. At this point, I had pitched a complete game, but if we were forced to go to extras, I'd have to bring in another hurler. My arm was weary and we were still down a run.

I was leading off. I must have been nervous because I swung at the first pitch and grounded into a come-backer. Then I took over coaching first so my teammates wouldn't hear me cursing myself for being so impatient. One down. Following me, Jaxxx stepped in but for once he wasn't wearing his walking shoes, because he too picked on the first pitch he saw. He must have liked it because he almost came out of his cleats taking a big cut. He hit it on the screws, but the blur it became ended its short life in the third baseman's glove. The hardest hit ball all year by the boy from Jamaica but he only took one

95

step out of the batter's box before stopping and shaking his dreads in disgust. Two down and now it was up to the bottom of the order.

Ella Rose came up swinging her bat around like she knew something the pitcher didn't but took two weak swings without making contact. Our season was down to a strike. The third pitch, also a swinging strike, turned our luck around when it landed in the dirt and skipped by the catcher. "Run, Ella!" I yelled from the coaching box. "Run run run run lay doo run run!" While she may not have been much of a threat at the plate, she was the fastest runner on the River Otters. By the time the catcher had retrieved the ball, she was standing on first, panting and getting a hug from her Captain. The tying run was on base.

And our shortstop was striding to the plate. One of the most amazing things about my sidekick is that, even though she hasn't racked up a single base hit all season, her grin, when she's stepping in, always says, "You'd better pitch around me, mister (or mizz), if you know what's good for you." She was kind of sketchy on geography and probably had no idea where Sumatra actually was, but wherever it might be, she truly believed she was going to clobber the next offering halfway there.

All the Otters were cheering her on.

"Pick out a good one, Izz, and give it a ride!"

"Take him deep!"

"Rough him up and run him out of town!"

"This bum's got nothing, Izz. Turn one around!"

As always, she was ready to let it rip. Crouching down in the box, she clawed with her cleats in the dirt, like a bull about to charge. She waggled her bat in a menacing manner. Then she dug in and dared the pitcher to be so foolhardy as to put one over. He challenged her with two fastballs. Twice she swung, and twice she stirred up quite a breeze. In truth, she has a real pretty swing. The problem is getting it to what's called *intersect* with the flight of the ball. Her eyes know what to look for and her hands know what to do. It's just that her hands and her eyes don't know what they know at the same time. As I say, she's only seven.

For the second time, we were down to our last strike. The cheering died. We were all holding our breath, wishing time would stop. Izzy remained totally casual. She stepped out of the box and

96

looked down to me at first. Just to give her a little time, I touched my cap and my uniform shirt and my nose and my ear in a bunch of made-up signs that meant absolutely nothing. She nodded as though she understood and stepped back in. I had to watch but I couldn't watch but I watched. Confident of Izzy's inability to make contact, the Goofballs' pitcher chucked one in medium speed right down the middle. Maybe it was because she had looked down at me, but Izzy changed her strategy. Instead of swinging from the heels, she took my advice and sort of poked at the pitch, as if it were pestering her. The ball and bat met and the ball decided to go away. It didn't go very far or very fast but it went to a very convenient place, squibbing down the first base line and past the astonished first baseman and out into short right field. I even waved at it as it went bouncing by. There was so much spin on it that it curled into foul territory. I wished I had the not-a-flute then to wave her on to second but I settled for pinwheeling my arm. Ella Rose was tearing around the bases, her cap flying off, feet barely touching the ground. There was no call for her to slide into third because the Goofballs' first baseman and right fielder, in trying to run down the ball, had collided and fallen to the ground. Ella scored without a throw. Izzy didn't know what to do. She had never been on base before.

"Pretend you're Holy Toledo!" I yelled and that seemed to be the right thing to say. The Goofball's second baseman had finally picked up the ball, but she didn't even make a throw home. There would have been no point to it. Izzy scored standing up and we mobbed her at the plate.

People were pouring out of the stands, and my Poppy being lowered from his palm tree. Everyone wanted to congratulate the pennant winners. It was a good feeling after 51 games to know there would be even more. My Poppy let all our friends and neighbors have a word with me and then came over and gave me a big squeeze.

"I think your glove brought me good luck," I said.

"You didn't need luck, Little Coconut," he said. "You are a ballplayer to the bone." I was looking for Mister McKeever and thanking him in my heart for teaching me the grips for both of my breaking pitches, and just then it hit me. It didn't matter that I wasn't going to be a detective. It was like Izzy said: I made the scroojie

97

work. And that meant that I had made *myself* into a fadeaway machine! So even though I might not be a private eye, maybe I was on my way to becoming a great inventor, just like Mister Wheeler!

What I had said about Holy Toledo! gave me an idea. My sidekick had so loved her first time of being tall in the saddle. I knew she would be up for a second. "Let's ride, Mizz Izz," I said. I couldn't think of a better way to celebrate winning the big game. "Let's mount up."

We started to walk away from the scene of one of the greatest ballgames ever played when the tall weirdo in the furry animal suit walked up to me and said, in a deep growly voice, "Hello, Wilder. I'm Otto the Otter, your new mascot. Can I have a hug?" I thought this very strange. We weren't supposed to have a mascot. I had heard that some of the teams in the bigs have mascots but they sounded totally bogus to me.

"I'm sorry, Otto," I said, "but if you're trying out for a job, you'll have to talk with my father, the king? He's in charge of such things."

"I already talked with your Poppy," said Otto, in the same growly voice. "He said it was OK for me to grab you up and *attack your tickle spot!*" The big furry weirdo pulled off its head and shook out its long blonde hair. Then this very beautiful not-an-Otter grabbed me up and started to kiss and slobber on my tummy. I didn't know if I could stand to be so happy. My Mumza had made it back for the big game and I wasn't about to let go of her.

"Sorry, Izz. Can we save the horseback ride for when we win the Crown of *Quietude*?" My timing was very good. Mogu Mogu had come down out of the stands to congratulate my shortstop on driving in the winning run. She had pretty much forgotten about her starting pitcher.

"Sure, Cap," she said, "Whatever you say," her eyes trained on the cute Hawaiian boy. Lucky me.

Chapter Twenty-Two

"It's some kind of metallic polymer," said Jake. "I'm neither a metallurgist nor an interior designer, so I'm on shaky ground here, but I expect its function is purely decorative. That is, its *original* function. You would use this stuff in arrangements around the house instead of real bamboo in order to keep aphids and mites away from your living room." He studied it for another few seconds. "I think it was designed for interior decoration...until..." He held it up to the light, "it was retrofitted. Watch closely." He held up the stick and placed a fingertip at either end, then pressed both inwardly. With a barely audible clicking sound, the two joints on the faux bamboo jumped open by no more than a quarter of an inch. Jake caught my eye to make sure I was paying attention, and actually said, "Voila!" as he turned the ends of the stick. They turned easily and he was able, with little effort, to pull them off and set them down one at a time, leaving only the central portion. "It's spring-loaded," he said, holding up the interior section for me to see into. It was empty, as empty as the recently cleaned barrel of a rifle.

"It's empty," I said, as alert a champion of the obvious as ever.

"What were you expecting?"

"I don't really know. It's an ingeniously designed hiding place, right? A lot of thought has gone into it. First, it was made to look like something that was made to look like bamboo, though it wasn't. It was made to look, upon closer inspection, like something you would use to decorate the interior of a home, one which would be taken, by the casual eye, for bamboo. But it's actually a hiding place. So why isn't it hiding something?"

"Damned if I know. But I would wager that it has been, and recently too."

"Why do you say that?"

"Because, though we have no physical evidence to substantiate it, my theory would go something like: You say Wilder and her friend found it in the water trough by the Pirate's lair. Correct?" I nodded. "Well, since no one would go to the trouble of putting this gizmo together except, as you say, as a hiding place, it follows that whatever was hidden in it was removed by one of the hiders (i.e., the fortune hunters), before tossing it into the trough. It had therefore become obsolete and was surplus to requirements."

"Unless he ditched it there thinking to return and fetch it. Branches frequently fall into that trough, making it an ideal hiding place for such a hiding place." Jake frowned in concentration.

"A possibility, I admit. But if that were the case, it would probably still be in there. I would speculate that the two from Barney's Beanery, following the plan they shared with Mister Smirnoff, went to a location with which they were familiar, a domicile probably where this remarkable piece of craftsmanship—what does Wilder call it, the 'not-a-flute'?—was sitting around looking perfectly innocuous, liberated it, and on the way to wherever it pointed, the female member of the duo did in her cohort, made off with the not-a-flute's contents—a tightly rolled map, or diagram of some sort, I assume—and is now at large, freed from the onerous obligation of a two-way split of the loot."

"So instead of looking for two people we won't recognize, we're only looking for one?"

"Yes. And we know to look for a woman."

"Thus inserting the invaluable phrase *cherchez la femme* into the discussion."

"Right. It's like when the P.I. says 'plus expenses.' to the client. You have to find a way to work it in."

"Just so. My guess is that the deceased somehow tumbled to his partner's deadly intention and fled. Maybe there was a quarrel en route or maybe she had planned it all along. Whichever, one was equipped for a fight, the other only for flight. The latter took off, on foot, though apparently not fast enough. While fleeing, he must have tossed the not-a-flute into the trough, hoping to retrieve it after escaping from his would-be assailant. Or, as you suggest, removing the contents and tossing the thing into the trough to serve as a red herring that might slow down his pursuer."

"So the real question is still whether the contents were in the not-a-flute when it became, for want of a better name, a not-a-float?"

100

"That's anyone's guess."

"Well, your reconstruction could account for the not-a-flute being empty, but it tells us nothing about who might have emptied it. It definitely wasn't on the body."

"I would suggest that it was emptied by *la belle* herself, she who holds the other half of the puzzle, the map to which the contents of the not-a-flute is supposedly the key," put in Creole.

We were holding this confab in her tower. She walked out of her tiny kitchenette in a floor-length Canterbury nightshirt with her long blonde hair piled atop her head, held up by ingeniously inserted chopsticks. She was sipping from a mugful of one of her delicious fruit smoothies. If you like fruit smoothies, *Quietude* is the island for you. She pointed at the not-a-flute.

"I believe I saw that thing the other day at Buck O'Neil Field," she said. "PW was using it to coach third, I think."

"That's right. He was. Then he carried it off on one of his mysterious walkabouts. Wilder, who found it first, was then reunited with it at a movie party I held for the River Otters at the palace a few nights ago. PW attended and brought it with him."

"And you got it from her?" I nodded. She sipped thoughtfully and let Jake kiss some excess smoothie off her upper lip. "But I have the feeling I've seen it somewhere else, too."

"Do you remember where? It could be important, Brat."

"No. But don't worry, Boss. It will come to me."

Chapter Twenty-Three

"Can you stay for the championship, Mumza"

"That's the plan, Booski. I'm all yours until the River Otters have vanquished their final foe. Who is it going to be?"

"We don't know yet. Tomorrow, the Leeward League is having a one-game playoff, just like we did in the Windward League. It's between a team called the Jumping Jehoshaphats, from a village called Zip-a-Dee-Doo-Dah, and the Gee Willikers from Lackadaisy. They have some crazy names over on that side, don't they, Mumza?"

"That they do, Booski. Did you miss me?"

"I missed you like nobody's business, Mumza. I wished and wished you would make it to the playoff game. I wished on Brigitte's hood ornament and on the Southern Cross and on the not-a-flute and on Holy Toledo's nose. I wished on pretty much everything you would make it back on time and then you were here and I'm still having goosebumps."

"I was awfully glad I made it. It was a close thing. Have you been keeping up with your homework?" My Mumza was an excellent student in high school and college back in Florida in the days before me. My Poppy says when he was in school, he majored in staring out window which is how you get to be a poet. I take after both of them in different ways. I've been doing pretty well on my homework while she's been gone, but I'm still kinda weak on some subjects. She gives me lots of assignments and tests which is okay I guess but it *is* baseball season and I *am* the team captain, so she shouldn't expect me to do ALL of them.

"Izzy helped me study for the exams and I finished them and gave them to Poppy." I said, hoping he had forgotten they were in the trunk of the banyan tree. Some of my answers might have been the right answers but only if the questions were different.

"I'll look them over in the morning. I could use a good night's sleep first. How are Holy Toledo! and Tickety-Boo?"

102

"They're swell, Mumza. And they're becoming best friends. I'm going to ride Tickety-Boo over to the leeward side when it's time for the championship. You could ride Holy Toledo! if you'd like." She was pretty good on horseback, my Poppy not so much. He told me one time that he'd mount up as soon as *fierce bands of hostiles began to fire flaming arrows at him,* whatever that might mean.

"I'd be honored, Booski. How is your dad going over?"

"Oh, he'll ride in Brigitte, I expect." He wouldn't go very fast though. He likes the sound of the surf splashing against his white sidewall tires, so he drives very slowly. One time we had a race with him driving Brigitte and me riding Holy Toledo! and I blew him away.

We all slept at the cottage and Holy Toledo! came to the window the next morning and *nickered* at me to wake up. *Nicker* means sort of the same thing as *whinny,* but it's softer and quieter, as though my horse is doing what's called *speaking in confidence* to me. It's my favorite way to wake up. He smells like his regular horse self but with a little bit of lavender from the garden mixed in. I reached into the Quaker Oats carton I keep by my bed and pulled out a handful and fed it to him. He ate the oats and licked my hand and nickered and I was awake as ever can be. My first horse was a rocking horse made for me by one of our master carvers when I was real small. Her name is Sally and she still lives in my room at our cottage. One time while Holy Toledo! was watching through the window, I pretended to feed some Quaker Oats to Sally and my Arabian stallion reared his head back and sort of snorted, as though I had displeased him.

At the palace, I sleep in the guest room. But at our cottage I have my own room with all my kid stuff in it. My twirly mobile hangs from the rafter, my giraffe hand-puppet named Gladys is in my toy chest (they tell me I named her Gladys but I don't remember so why I chose that name or the name Sally for my rocking horse, these things are mysteries to me). I have two other stuffed giraffes because my Poppy says giraffes remind him of my Mumza. One is called Little Bonny and the other, a really big, practically life-sized one I got in a mail drop when she came floating down out of the sky on her own parachute! She is called Big Bonny. I still have my nesting dolls and puzzles and my books and all my soft blankets with the shiny satin

103

trim and my first swim fins and my first little belly board and a game called Parcheesi and really my whole life when I was little. The one thing that isn't there is my pocket watch. Now that my Poppy and Mister Buchanan have the not-a-flute, I was back to wondering about my watch. I think Izzy has forgotten all about it. My dad says they figured out how to crack it, but it was empty. Dudsville, he says. So maybe I can get it back. Then I could give it back to PW and he could use it to coach third in the Championship Series. I'm thinking it's good *mojo*, a word I picked up from Mogu Mogu. Baseball players are very superstitious. For instance, if we win a game, Izzy has to wear the same hair tie until we lose a game. Even Walter, the oldest and most serious of the River Otters, if he gets a hit won't change bats until he strikes out. Ella Rose always hops over the baseline chalk when she's coming in from first. Tobias, the French boy who's our left fielder, refused to stand under the waterfall with us while we were in a winning streak and everyone moved away from him in the dugout but really he didn't smell any different. He told me he takes baths in the little creek that runs by his house.

My Poppy came in to say good morning. He always looks so happy when my Mumza comes home. I think it's because they get to hold hands all night long. They really like holding hands. My superstition is keeping my glove on *my* hand all *day* long on game days. I bet I'm the only girl in the world who ever rides a horse while wearing a baseball glove. He brought the not-a-flute with him and showed me the trick to opening it. I should have figured it out before. I almost told him about the lost watch, but I just couldn't do it. Maybe I can wish on Brigitte's hood ornament to find my watch. The hood ornament is a silver statue of a woman with a sort of cape streaming back from her as though the wind were blowing it. I call her the Spirit Lady. If I kept won-lost records for wishing places, she would come in first, so many things I've wished for on her have come true.

104

Chapter Twenty-Four

Creole, Jake and myself were strategizing in the Idyll Dipper, trying to put together a time line: The treasure hunters had found the not-a-flute at a pre-arranged location and had it in hand, however briefly, before treasure hunter number two had slain number one. They alone would have known how to crack it. At least, one of them had. We had to assume that they, or an associate with whom they'd worked, had designed it. Then Wilder and her sidekick had knocked around with it for a while, but hadn't known it for what it was, much less whether it was empty or how to find out. Then PW had taken possession. My Bushman friend had held onto it longer than anyone. I had no reason to think he would hit upon the abracadabra of the thing. It was a techno-gizmo and he a hunter-gatherer who descended from the first people of earth. When Wilder had shaken it out of her ball bag, it was slightly scratched, but not dented or broken. That left me back with the first treasure hunter, who must have, while being pursued by his partner, opened the not-a-flute, secured the contents and tossed the no longer needed device into the trough before being run to ground by the killer. Maybe he hoped his partner would spot the not-a-flute in the water and stop to open it, giving her quarry time to make a getaway. So the partner must have secured the contents to use for its intended purpose, right? It made the most sense to quit wondering about who had done what when and/or to whom and start a quiet manhunt.

Creole sashayed in with a steaming pot of tea (she was the only woman in the country who could truly sashay, I sometimes wondered if was an inherent, perhaps inherited, trait or if she practiced in front of a mirror) and gave me a look. The fact that she made eye contact with me before her sweetie told me that she had jogged her memory to good effect.

"What news, Brat?"

"It came to me, Boss. Do you remember when we were visiting one of the good ladies of Daffadowndilly, the one named Bess, on our way to the mystery spot where Poppy Tobago's stalker brother, who didn't actually exist, had supposedly camped out with his imaginary lover?"

"I thought we agreed never to talk about that."

"I'm sorry, Boss, but you said it might be important."

"OK. You're forgiven."

"Well, it was in Bess's cottage that I first saw something that looked like that not-a-flute thingamabob."

"Do tell."

"I remembered that part of the charm of her cottage was in its many decorations. One of them, set against a wall, was a little stand of this black bamboo. At least, I thought it was bamboo at the time. It was the only tropical touch in an otherwise typical English country cottage. That was why I took note of it. Anyway, it was definitely the same stuff. Do I get a raise?" Another old joke. No money, so no raises.

"No, Brat, but you get a bonus." I would have to tap the discretionary fund, i.e., McKeever's offshore bank account on Maui, but I didn't think he would mind. "As soon as we get past this case, I'll send you on a shopping spree in Papeete."

"Hotdamnboyohboyandwowsers!" she said and lapsed into the arms of her fella.

As sweet as it was to have my family back together, I couldn't help knowing there was a murderess in our midst. I didn't believe she meant harm to any of *Quietude*'s children. As far as she knew, we were unaware of the treasure that had been lying around here for a few hundred years. The only tip-off would have been the presence of the émigré whom I'd been keeping under wraps at the Doubloon. All we had to do to avoid further bloodshed was to leave her alone. But that would mean abandoning our rather Quixotic quest. I decided not to make a final decision until I had apprised Bonny of the situation and we had spoken with the good ladies who had done so well by the village of Elsewhereville.

"To Daffadowndilly we go."

We swung by the cottage to pick up Bonny and see if my Little Coconut felt like venturing out. "Wilder Kathleen, your Mumza and I

106

and Queenie and Mister Buchanan are heading up to Daffadowndilly to thank the good ladies there for sewing your uniforms. Queenie is taking them some of her mango marmalade and your Mumza brought home some tea cozies—"

"Whatever they might be." she said.

"Right. Would you care to come along?"

"I don't think so, Popster. I see on my table that my Mumza left some more assignments for me. I saw some markings in red pencil, which means I got something wrong and now I have to get ready for *a make-up test*. A make-up test," she explained, "is when you flunk a test the first time around, not a test for putting make-up on your face. Make-up, in case you don't know, is this gunk that women out in the great world put on every day but I find it kinda creepy. Why don't they just want to look like themselves? Could you leave the not-a-flute here? I'd like to keep it in my toy chest."

"I don't see why not. You do have a perfect right to it, having found it in the first place."

"Thanks, Poppy. And could you please extend my fondest regards to Bess?"

"Betcha, Little Coconut. Now go hit those books like a batting practice fastball."

As usual when we went out walking, Creole had been familiarizing me with the names of the trees and flowers we passed along the way. I recognized the trees as trees, and knew the flowers for flowers but left the nomenclature up to her. Why bother having a honey-dripper of a secretary with a world-class memory for all matters floral and arboreal, after all, if she isn't going to help you conserve your dwindling brain cells for important stuff like obscure baseball statistics and the names of old doo-wop groups? But now that she and Bonny were up to speed on the case, she had morphed into detective mode. You could tell by her hat. She'd traded her bonnet for a stylish fedora and carried the gardening shears, cleaned of blood, in a belt at her waist.

"If they found the map on a previous visit and squirreled it away, their plan being to utilize it now, why didn't they use it in the first place?" said Creole

"That's one of the things I hope to learn when we reach

107

Daffadowndilly," I said, holding to Bonny's hand. My other hand was clamped around Cassidy McKeever's' blackthorn walking stick. I had borrowed Wilder's approach to borrowing and borrowed it from him permanently. My beloved, like my secretary, is a vigorous walker with an insatiable appetite for natural wonders. She must find kinship in them, being a bit of a natural wonder herself. The two of them had been hiking partners for years. My best chance for keeping pace with them was to stay firmly latched onto Bonny, knowing she wouldn't let me collapse into a pathetic heap and end up as old poet granola for the wild boars. "Though we must proceed indirectly. Clearly, the good ladies are unaware of their part in this play." The best lead we had had come from Wilder, who told me about the fellows she quoted Bess as calling "soldiers of fortune." I had long wondered how the little cottages of Daffadowndilly had been constructed. Leave it to my nine-year-old daughter to find out.

"So we don't think they're in peril?" asked Bonny. "They were unwitting accomplices in the hiding of the not-a-flute. Would the treasure hunters, now treasure hunter singular, wish them harm?"

"Probably not," put in Jake. "The lone hunter will be wanting to go about her business as stealthily as possible and somehow get off island with the spoils."

"I would still like to have an idea as to why they chose to return for the treasure," I added, "rather than hauling if off immediately after they first found the map."

"Exactly what I was getting at," said Creole. "Oh, that's an ylang-ylang tree [ee-lang ee-lang] formally known as *cananga odorata.*"

"I was just about to say that," I said, thinking that if you added another ylang, *ylang-ylang-ylang* would sound about right for back-up singers on a long forgotten doo-wop tune.

When a clearing came into view and the curious sight of smoke curling from a chimney—our climate makes a fireplace unnecessary, I took the one before us as a token of homesickness—I began to recognize the little village of Daffadowndilly, a settlement of brave older Englishwomen who had found companionship in one another's company after losing their husbands and finding common cause in the raising of the flowers which give the place its name. They had traveled more than halfway around the world to make a new home in

108

a place that, with the exception of it being an island, could not be more different from the green and pleasant land of their birth. They must have seen us coming from a ways off, for they had lined up, and, leaning on their hoes for support, dropped a sort of chorus line curtsey as I approached. I guess Wilder had blown my royal cover.

"Bess, I confess I played a small trick on you the last time, well, the only other time I was here in Daffadowndilly. I failed to mention that I'm the, um, king. My secretary, whom you know, colluded with me in this imposture. I didn't want to make you nervous." The truth was that it would have made *me* nervous. We were seated around a hard wood table decorated with a lace cloth in her parlor sipping Early Grey tea. Well, everyone else was sipping it, I was blowing on mine now and then, tilting it toward my mouth until it touched my lips and setting it back down.

"That was considerate of you, your majesty. I only realized your standing when I met your daughter, the horsewoman and baseball player. I was put in mind of those old stories wherein the king or queen goes about in tatters among the common people to, as they say, take the temperature of the nation."

"My daughter loves those stories."

"And I love her. We all do. She will be a fine queen, though I hope that I will not live to see her coronation, for it would mean the end of your majesty."

"Dear Bess, if there were a Nobel Prize for kindness, you would be on the next flight to Stockholm." I began to think I should get out more. "Wilder, who loves her new uniform, by the way, mentioned to me that your cottages were built by a band of wanderers who were passing through at the time, it must have been, what, nine years or so ago?"

"That would be about right, I should say. They were strapping lads, and hard working. They not only performed all the labor of construction, but followed to the letter all the ordering of the materials we asked for. We showed them photos of our homes back in England and they were able to duplicate them quite faithfully." I pointed at the small stand of supposedly black bamboo arranged in clay pots against the wall opposite us.

"I can see that. Though that business over there, while handsome and a nice island touch, seems a trifle incongruous in these surroundings."

"I suppose it does, though I'm so used to it I only think of it as part of my home. One of the 'slow nomads,' as I always think of their band, thought it might be a nice way of staking our claim to belonging here. I've come to love the way it shines in the lamplight at night."

"Do you know what became of them, the slow nomads?"

"No, though I have wondered. As I was telling Wilder, one of them returned recently, accompanied by a lady friend. He said the old crew had lost track of one another over the years. It saddens me when old friends are parted, though I suppose we all lose one another eventually. We start our lives as wayfaring strangers and as wayfaring strangers do we depart." Creole and Bonny chose that moment to present the gifts of marmalade and tea cozies, a felicitous bit of timing since it turned the mood a touch merrier. While they were chatting, Jake and I wandered over the faux bamboo and studied it, trying to look no more than mildly interested. Jake, shielding his hand with his body, pointed to a spot that looked as though the symmetry of the arrangement had been interrupted. I took it to mean that it was where he believed the not-a-flute had been stationed until a few days past. I nodded my agreement. We returned to the table and prepared to take our leave.

"Do you know if he is still on-island, your benefactor? I'd love to give him a formal greeting and congratulate him on the good work he and his companions did for you ladies." Of course, I was really asking if she thought the woman was still among us. I couldn't bring myself to frighten her unnecessarily by giving her the bad news about her old nomad.

"I'm afraid I do not, majesty. I remember the gentleman quite clearly from the lads' earlier journey out. I couldn't remember his name, though. I think it was the name of a poet, or perhaps a Biblical prophet. I'm afraid my memory is not what it once was."

"And his lady friend, was she a part of the original crew?"

"Oh, no. They were like a squadron of paratroopers preparing to be dropped behind enemy lines. Rough and ready fellows. A woman would have stood out rather dramatically."

110

"Oh, Bess," spoke up Creole, pulling the gardening shears from a little scabbard at her belt, "I found these a little way down the trail. I thought they might be yours."

"They are indeed, dear, and I've been looking everywhere for them." She gave a little blush of pleasure. "First people start wandering off, then they are followed by implements. Perhaps the shears were doing a bit of pathfinding on their own."

"I fear we must away, dear Bess" I said. "But Wilder, who is busy with academic obligations, asked me to give you her fondest regards."

"What lovely manners she has. And do congratulate her on the River Otters winning of the pennant."

"I will. I think the snazzy uniforms made all the difference. If any of you ladies would care to attend a championship game on the leeward side in a week or so, I would be happy to convey you thither in my motor carriage."

Chapter Twenty-Five

My Poppy says that people like me who were born at sea are fearless and ever ready for adventure. I think he might have made that up, but I always believe it when I start to be afraid of something, like spiders, not the big spiders we have here in the interior, they're kinda beautiful, in a spooky way, but the little bitty ones I mentioned earlier, they crawl around on the jukebox, it's creepy. I start to think they're going to crawl right into me and then I remember that I was born at sea and I feel better. As for being ready for adventure, I guess that's true. The next big one will be the Championship Series. We had won our first pennant, well, really, the Windward League's first, since this is the first year we have played. Now it was time to capture the Crown of *Quietude*. We were in the middle of a week off now that the kids from Zip-a-Dee-Do-Dah had won out over the Gee Willikers. We had never played at Paradisiac's Park and I wanted to take a look at it before our series began, check out the foul lines and get a feel for the mound.

Izzy and I and PW were hiking over there but I thought we needed to pick up the pace if we were going to be back in time for batting practice at Buck O'Neil Field. Walking with PW always teaches me really cool stuff. He will stop at a tide pool and examine every living thing. He's like a scientist from another world. I cannot tell what he is learning, but it makes me want to study things the way he does. Everything makes him laugh. I like to think when he is studying things that his laughter goes into the things he studies and makes them happier altogether. He becomes old friends with everything he finds.

I was lugging my ball bag, feeling like a little girl hobo I read about in a book one time. But my feet were starting to hurt and I began to wish there were a train I could hop to the leeward side. Izzy and I struggled on bravely, trying to work up a new cheer for the championship. It's not so easy finding rhymes for *Jehoshaphats*. I saw

PW leap up at the sight of a daytime moon in the sky, the same color as the surf at our feet. PW grinned up at the moon and his smile was like its little brother. He broke into a dance, grabbing Izzy and me by our hands and twirling us in circles with the wavelets breaking around our ankles. I accidentally dropped the ball bag and PW leaped to grab it out of the water before it could float away.

As he lifted the bag from a whitecap, the not-a-flute came out the top and was on its way to Hawaii when he snatched it out of the water. He made it into a part of his dance with the moon, and then pointed it at me, using his other hand to flash me some of the sign I've been able to teach him. My Mumza taught me to sign in my infancy, before I could even make words out loud, and I've been showing him since then. I don't really know if he gets what I'm twittering, since he's not into learning English or any other spoken language and the words and letters are sort of English finger-speech. But he does seem to be delighted by the idea of chattering with his fingers. Maybe he can tell what I mean by looking at my eyes, I can't say, but sometimes he answers, and the answers always make sense. Izzy can't even understand baseball signs, so she looked at me to see what he was saying.

PW stood in the backwash of a little wave and took a stance like a hitter in the right hand batter's box. He spread his feet and held the not-a-flute up like a bat, over his shoulder and cocked behind his neck, as though waiting for a pitch that could decide the big game. After a second, he raised it up even higher and then his eyes grew wide and he turned his head around and looked really ticked off at an imaginary umpire, who, I guessed, had just called PW out on strikes. He stomped around in the water, raised the not-a-flute and brought it down over his knee like a bat he wanted to bust. But it never really touched his knee. He held it out to me. The message he had sent me with his fingers had been *Watch*. His little pantomime in the water, which I knew from the times he was bummed out by the umpires on Buck O'Neil Field, said *Look in the not-a-flute*.

I took a deep breath and went through the steps: fingers in the ends, press, wait for the click, twist both ends and *presto!* as they say in the old stories. I handed the ends to Izzy and peered into the middle piece. At first I thought it was empty, which would have been a mean trick for PW to play on us. It was the first time that Izzy had seen the bamboozler cracked open. "Is there a prize inside?" she said. "Lemme see. Lemme see." She leaned in, so excited she could barely breathe. I don't know what I was expecting to find. If you've been listening to *1001 Tales of the Arabian Nights* half your life, anything seems possible. A gigantic genie might curl up out of the not-a-flute and take shape in the air over our heads. A dragonfly might slide out and hover before us and dart away. If I was expecting anything, it was that it would be just as empty as when my Poppy had shown me how to open it a few hours before. It had been in my toy chest for a little while and then gone into the ball bag. But if it was empty, why did PW want me to crack it?

"Cool your jets, Izz. It's probably just PW *winding us up*, as the good ladies would say."

I stuck my finger in and felt something sharp and papery. I poked at it a few times and pushed it far enough that I could take it in my fingers and slide it out all the way. A piece of paper not quite as wide as the not-a-flute itself, it was rolled up and seemed to call for a *Hear ye! Hear ye!* A *Hear ye! Hear ye!* is a thing my poppy does when he has a decree he wants lots of people to know about. He has Laurelai write the decree on a bunch of different scroll-y things with wooden ends and sends small boys running to the different villages to unroll the scroll-y things and call out *Hear ye! Hear ye!* to make people gather round. Then they read out the decree. The small boys get pearls for their troubles. Most of the decrees are kind of silly if you ask me. One said that no one was allowed to wear a necktie, whatever that might be, in the presence of the king. On Jackie Robinson Day, he decreed that everyone in the country had to do something 42 times. 42 was Jackie Robinson's uniform number in the bigs. It didn't matter what you did, just so you did it 42 times and thought about Jackie Robinson. It was on the honor system, which means you can't fib, you have to really do it. I think everyone obeyed the decree. My Mumza was here that day and she took 42 sips of Chardonnay, marking each one down in a notebook. I threw a tennis ball 42 times against the wall of the bunkhouse in our cottage where I have sleepovers. We don't have tennis courts on *Quietude*, so I don't know where the ball came from. I asked my Poppy what he did 42 times on Jackie Robinson Day and he said he thought of all 42 of the islands where he and my Mumza have played their twirly girl game. Like I say, I can never tell when he's kidding. 42 is LOT of islands.

But I really like his new decree. It announced a new contest for our first ever creek-naming. We ran out of rivers to name, so now we're going to start on our creeks. I know the creek he picked out to be the first and I've already thought up a good name. I won't say it now because I'm a superstitious ballplayer and always afraid of jinxing things. I'll just say that creek is kind of *dawdly*.

But this scroll-y thing wasn't a decree. It didn't say anything. What I mean is it didn't have any words on it. But it did have some pictures. It was confusing because the paper seemed old, but the pictures didn't. So they seemed like new pictures made in olden times. One time, my Mumza showed me in a schoolbook what are called *colored plates* of maybe the first pictures ever, cave paintings in France I think. The pictures on the scroll-y thing were sorta like those paintings, they were in that kid stuff-style, the way little kids make drawings in crayon of how their mom and dad and their own self in the window of a house look like with a big round yellow sun in the sky. But the paint didn't look old. It wasn't all hard and cracked like it had been around since a long time ago. In fact, it looked familiar, as though I might have painted it myself when I was little but I didn't. I probably shouldn't have touched it with my finger but I did. That was when I realized it wasn't paint but chalk. When I tried holding it sideways to see what the picture was about, I could tell that it wasn't a painting but some kind of strange map.

"Give it here, Cap," said Izzy. She unrolled the map and looked at it closely. Then she rolled it back up and peered through it like a spyglass. Then she unrolled it a second time and looked at it even closer than the first time. "A*ha*!" she said, putting a little topspin on it. I had told her that if she ever wanted to be a private eye, she must learn how to say a*ha*! and hold her index finger in the air.

"What mean you by this a*ha*! young shortstop?" I said, because it sounded like something a detective would say in a story. "Has this map spoken to you in the voice of a bygone world?" I wasn't sure what that meant, but it sounded good and Izzy looked very impressed.

"No, Cap, not really," she said, giving me back the map. "I just thought it was kind of pretty. I like all the little pictures."

115

Because I had walked all over the island with PW, I sort of understood the map. It wasn't a map of *Quietude*, not like the big fancy one my old friend Futon had made and hung in the library of the palace. It was more of what you might call a *confidential* map, a picture of our travels together. We have walked and fished and cooked our catch and dug clams and crabbed and hiked and hunted and swam in rivers and in the ocean and climbed mountains and surfed and canoed and dove the reef and did somersaults down sand dunes and had footraces and had zip line races too. When I was seven, I made a zip line with nylon rope and a picnic basket I sat in. It runs from the palace down to our cottage. I have to keep using bigger and bigger baskets for me to ride in because I keep getting bigger. About a year ago, my uncle John helped me put in a second zip line that runs what's called *parallel* with the first from the observation tower of the palace, a little platform for my Poppy's telescope, down to our family home. Now PW and I can say *one two three go!* and whiz off to the cottage side by side, me in my biggest basket ever and PW in a little boat he made out of tree bark. When we're having zip line races, we call ourselves Zoom and Whoosh. We take turns. Sometimes I'm Zoom and sometimes Whoosh.

His map was like a little movie on paper showing where we have wandered around. But not all of our places, only six, plus a little drawing of Buck O'Neil Field. It had the bases, home plate, a stick figure in a third base coaching box and the tall palm tree behind home from which my Poppy watches me pitch. Those were the only places marked on the map. I knew them all well, these places where my friend and I had become *masters of adventure*. Suddenly, I recognized the chalk, from its colors. My Mumza had brought it home for me from one of her White Ops trips. In the great world, children use these chalks to make outlines for hopping around games on pavement. On *Quietude*, we don't have pavement, so I used the chalks to do what's called *blazing trails*, to make sure my friends would know how to find me if there was some kind of emergency, like if Izzy had misplaced her baseball glove or something. The colors were a very pale blue, yellow, red, green and white. One of my best inventions (though maybe it doesn't count as one) is that I thought up a system of meanings for the different colors and taught them to my friends, especially to the River Otters. Green means *Keep Going*, yellow means *Stop and wait, I'll be coming back,* blue means *Meet me here tomorrow morning,* white means *fast water ahead,* and red meant *Danger, beware!* (if I knew there were wild boars in the area). At least, that's what they were *supposed* to mean. I don't think anyone but Izzy ever learned them. Well, she tried to. She was so used to getting lost, she figured she needed all the help she could get.

This map hadn't been in the not-a-flute before now. No one but PW could have made it, and no one else could have put it there. I keep the colored chalks in my toy chest at our cottage. He must have found them there and used them to make the map. That was all I could figure out about it. Was it a present or a lead? Had he made it for me the way my Mumza makes the photo albums we look at together whenever she comes back home? Was I supposed to use it to find something or use it only to remember our adventures? I looked at PW and moved my right hand flat under my chin with the fingers spread out, moving it toward him in the sign for *thank you.*

"Does that mean he's supposed to steal second on the next pitch?" asked Izzy, who's not so hot on signing. I showed her the map again, pointing at our ballpark.

"What do you make of this, Izz?"

"That's Buck O'Neil Field!" she said. "Maybe this map is supposed to show people how to get to the Championship games." With the exception of her crush on Mogu Mogu, baseball is pretty much the only thing on Mizz Izz's mind these days.

"Yep. That's where we throw it around the horn, all right." I agreed, wondering why our park was on the map. All the other places were secret ones that only PW and I knew about. "Do you recognize this chalk?"

"I saw some on the trees in the interior one time," she said. "I thought maybe it was some kind of coyote writing." I guess, in the heat of the pennant race, she forgot all about trailblazing. I looked at PW, who signed *you're welcome,* one of the signs I taught him. I never told him the color code of the trail blazing marks I leave on the tree trunks, and he wasn't with me when I left them. PW always knows where he's going anyway. It's like where he is going is waiting for him. He knows things in ways other people don't, like he's a person and a smart, funny animal at the same time, a bottle-nosed dolphin maybe.

117

I noticed that the places on the map, if you started on the left side like you were reading a book, went from the west side of the island, where we were now, east to the Grieving Widow, with two farther north or south and then circled back around. The first place you came to was a spot drawn in blue. It was on the rocks down by the south shore where a big blow-hole goes hugely kersploosh every few minutes. *Three, two, one, blast-off!* and the water explodes into the sky and when it comes down you get soaked if you're standing close by. PW had drawn blue lines going up all crazy like so you could tell it was the blowhole. When I told Izzy about the blowhole, she said she'd like to sit right where the water rockets out and go shooting up into the sky herself. I told her she might not like coming back down so much. I studied the map and let it blaze a trail in my mind. Altogether there were six places marked in chalk, plus Buck O'Neil Field. PW pointed at the blue blowhole picture.

Did he want me to go to the blowhole? Would my pocket watch be there? Was I supposed to go to all six of the places on the map in order? Was something waiting for me at each place? I could check out Paradisiac's Park later. Right now we had to get to batting practice. In the morning, I thought maybe I could visit the six places and try to figure out why PW had made me this map. At the moment, I barely had time to get to the cottage and put on my uniform. Izzy didn't need to change because she never wears anything else these days. PW would be going with us to pitch batting practice so I could save my arm for the big game. It was Buck O'Neil Field, ahoy! as the Captain would say. I looked at the drawings again, memorizing the six places.

PW, who hadn't brought his board, was body-surfing. After you've known him for a while, you begin to think he could surf on anything: sunlight, a tidal wave, maybe even a waterfall. Sometimes, for fun, he jumps in one of our rivers and lets the current carry him downstream. He's happy no matter where he ends up. I felt like I was about to jump in a current myself, with no idea of where it would be carrying me.

Chapter Twenty-Six

We had repaired to the Doubloon for a confab cum search party when Jake and I began to feel parched. My secretary keeps wine but no liquor in her tower, except for when she's preparing for one of her legendary girls night out brawls. We were taking another of the meetings I'd begun to think of as The Newshound Meets the Boozehound. Jake, used to dealing with temperamental actresses, a class of people comfortable with straying from the truth in search of a larger truth, was the ideal handler for Mister Smirnoff, who had slipped effortlessly into the enviable role of sugar-uncle-in-residence, reminding me more than a little of Walter Huston at the end of *The Treasure of the Sierra Madre.* (1948). Our cocktail waitresses, some of whom have opted for *Quietude* citizenship, others drifting through on semi-vacations, playing equatorial jumprope, hemisphere-hopping their lives away for as long as youth allowed, dancing most nights to a standstill and exchanging their services at the saloon for handy-man work, produce, hauling, building, fishing and surfing lessons, were fluttering around the émigré as though he were a shared patient whose very life was hanging by a thread. When Marlowe, today in raggedy old pink pedal pushers and flip-flops, saw us come through the swinging saloon doors, she pulled Smirnoff to his feet, smoothed his shirtfront, ran her fingers through his hair, didn't bother with the necktie he had taken off and stuck in his pocket, and steered him protectively over to the bar. His suit jacket had been wisely set aside and trousers abbreviated at the knee. The Russian had gone native in record time. A new barmaid with the memorable name of Shiva O'Malley prepared his Grey Goose and tonic without being asked.

"Death to traitors!" said Mister Smirnoff, raising his glass and rendering it half-empty. "Excuse me, I have been meaning to make of you an inquiry."

"Inquire away."

"Please do not misunderstand me," he said. "I am whole-hearted in my appreciation of your hospitality. But *I* do not understand. If you have no use for money, how can you continue to produce this mighty river of refreshment? Surely, an economy based on free drinks cannot long endure, as one of your presidents once said, I think."

"Ah, I see. I thought Jake would have explained that. We own and operate a floating nightclub on a ship in a harbor off the coast of southern California," I said. "It's called BBNGs. Perhaps you've heard of it?"

"Da, heard of. Rumors have reached my ears. I thought they were what you call urban legend."

"No, it's quite true. It's a gentleman's club where young ladies from all the islands of Polynesia dance the dances of their native isles to the accompaniment of island music. *Quietude* acts as a sort of recruitment center and talent scout for dancers. Women from here and from our neighboring islands find work at the club, which in turn finances scholarships for them at various universities, and the club reciprocates by sending big shipments of liquor back to us." Mister Smirnoff shook his head in amazement.

"This system beats holy living crap out of communism," he said. "Is more revolutionary too."

BBNGs stands for bare-breasted native girls, a phrase which warms the hearts of all right-thinking men. My brother and I and Cassidy McKeever had cooked up this idea when it occurred to us years ago that we needed to find a way to keep body and soul on speaking terms. We were all put off by the ambience of regular strip clubs, those loud, pounding sweatboxes where heavy metal vied with the bellowing of belligerent coke-heads. We still loved to look at ladies in their natural state, but found breast implants to be a violation of the natural order. Thus had BBNGs been born. We remodeled our old full-rigged frigate, *Heather & Yawn*, turning it into a floating roadhouse, and now a man could find an evening's peace by taking a short ride on a luxurious motor launch to a land of sea-going enchantment. The dancers were neither up for sale nor up for grabs. The vibe was as mellow as the music and the customers well behaved. My old friend Captain Primo had been the resident bartender there for two years now but he was headed home soon to be reunited with his horses and his old crew. I needed to decide on a replacement for him at the club.

120

It was due to BBNGs that the nation of *Quietude* had been born. Initially, we'd had trouble hiring enough dancers of Polynesian origin and ended up taking highly publicized "audition expeditions" throughout the various island chains of the Pacific in search of talent. On the third of those voyages, we stopped at an uncharted island somewhere in the vast warm water Siberia between Tahiti and Papua New Guinea. Truth to tell, we were off course and lost. If there'd been a gas station in the vicinity, I would have stopped and asked for directions.

We dropped anchor and went ashore in longboats to top up our water bags and hunt game birds to replenish our dwindling larder. Soon we met the old chief who I think of as the true father of *Quietude*. He was lonely and thirsty and we did what we could to lend him a hand and raise his spirits. Months later, back in California, we learned that he had passed away and, to our great surprise, left us his island. We decided to start our own country and to call it *Quietude*, insisting it always be writ in italics because it seemed quieter that way.

A minor spasm of fractiousness had broken out as to how the woman and her late fellow hunter had arrived without any of us noticing and where we should begin our search. "We're wasting valuable time," said Jake. "It matters little how they came among us, separately or together. The man, sad to say, is here to stay. We don't even know if the woman has the map. Hell, we don't even know if there *is* a map. All we know is that there is a contrivance which might have held such a map. Since the contrivance was empty when we happened upon it, it's safest to assume they got to the map and she may now be following it. She may already have found the treasure and be waiting for the chance to skedaddle with it. I say we spread out and begin to cover some ground."

Cassidy McKeever, my old friend who rarely leaves the big cave he calls the Hibernaculum, chose that moment to amble up and lift his left arm in the air at Marlowe by way of requesting liquid sustenance.

"We could gather about a hundred people together, join hands on the beach and walk slowly across the entire island," he said, "though that would be a rather exhausting way of meeting girls." I think he was just waking up. Marlowe brought him his usual, a Jameson's on the rocks and he thanked her with his famous big grin, his once black

121

but currently silver Zapata mustache rising like a lifting tide. He took a long swallow, set the glass down and went on, "Or, you might want to make tracks over to the Grieving Widow and fan out." Jake was suddenly on point.

"Why?" he said. "Did you see someone?"

"I did," said Cassidy. "I was performing my morning ablutions—" His cave is fronted by a waterfall, a set-up which solves all his laundry problems. In the morning—*morning*, in McKeever-speak means whatever hour he finds himself conscious—he makes a libation without water and stands under the fall in his old clothes, letting the descending curtain make pale his morning cocktail and soaks and sips and contemplates until he feels clean and ready to re-enter the comforting gloom. Then he hangs his clothes in the trees to dry and ambles back into his lair. "when this forest creature stepped into my sightline. At first, I thought I was still dreaming. I often dream that I'm standing out there, but usually the people I see are people I know, or used to know, long ago. The forest creature, who was clearly a human woman, though she looked like she had just transformed herself from a fawn, was unknown to me. I would have remembered."

"What can you tell us about her? You say she was headed toward the Grieving Widow? Can you describe her? What was she wearing?"

"She has long black hair, all the way down to her hips," he said, enjoying the recollection. "Tall, about five-ten maybe five-eleven. Very long legs. As to clothing, it was not the eminently casual, half-naked look we've grown accustomed to around here." He stopped to reflect. "In fact, her outfit is probably why I saw her as a recently transformed fawn. She was in buckskins." His long hair was still wet, he hadn't even taken the time to tie it back in a pony tail. And his faded old pale blue work shirt still damp. He must have walked straight over after his vision of fawn woman.

"Buckskins, you say?" Creole began to pay closer attention. She was used to being the only woman on-island with noteworthy ensembles.

"Yeah, dark gold buckskin shorts, rolled up one turn and cut very low, and a matching buckskin vest, with fringe. Buckskin fringe. Only one button buttoned. Buckskin moccasins. No headgear."

"Did she notice you?"

"I don't think so. I was standing under a waterfall about fifty yards from her. She never even turned her head."

122

"You seem to have gotten a pretty good look at her."

"It's my super-power. When I look through a waterfall, there's a magnification factor of ten." McKeever and I always fell readily back into our old sideways conversational rhythms, no matter how long he'd been in seclusion. By this time, he'd pulled his borders in so close that the ingeniously joined driftwood bench he'd fashioned above the little swimming beach about an eighth of a mile from his cave marked the outer boundary of his territory. Once a great walker, this last outpost, which we used to refer to as "girl-watching headquarters," allowed him to sit and sip his Irish and study the sea. He never tired of watching the waves coming in. It's good to have one thing in life you know won't fail.

Even his visits to the Doubloon had grown infrequent. On the occasions when his big hands pushed against the swinging doors and he came through in his slow bearlike way, conversation stopped and both men and women turned to him. It was as though Bill Hickok had walked out of the smoking train wreck of the past, having worked up a powerful postmortem thirst.

"Was she holding anything?" He waffled his brow, going back to the moment.

"No. Her hands were free." His eyes shifted, as though he were peering through the waterfall again. "In fact, she had her thumbs tucked into the pockets of her shorts as she walked. She wasn't walking with any great sense of purpose, though, more kind of aimlessly."

"Any other distinguishing features?"

"She has a fine jawline and a very cute tummy." Maybe I should order one of those prescription waterfalls for myself.

"It has to be the lone surviving treasure hunter" said Creole to Jake. "No other dame in all the land has such a get-up." She seemed a bit miffed.

A day earlier, we would have been the woman's competition in a treasure hunt. Perhaps we still were. But now that we'd stumbled over and laid to rest the handsome stranger, we were also one very weird posse.

"Let's walk-a-hula, babies," I said. Cassidy raised his glass at Marlowe.

"Can I get one to go?" he said.

Chapter Twenty-Seven

Early the next morning, Izzy met me at the cottage, wearing her River Otters uniform, her glove on her left hand. "Game one isn't until tomorrow, Izz," I said.

"I know, Cap," she said. "I just want to be ready in case a foul ball comes our way." She pounded her hand in her glove and glanced around, as though foul balls were a kind of bird that might appear anywhere.

I gave goodbye kisses to my Mumza and my Poppy, who were still sleeping, stowed PW's map in my toy chest so Izzy couldn't lose it and no one could take it away from me, fed Holy Toledo!, made sure Tickety-Boo had plenty of water and let her lift me up on her trunk which is how she likes to say aloha, and we headed out for the blowhole. I had left the not-a-flute with PW so he could use it to coach third the next day at the first game against the Jumping Jehoshaphats. I was in an old shirt that my pitching coach had given me and my vest with the pockets for my watch. I thought maybe it would help me find the watch before my Poppy knew it was missing. That was why I had borrowed a fedora from the king while he was asleep. Private eyes don't wear baseball caps unless they're *undercover* as baseball players.

Our destination is like a field of jaggedy big pointed rocks made out of real old lava on the south shore where hardly anyone ever goes. It's what's known as *desolate*. Near the edge of the field is the blowhole. Under the rocks is a cave and when the roof of the cave got old and tired and collapsed, it made a hole for the rushing seawater to go charging into and giddy-up all the way into the wild blue. If you are careful, you can get very close to the blowhole. PW can get closer than me, so close that when it erupts, he has to pull his head out of the way at the last instant to keep from getting blasted. The waves crash against the rocks like the sea is trying to give the land what my Mumza calls a *tongue-lashing*. I won't even ride Holy

124

Toledo! here for fear he might put a hoof wrong and break his leg. I was wearing reef-walkers so my feet wouldn't slip. Izzy, a sure-footed shortstop, was wearing her cleats. They're made of hard rubber, so I thought they would help her keep her balance. The blowhole is only about twenty feet from the drop-off, where if you fell it would be into the sea and say your goodbyes to *Quietude*.

A few stubborn blades of grass push up through the rock, not enough to interest an Arabian stallion. But the grass's only company, a pandanus tree about thirty feet tall grows all by its lonesome across the way. On his map, PW had drawn a line going up close by the blowhole and I thought he must mean this tree. Nothing else in the neighborhood was going up unless you counted the kersplooshes from the hole itself.

I know about this tree and a bird that lives in it. The bird is called a *red-moustached fruit dove*. Queenie told me about how they used to live in the Marquesas where we got the grass I make hay from. But the doves became *extinct* (which means there aren't any more, sort of like the Negro Leagues in the bigs) because of great horned owls and rats and cats that people brought there on ships from out in the great world. Everyone thought they were goners, but then Queenie saw one in this very tree! Which means they survived to live on *Quietude*! No one knows how they got here. I guess they flew. I had no idea why PW sent us here, if he did. But that line must stand for the tree so the tree must be why we were here.

"Do you think you can climb up to the top of that pandanus tree, Izz?"

"I can climb anything, Cap. Whattaya want me to do when I get there?"

"Look for something that doesn't belong."

"Like the bamboozler in the pirate's watering trough?"

"Exactly. If you find anything, bring it down." She took off her glove but left her cleats on and shinnied up the tree until she reached the branches at the top that look like a palm tree's but they're really not. This tree also bears a kind of fruit that looks like a pineapple but it really isn't. It's sort of a tricky tree. Izzy's head was hidden by the branches, so I couldn't tell what she was doing. But a tree only goes up and down, so at least I knew she wouldn't get lost. I prowled around the base of the tree looking for clues.

When she got back down, she did what's called *doffing* her cap (it just means you're taking it off) and bowed to me like she does to my Poppy.

"Find anything, Izz?'

"Betcha." She reached into her cap and brought out a piece of paper. It had two straight edges and a raggedy part that looked like it had been torn out of something larger. There was a drawing, in ink, of up and down water, waves meeting the edge of an island. Lots of water and just the edge of land. That was all.

"It was in a nest up there," she said. "Under an egg. No bird. I was glad there was no bird, because it might have scared me or I might have scared the bird. How'd I do, Cap."

"Solid, Izz. But It's only the beginning." I told her about the fruit dove and she said it must be a make believe bird because real birds don't have mustaches be they red or any other color. Then she asked if we could put baseballs on the blowhole and make our own pop flies. It was time to get her out of there. I went to the place in my mind where I had memorized PW's map and read it from west to east. The next stop was a pig-trap deep in the jungly interior. "Stick close to me, Mizz Izz. I'm taking you to a place no middle infielder has ever gone before."

PW and I had helped to make the original trap for Mister Buchanan when he needed one for our movie. We had bent back a palm tree at the edge of a shallow pit covered over with branches, held the tree in place with a rope and attached a machete to what's called a *trip-wire*. When the pig tripped the wire, a noose closed around his leg, he swung up into the air where the machete sprang out and cut his throat, though in the movie, it accidentally cut the throat of a man instead. It was all pretend and the man was OK. The movie trap was very complicated, so that there could be lots of blood and action. When the movie people left, PW and I had had replaced that trap with a simpler one with no pit and no machete in the hope of catching a wild boar someday and having a pig roast on the beach. Ours still has a bent down tree and a noose, which could catch a shortstop or even a starting pitcher and hoist her up into the trees where it would be hard to cut her down unless you have a machete. Everybody knows where it is and not to step into it. The movie trap

126

was kind of gross and gruesome in a cool movie way, it went s*nappety-snap* real fast, but ours was probably better, except it would only work if you put down some kind of food that wild boars like to eat (and they, like Tickety-Boo, will eat pretty much anything) so one would stop for a snack and before he knew it be hanging upside down. No one ever remembered to do that though, and that's why we had never caught a wild boar so far.

We looked all around the little space between the trees where the trap was set. Even though I now knew to look for a piece of paper that would fit against the piece of paper from the blowhole, I had no luck finding one. I checked PW's map in my head again. His drawing showed a bent back tree and a noose, nothing else. Izzy sat on the ground, looking bored. I could only think of one more thing to do.

"Stand back, Izz. I'm going to set it off." I found a fallen coconut on the ground and rolled it toward the noose, but it rolled a little too far. Izzy got the idea and found another one. She rolled hers toward the noose but it stopped just short. We needed to stand back so the rope wouldn't lash us when it went up. We kept rolling coconuts trying to get one just right so it would set off the trip-wire. Being ballplayers, we're both very competitive. As a pitcher, I felt I was better qualified. Izzy, being from Australia where they play a game called *cricket* where you sort of bounce the ball on the ground to a *batsman*, thought she was bound to win. On my eleventh coconut roll, I landed it dead center. The trip-wire went off and the tree went up to be with its old friends the other trees and I hurried to the spot that now was safe. I noticed that the pile of mushrooms I had left to tempt the wild boars had been replaced with a layer of dried leaves. Under the leaves I found the paper.

Our next stop, according to the map in my head, was an easy one. PW had put a part of the old map in a letterbox he and I had made around the time of my trail blazing. I left letters there for friends, and some of my friends left letters for me. Izzy once left me a letter that said, "Cap, This is fun, like playing catch with letters. Peace and love, your devoted short-stop." She got that peace and love thing from my Poppy. The mailbox was kind of like a little hut for a bird, if birds lived in huts. PW set it in a tree wedged into the crook of a high branch. It looked so much like a part of the tree that you wouldn't notice it unless you knew where to look. The part of the map from the pig trap had fit perfectly into the first. It showed a larger section of the island, with a few landmarks. Part three, tucked into my letter box, showed a wavy line that I thought was a river and then a drawing of brown lines going up and a lot of little white streaks above them. I thought it meant a rain forest. I checked the map in my head to see if it was like the map we were putting together, but they were totally different. The places where PW had hidden the sections of the other map were leading me in a sort of circle, one that would end close to our cottage. Maybe he wanted me to go home when we had found all the parts and put them together? Then I could put the map in my old toy chest where it would be safe, even though I didn't know what it was for. I had seen no sign of my pocket watch.

Part four of the map in my head led us across a different river, the Scheherazade, to a wide meadow where Holy Toledo! loves to graze. When I was very small, PW and I had robbed a beehive in this meadow and taken the honeycombs to my Mumza to put together with peanut butter at our cottage. It was PW's first peanut butter and my first honey. Afterwards, Holy Toledo and I would stop here sometimes for him to have lunch. I would pass the time lying along his back and listening to him munching the fresh green grass, happy to be alive and on horseback. I knew we were in the right place because PW had drawn a stick figure me on a four stick-legged Holy Toledo! and the long grass in green chalk with trees all around. But since Izzy was with me instead of my stallion, I knew the hiding place couldn't be in a saddle bag, so where was it? Thinking back on the afternoons I had spent here with my horse, I remembered how carefully he had stepped. When he runs or walks, you'd think he would be looking ahead at where we are going, but he also looks down to see anything that might make him stumble. In this meadow, he always plays a little game with me when we come to a spot that he wants to go around. I think it's an old *den* or *burrow* where some small animal made its home long ago. Holy Toledo! would stop, whinny, back up a few steps and then walk slowly around the hole, looking back at me over his shoulder.

I felt like I should dismount and look around, but since I was on foot, I settled for crouching while I walked, studying the ground for holes. Izzy imitated my crouch, even though she didn't know why.

"Are we checking for *venomous serpents*, Cap?"

"No, Izz. Looking for holes in the ground." She walked alongside me in her crouch as I walked around in my own, her hands clasped behind her back. Then she tripped, not being a keen-eyed Arabian stallion.

"Lost my footing, Cap." For once, her losing something was a big help. I pulled her to her feet and studied the spot that had tripped her up, getting down onto my hands and knees to take a closer look. I thought it was the same hole that Holy Toledo! so carefully avoids. Even though it was kind of creepy, I reached my hand down into the hole, fingers first, then wrist, and finally all the way up to my elbow. No snakes bit me but my wiggling fingers found, rolled up, part number four of the map that the map in my head was guiding me to.

Part Five took us across three creeks to a spot I think is magical. All by itself on a high hill overlooking the sea is a huge old flamboyant tree, its thousands of bright red flowers *bestowing* shade as wide as our center field. I think it's the only one of its kind in the whole country. My Poppy calls it our *Quietude Christmas tree*. PW and I used to play a game here where we each stepped off a hundred paces in opposite directions and I would give my special whistle through my teeth and we would race back and the first one to touch the tree was the winner. One time (I was still pretty small) I got there first and hid in the knothole near the bottom of the trunk. I thought I had really fooled him until I got splashed in the face by an ostrich egg's worth of water. PW is really hard to fool. On his map, I could tell the flamboyant tree because it was drawn in red chalk and was way up on the hill. From here, you can see a long ways, but I like to lie under the tree and look up through the red flowers at the clouds if there are any clouds or just the blue sky and wonder about stuff. Right now, I didn't have to wonder about where to look for the next piece of the map. It was right in the knothole. When I reached in and pulled it out, Izzy looked at me like I was some kind of magician.

I closed my eyes and looked in my head at PW's sixth and last drawing: a witch's hat shape for a mountain, a line showing how far up the mountain we should go, and on the line, a spiral shell. There's a kind of shell called a *conch*. In Florida, where my Mumza is from,

129

they pronounce it *conk*, like you would accidentally conk a batter on the head with an inside pitch, which is called a *beanball*. But here we say *conch*, which almost but not quite rhymes with *lunch,* which you could make out of the mollusk that lives in the shell if you wanted. The small boys use them when gathering villagers for a *Hear ye! Hear ye!* You blow into one end and it makes a sound sort of like the foghorn I heard one time in California. PW and I have one that we use when we walk to a place too far for my whistle to reach Tickety-Boo but I want her to come and rescue me. She hears it no matter how great the distance and always finds her way to her mistress. PW showed me how to do it. It's a big shell, you need both hands to hold and blow into it.

We keep it at a little clearing about halfway up Mt. Elmer, our *dormant* volcano. Dormant means it's not quite extinct like the people in the Marquesas feared the fruit doves were but isn't wide awake either. It could still blow its stack any old time but probably won't. I don't try to hike all the way to the top, halfway is plenty for me. The first time we went there, PW told me, with sign and pantomime, that the night before he had dreamed of a wild horse in this clearing. *A wild horse!* Where could it have come from? All of Captain Primo's horses are accounted for in the corral by the *Naughtylass.* It was a mystery. The mountain climbing had made me kind of tired, so I taught Tickety-Boo to come to me when I blew into the conch shell, figuring the next time I went to look for the wild horse, I could call my biggest girl and she would carry me back down. I didn't want to call her now, though Izzy was starting to look like she needed a hammock real bad.

"C'mon, Izz, it's our last stop for the day. Then we can go home and rest up for the game."

"Can you carry me, Cap?" she said. "I could be like a piggyback-pack." I didn't want to send her home by herself. She would get lost and I would need to find a new shortstop.

"No, Izz. But here's what we can do. You wait here and I'll come back for you. We can have a sleepover at the cottage. Okay?"

"Sure thing, Cap. I think I'll just curl up here and take a little nap."

Finding the shell was no trick at all. We keep it under a rock ledge that juts out a little ways from the mountain right where you can sit down to rest. That's what I did, sat down on the ledge, reached underneath and pulled out my elephant summoner. Now came the hard part. Even more carefully than Holy Toledo! steps around that abandoned burrow, I eased my fingers into the shell, using them like tweezers, and ever so slowly pulled out the paper, stopping many times to make sure it didn't tear, taking deep breaths when my fingers slipped and starting over until I had in my trembling hands the sixth and final part of the map. I was concentrating so hard, I even forgot to look around for the wild horse.

I had expected the last part not just to fit into the others, but to be like the last piece of a puzzle, the piece that explains the whole picture. It did fit but it didn't explain anything. I was keeping the pieces of paper in a waterproof pouch tied around my waist, but I was also keeping them in my head alongside of PW's map, the one we'd been following. I didn't want to take them out here where the wind might snatch them from my hand or a sudden rainstorm drench the paper. But just from glancing at the separate parts, I had a pretty good idea of what the map was about. It was an old map of my homeland. The rivers and the rain forest and the mountains were right where they would be if I had drawn a map of *Quietude* myself. But this map was so old I was pretty sure it had been drawn before there *was* a *Quietude*. Way back when. Half past the dawn of time, as my Poppy would say. I came back down to find Izzy sleeping at the side of the trail, her glove under her head for a pillow. I wished I could invent a way to toss her to our cottage as softly as a routine throw to first and the cottage could catch her safe and sound as a ball in the pocket.

"Wake up, Izz. It will be dark soon."

"Okay, Cap. Did you solve the mystery of PW's treasure map?"

"Sort of. His map isn't a treasure map, Izz. It's a map *to* a treasure map. A map like a puzzle but even if you put all the pieces together, you still don't know what they mean. Right now it's time to go home. Upsy-daisy." We shuffled and skidded down the trail. I didn't know if either of us would be able to sleep. We might just lie awake all night, talking about the next game.

131

Chapter Twenty-Eight

As we walked, I began to wonder about motive. Nine years lay between the first visit of the men whom Bess called the "slow nomads" and the reappearance of one of them, with a woman in tow. Why the long wait? And what had become of the others? As to the wait, I had to admit that we weren't exactly burning up the trail ourselves. Three days had gone by since we'd discovered the body. Well, we were a posse on island time, after all. Plus there had been the big game and the necessary visit to Daffadowndilly. For all we knew, the woman might have met up with her boatman and be halfway to Chile by now.

"If you don't know *what* it is and you don't know *where* it is and you don't know how it got to wherever it is, why do you think it exists?" said Cassidy. It struck me as a reasonable question.

"Because so many people are looking for it. Even you are looking for it."

"I'm looking for a girl with a really cute tummy. A navel that begs for a jewel." Only a few minutes in and he was already getting into the spirit of the case. What form did I want the treasure to take, I wondered? Sea chests overflowing with the gems of diadems? Diamonds in such profusion as to fill big sugar scoops to overflowing? Pieces of eight multiplied into infinity? I hoped it would not take the boring contemporary forms of bearer bonds and/or tech patents. Where would be the adventure in that?

We were four in number: McKeever, myself, Creole and Jake, a quartet in search of a tall brunette who couldn't be called a damsel in distress, not after having been a party to the puncturing of the handsome stranger with a pair of gardening shears. I tried to stop picturing her sitting atop the fellow, the implement raised overhead, about to become a deadly weapon. I had considered enlisting the émigré, but he begged off by showing me a nasty looking bunion he propped against the bar rail. It looked painful enough, though I figured the sight of the murdered man's body had probably done more than the bunion to dissuade Mister Smirnoff from further venturing out. I had asked of Bonny that she hunker down at the cottage, taking a homebody day. "Is Wilder safe?" she had asked. She wouldn't have worried on her own account.

"I think so," I told her. "A curious aspect to this case, or fortune hunt, is that the only person who might have been in danger has already been dispatched. But if Wilder shows up here, don't let her leave."

Unlike the environs of our cottage, on this side of the mountain, some of the falling water led downward to the openings of underground caves. Not many, and most were quite small. Wilder had told me about them, saying they were great places to play hide and seek, but I hadn't paid much attention. Creole, leading Jake by the hand, had found a kind of stone slippery slope and bid us follow. What was it Hunter S. Thompson used to say? "Buy the ticket, take the ride"? Fortunately, I was in shorts and a t-shirt which would dry out quickly, so I had no choice but to trust my secretary and plonk my royal ass down in a warm trickle flowing through a narrow channel over smooth rock which carried me rapidly along into a dark cavern. It didn't take long to learn that the cave was the first in a series, one opening into the next. The caves had been created over centuries by geologic upheaval, erosion and moving water, but no water dripped down into them. They were water-tight, apart from the big rivulet we had ridden in on, which, after gliding through, connected down below, I thought, to the Not a Care in the World River. I realized it might be the ideal spot for a wine cellar. The one the lady of the cottage had wanted beneath the cottage could not be dug. The soil of a volcanic island is too shallow and we weren't about to blast through rock. But, despite the warm water flowing through it, this cave was cool, maybe the coolest spot on the island, cool and gloomy, just right for the aging of vintages from the valleys Napa and Loire. It was also reminiscent of a salient feature of our cottage.

These chambers were, to the mind of a boy who'd cut his teeth on tales of skullduggery and derring-do, ideal spots for stashing a treasure, though I couldn't think how. They just felt like the sort of place that buccaneers on the run might find suitable to their purpose.

133

But all the surfaces were solid rock, you couldn't *bury* a treasure here. You'd break the blade off your shovel. And she whom we sought wasn't hiding here. When we reached the third and last cave in the series, we soon realized there was no point of egress for anyone not purely liquid, so we returned to the slide, where Creole and Jake scrambled partway out and reached down to help their dilapidated liege. The two of them, working together, were able to haul me from the cavern. Twice I scraped my head and lost my straw Stetson to the low ceiling of the passage. McKeever had wisely waited on the surface to act as a lookout.

We reassembled, spread out and kept tracking south to southeast. Five minutes later, we were within sight of the largest waterfall on this side of the Widow. We were walking, as quietly as possible, through a dense fern forest on a trail made by my subjects' footsteps. The fall itself spilled exhilaratingly down about eight hundred feet, white and free-flowing as the hair of god's godmother.

A closer look revealed why the water might have been in such a hurry to hurtle toward planet earth. Standing on a stone ledge at the bottom was fawn woman, face raised to receive the liquid benediction, feet spread, hands cupped to catch a few sips which she brought to her lips and drank. She had left on her buckskins, and they clung to her curves with admirable fidelity.

When she stepped out from under the water and stretched, I fancied I could hear a crucial portion of the moisture leaving her vest and shorts. I couldn't really have heard such a thing. It's possible I have an over-active imagination. "What do you think would be the word for when water is being pushed out of a woman's buckskins by the woman underneath the buckskins?" I asked McKeever. It's just the sort of thing he tends to know. He rolled his massive shoulders and concentrated mightily for a moment.

"Squilching," he said. But he looked troubled. "No," he said, "Squenching. Squenching is better." As I say, he doesn't come out of his cave often, but when he does, he makes it count.

"Perfect" I said. "I should make you Lexicographer to the King."

"A groovy honor, Mister High, but I must decline. Sounds like a lot of work and I'm trying to learn how to relax." What a country. Our guest tilted her head to the side to twist and squeeze her hair by way of drying it, then piled it atop her head in what women call a "messy bun." I felt McKeever's attention ratchet up when she shifted her weight. A renowned ladies' man in his heyday, he had survived several embattled marriages, helped to raise three children and retired from the romance wars with his brains no more than moderately scrambled, then repaired to the hibernaculum to lick his wounds and think the world over. I had no idea what he got up to in there. Wilder might know. One of our barmaids had once asked him the meaning of the word "spelunking" and he'd taken her back to the cave for the night to demonstrate. The next day, she looked very relaxed. I never spoke to either of them about the encounter. So far as I know, it had been the only time he'd enjoyed female companionship since we'd set up shop a dozen years ago.

As for me, I thought of the long simmering tears of the Grieving Widow, somewhat illogically, as Bonny's private reservoir. I felt proprietary toward them on my beloved's behalf. What was this long drink of water under an even longer drink of water doing poaching my lady's nearly amniotic fluid? Well, she was on the other side of the mountain, so maybe I should cut her some slack.

We stepped out of the fern forest and walked slowly toward her. For a second, fawn woman did resemble a forest creature. She looked startled—as who would not come upon unawares in such surroundings?—and I feared she would bolt. But she stayed in place, as though rooted to rock, wary and watchful. The waterfall was thunderous and rendered calling out a greeting impractical. I think it was my secretary who first caught her eye. Creole lifted her right hand and waved, a simple gesture but, accompanied by a smile, it seemed companionable, almost sisterly. The rest of us stood still and tried not to look either threatening nor afraid. The woman wasn't armed with anything other than the charms which had first caught McKeever's eye back at the Hibernaculum.

She walked toward us, steering straight for Creole. When she got within a few feet of our party, my secretary held out a hand. Fawn woman took it and held it in both of hers. It was as much a brief embrace as a handshake. Their eyes met and some female tumbler fell into place, an exchange of information I wasn't equipped to receive or interpret.

135

"I'm Clementine," the woman said. "I wonder if I might trouble you for directions. You see, I'm quite lost." She seemed totally out of it. She turned to Jake. "You're welcome to take me into custody." Jake looked at me.

"We don't have any custody," I replied. "You'll have to settle for being taken into a saloon."

Chapter Twenty-Nine

If a stuffed animal could snore, it would sound like Izzy in her sleep. It's like a purr that snuck out of a cat and made its way into a shortstop. She was doing a better job of resting than her team captain. I knew I should be concentrating on the upcoming game, but I couldn't stop thinking about the map. After Izzy dropped off, I stayed awake, took the six pieces from their waterproof pouch and laid them out on my Scrabble table. All six parts fit together perfectly, their ragged edges smiling into each other. Should I tape them into one big piece? My Mumza brought me what's called *Scotch tape* one time, though it's not from Scotland but the US of A. I decided to leave them separate. A harder decision was what to do with the other map, the one PW had made for me, which was now living in my toy chest. Should I tear it up or burn it to keep it away from, well, I didn't know who? I could not bring myself to do it, at least until I could learn whether he was just playing some kind of game with me or maybe it was *a matter of life and death*. It wouldn't make sense to anyone else if they should find it. Even if they were to visit the six spots, I had gotten there first so they could find nothing. And it was mine! An original PW! Maybe the only one of its kind, like Brigitte, my Poppy's 1932 Rolls Royce Phantom II woodie.

The map spread out before me was a very simple one. But if you hadn't lived here your whole life, you might not understand it because there were no words on it and only one color, black. On the left side was a lot of ocean, with little dots that must mean other islands, some near to here and some far away. Lots of little dots spaced far apart, with wide spaces of water in between. You could tell it was water because it was drawn in waves. Then parts two, three and four had drawings of rivers and mountains and forests in the middle of the map until part six which was the south side of the Grieving Widow around the bend from my Mumza's waterfall, where there are a lot of small caves where I used to play when I was little.

The caves are spooky beautiful like the big spiders in the interior. There's a waterfall near them much bigger than the one my where my Mumza likes to have her Chardonnay picnics. Her waterfall is sort of a little sister to the big one by the caves, which thunders down from the heights and if you're inside one of the caves, the sound *reverberates* like crazy and you think you're going *over* the falls or something. I like that word *reverberate*, it sounds like you could play it on a bongo drum.

That big waterfall was drawn high up on the south side of the mountain and going down to the caves. There were no names of places on the map, only four arrows to show how to hold it right side up. And there were no drawings of the leeward side of our island. It ended at the Widow. The whole map was very dark, so I wondered why the caves, where I used to play, seemed darker than all the rest. Could a shadow fall over something from inside of it?

Chapter Thirty

The émigré, McKeever, Jake and myself had gathered early in the Doubloon, making ready to interview our guest. A few minutes later, Creole and Clementine strolled in arm in arm. It was primarily my secretary's faith in the fawn woman that inclined me toward believing, if not in her innocence, at least in her right to a fair hearing. She had wandered on her own in a mild state of shock for three days, living off the land, too benumbed of mind to give a thought to the treasure she had come here for. So my secretary had told me in a hushed and hurried private conference. We couldn't lock the woman up in any case so we might as well hear her out. I shy away from the word "vibe" as well as the word "intuition," but I shared whatever sense my secretary had gained of Clementine when first their eyes and then their hands had met.

Creole was in a kimono, purple, blue, red and burnt orange on an ivory background, and ballet shoes, with her hair loose and flowing. She had acted as Clementine's wardrobe mistress, draping her in loose-fitting white gauze harem trousers and a flimsy red silk halter top. I never cease to be amazed by my secretary's magic steamer trunk. I don't know if there actually *is* a trunk, only that she owns such a rich variety of clothing it's as though all the world were her walk-in closet. You never see her in the same ensemble twice. When women first arrive in *Quietude*, they dress as they are used to, or as they would on any tropical vacation. But in time, both the heat and the force of conformity have most of them discarding their tops. But it takes a while. It makes for a topsy-turvy world in which our menfolk, inured to the sight of bare-breasted ladies, find those who are clothed to be the height of provocation.

Creole led our guest to a table in the corner which could accommodate the six of us. Marlowe furnished every one but McKeever with coffee. Cassidy is trying to kick caffeine so he stuck with Jameson's and water. Clementine looked, if not entirely composed, at least

139

somewhat rested and less ready to jump out of her skin.

"Good morning, your majesty," she said. Creole rolled her eyes in a way that only I would notice. As the former queen and my longtime fellow PI, she, like my daughter, finds my royal stature to be mostly good for a laugh. I once overheard her telling an old friend that "the king has a built-in jester." Well, better that she found me funny (or even laughable) than a fuddy-duddy or a potato head.

"Good morning, Clementine. Your name was permanently installed in my head even before we met, thanks to the old John Ford movie." She clapped her hands, sorrow banished for a moment. "My father loved that movie!" she said. "It was why he chose my name! His favorite part was when Henry Fonda said to the lady, 'I sure do like that name, ma'am, Clementine.' My dad said he knew right then and there what his daughter would be called." I'd been meaning to show *My Darling Clementine* (1946) to Wilder, who was already a big fan of *Shane* (1953). As a rough and tumble tomboy, she probably wouldn't identify with Cathy Downs as Clementine but might with Linda Darnell, as Chihuahua, thanks to their mutual abundance of dark wavy hair. Or maybe, as a horsewoman of renown, she would identify with the cowboys.

"You know Mister Smirnoff here, I believe, and Creole, of course. This is Mister Buchanan." Jake had fallen out at the palace, fearing that any male presence, no matter how benign, would not be entirely welcome at the Idyll Dipper. Better to leave the women alone to get to know one another.

"Call me Jake," said Jake. "I met Mister Smirnoff in Los Angeles shortly after you approached him looking for a boatman, which is why we both happen to be here. You couldn't have known that he would share your story with a journalist, or that the journalist's sweetheart—" he nodded and smiled at Creole, "made her home on the very island you were about to set out for. So you are clearly guilty of breaking the law of unintended consequences. The question we would like to answer is what other crimes you may have committed."

"If you're asking whether I took Dante's life, I did. But I assure you, it was entirely in self-defense."

"There was a struggle and the gardening shears went off," McKeever muttered to me under his breath. He used to write mystery novels.

140

"We were supposed to be working together," Clementine continued, "each bringing one of the two elements necessary to locate the treasure Mister Smirnoff here has already told you about. On the way back down the hill from that charming village, we suffered what, if you were given to understatement, might be called a falling out. It was really the continuation of a quarrel we had on the way up. What had begun as a disagreement in Los Angeles had finally escalated into all-out warfare. We were united in our desire to find this treasure—I made a promise to my brother, a deathbed promise, actually—but we held opposing views as to how it should be used—" She raised her right hand and held it flat against her chest, breathing hard, the gesture of one fearing the onset of regurgitation.

"Will you gentlemen excuse me for a moment?" She rose in her seat and Creole got up quickly to lead her to the ladies room. All eyes were on her as they made their way to the dames, all except my own which were on the émigré, whose eyes were trained on Clementine's rhythmically retreating backside. Because I am a heterosexual male human being, I assumed he was checking out her ass. I soon learned otherwise. The light of recognition, the one I'd been hoping for, dawned bright and clear, lifting him to his feet like an audience member about to start a standing ovation. I could almost feel his pupils dilating with excitement. He even set down his drink.

"That's it!" he cried. "I knew I had seen that face before, but I did not know where until I saw those shoulder, how you say, *daggers*. They spoke and it came to me."

"Blades. Shoulder blades," said Jake. "Where did her shoulder blades first speak to you and what did they say?

"In Moscow, the only time American circus came to town."

"Moscow, you say?"

"Da. It must have been twenty years ago. Is reason I didn't recognize her either in Los Angeles or here at first. She is now quite womanly of figure. In Moscow, she was a girl of about twelve, a slender child. She was dressed like a circus bareback rider, in a blouse that was flimsy and without a back, so that when she turned and walked away from me, I saw her own bare back, and her shoulder how you say *blades* made me think of an angel descended from on high. That is what they said to me, that an angel had tumbled into our poor world."

141

"Was she part of the circus troupe?"

"No. She was there with her parents, who *were* performers. I could not forget the occasion, though I would like to. It was the night her mother and father died. When she returns, ask her about her brother, the one she mentioned just now. This story is not mine to tell."

"Are you all right? Would you prefer to continue later?"

"No. I'm fine. I just needed to breathe until my stomach calmed down," said Clementine. While she had been in the women's room, Jake had fetched a glass of water, which she took a small sip on now. "Dante's death coming so soon after my brother's has my head swimming some of the time. I think I'm calming down and then it comes over me again. And it leads me back to other losses, ones I've lived with for two decades, but can never really get over."

"It sounds like you have a story to tell," said McKeever, who had been silent up till now. "Why not, as they say, start at the beginning?"

"Yes," she said. "I suppose that would be best."

"About twenty years ago, my brother Josh and his best friend, Dante, the man who died at my hands the other day, had been kicking around the world together after dropping out of college. I was staying with my mother's mother in southern California while our parents, who were well-known circus performers, followed that gypsified style of life wherever it took them. If the circus was playing nearby, I was allowed to attend, but they felt the disciplined routine of school and home and friends was too important for me to travel with them to far-flung parts. A rare exception was a date when their troupe had been invited to play at a venue in Moscow, at that time an extraordinarily rare cultural exchange. An *event*, as they say, lots of hoopla. Josh and I, since we were little, were devoted to each other, though our paths rarely crossed in those later years. I was even happier to see my brother than to watch my mom and dad. I met Dante there for the first time too. Our parents were trapeze artists, though they liked to refer to themselves as 'aerialists.' I had a red and gold poster in my room with lions and jugglers at the bottom and a picture of my parents at the top and a caption that called them 'Stars of the High Wire!' Unfortunately, they both turned into falling stars."

"Is that how they died?"

"Yes. Both of them. On the same day. One after another." What a splendid host I was. She had been among us for less than a week and in our first meeting, I had sent her back to the passing of her parents. A good thing I am the king and hadn't put in for the diplomatic corps. "He fell first, and was carried into the area under the big top known as the 'back yard' where the performers gather before going on, and an ambulance summoned. The ringmaster told my mother there was nothing she could do to help her husband whom, he claimed, had only had the wind knocked out of him, and that the show must go on. I've never understood why the damned show has to go on. What dreadful calamity would befall one and all if it didn't? I guess they'd have to refund the price of the tickets.

"So, anyway, she went up, in a state of mind I cannot imagine: dazed, sick with worry, her heart racing. Not surprisingly, she too fell, not thirty seconds into an act she had performed hundreds of times. The last time they spent together was in the ambulance which they shared. I don't know if either of them was conscious, but neither was alive when they reached the hospital." I felt I wasn't doing well by our guest and tried to catch Creole's eye. But she, like myself, had been stunned into silence.

"Circus crowds can be rather blood-thirsty," continued Clementine. "The appeal of the high wire and the trapeze, when you think about it, is in the hope, the hope which no one must ever mention, that someone will fall. Then the audience gets to enjoy that collective catch in the throat that's even more thrilling than a roller coaster." She tried to pull a smile, but it took effort.

"Anyway, it was a long time ago, and they died doing what they loved. I try to think of it like that."

I glanced at McKeever's whiskey glass and noticed that he hadn't touched his drink. He also hadn't said a word. Usually these days, his look is inner-directed, beyond the blankness of introspection, a kind of cliff-dive into deep solitude. He almost disappears. But as Clementine was giving us the lowdown on her life, his gaze never left her face. I took it as a good sign. I recalled the way he had looked at her as she fell under the spell of the warm water at the foot of the Widow. We'd been close friends for so long I could sometimes think along with him. To my surprise, it was Cassidy who first found his voice. "For someone who has lost her entire family," he said, "There

143

could be no better place to find respite than this island where you find yourself. You would be welcome to stay for as long as you like. If you found it agreeable, you might even consider making a home here." The corners of her mouth lifted and a soft light entered her eye.

"Thank you," she said. "It's a generous offer, and one which I will keep in mind. But first I should finish my story. If you decide I'm a murderess, you might not want me as a fellow citizen"

"Good idea," I said. "Can I get you a drink?"

"It's pretty early," she said.

"Not really, we're south of the equator." Her mind must still have been somewhat disordered, because my senseless remark seemed to make perfect sense to her and she requested a glass of white wine.

"It was at that circus performance in Moscow that Josh and Dante met the other four fellows they ended up kicking around with. In his letters, Josh told me about their globe-trotting, which had been extensive—Malaysia, Indonesia, Singapore, Sudan, Somalia, India, Thailand, Kazakhstan, and, as you know, the South Pacific, their last stop being *Quietude*—after they'd all been thrown out of, or just dropped out of, various universities in the States, none being cut out for academia. They all had a taste for adventure and were young, good with languages and good with their hands. They figured they could scare up a living wherever they landed, and they had. They did construction, did iron work, fought fires, chased girls, got into and out of trouble with the law, helped people who had gotten into scrapes of their own, found some missing persons, built some dwellings, took on perilous jobs, body-guarded and hired out as security for unsavory characters. I think they may have run some guns and may have muled some drugs—Josh kind of skirted the subject—and may have fathered some third world children. The way Josh made it sound, they were part Peace Corps, part Route 66, in search of what young guys are always looking for: sex and high old times. In a word, kicks. Sometimes they'd be strapped for cash, other times they'd be flush. Sometimes they stayed in student hostels, sometimes in luxury hotels. Sometimes they found work, sometimes they found themselves in trouble. They got good at different kinds of work and even better at getting out of trouble. They had only one

144

rule: stick together. They moved around the world like a small school of fish.

"Josh was twenty when they began their travels and twenty-eight by the time they ended up in Maracaibo, which is where he won the map in a card game, the map I brought here and then lost. A map of an island in the south Pacific, it was obviously old, but curiously incomplete. It had none of the usual markings of maps, no lines of longitude or latitude, no legend, no language at all. There was no way to attribute a nationality to its clearly amateur cartographer. There were only arrows denoting north, south, east and west, and sketches of what he took for the west coast of South America and the northern coast of what we would now call Australia, to give a general idea of where the island lay. To the west were a handful of dots, or dabs, which he took to be the few other islands and atolls in the vicinity. On the map itself there is no visual representation of treasure, no X marking a spot. There are wavy lines representing the rivers that you all know well. There are the peaks you have given names. At the time of the map's creation no Europeans had ever landed here, it was a purely Polynesian place.

"Josh's surmise was that the map was not so much a treasure map but a hastily drawn reminder to its creator of where the island lay. He maintained that the author of the map had visited the island in order to leave plunder and come back for it after shaking pursuers. The artist would have known where on the island he had cached the goods, but been uncertain as to whether he could find the island again. According to Josh's theory, the man had been sailing through rough weather, in uncharted waters, and landed here during a storm, aware that he was but a hairsbreadth ahead of the original owners of his ill-gotten gold. If the map's author and his crew had struck a ship on the open sea and relieved it of its chest of mad money, that ship might well have given chase and been closing in on the pirates when they reached your shores. If so, the ship's captain may have caught and hung the rascals shortly thereafter, perhaps in Maracaibo, leaving the loot in its hidey-hole somewhere on this island, unbeknownst to anyone living. There would have been no record of it, and the captain, satisfied that his gold was not onboard the looter's vessel, would have had to content himself with commandeering their ship and punishing the brigands who had taken his valuables. Just a theory, but the sort of thing all Josh's friends found stirring." I remembered Bess's name for the fellows who had built the good ladies' cottages, the "slow nomads."

"Did Josh and his crew have a name for themselves, do you know?"

"Yes, he mentioned it in a letter. They called themselves No Strangers to Danger." Jake chose this moment to break in.

"If the map was not in any obvious way, a treasure map, how did your brother convince the others to follow it here. For that matter, without any markings, how did he determine that it was a map of the island that would one day be called *Quietude*?"

"He didn't need to do much convincing. He had always been the leader of the crew and he was convinced that this map was what you might call "charged with significance." That was enough for the others to follow. They were a restless bunch, always looking for a sign or an omen pointing to their next port of call. They had named themselves No Strangers to Danger for a reason. Josh said there may have been warrants out for them in a dozen countries. They were quits with Maracaibo anyhow, the law closing in and the air of the South Pacific was air they hadn't breathed before. So they let Josh's half-baked theory guide them."

"And it guided them to *Quietude*?"

"Yes. Josh had read it correctly. Once they'd landed here and familiarized themselves with the terrain, he knew this for the island drawn on the map. His companions would have preferred lying around on the beaches, but he flogged them into hiking around seeking places where the supposed treasure might be hidden. On one of those hikes, they encountered the ladies of Daffadowndilly, who offered them room and board in exchange for their labor as builders. It was a sweet set-up, Josh said, because the work was challenging and gave him time to continue treasure seeking.

"By the time they'd completed the job, Daffadowndilly really was a village, that which had begun as an encampment. Along about then, via one of your mail drops, Josh received a letter from me. Most of my infrequent correspondence was the usual chatty sort about who I was dating and how I was doing in school. This one was different. It was, I'm embarrassed to say, a cry for help. I had gotten into a spot of trouble. I won't bore you with the details—there was a charismatic

146

older professor and a student-teacher conference and pretty much what you would expect might follow. Josh had always been devoted to me, even more so after our parents died. So he immediately decided to make his way to California to be by my side and settle the professor's hash. When he told his mates, they all realized they'd begun to miss their own families and decided jointly that it was time to go home.

"But before leaving *Quietude,* Josh took a meeting and performed a sort of ceremony with the other No Strangers to Danger. He hadn't found any treasure (the rest of them had pretty much forgotten the whole idea), but he felt he was getting very close, and wasn't ready to quit on the hunt entirely. So he solemnly divided the map into six parts and gave each of the fellows a part to hold. They were like promissory notes pledging allegiance to their return to claim the treasure one day and divide it equally among their number. But they must come together or not at all. Very Musketeer like, I know, but that's how they were.

"After they had returned to the States, the No Strangers found it impossible to settle down to pumping gas or selling shoes or working in convenience stores. One went into the Merchant Marine, one joined the Foreign Legion, which I didn't think still existed, another became a Navy pilot, one a safe-cracker in Hong Kong, one went to Ireland and became a cabinet-maker."

'Cabinet-making doesn't sound so dangerous," I said.

"It was in Northern Ireland."

"Ah."

"Yeah. He ended up making more coffins than cabinets."

"What did your brother turn his hand to?" asked Jake.

"Oh, different things. There had to be action, and at least a hint of risk. Stock car racing, bounty hunting, he was a cop for a while, on the bomb squad, no less. He had grown fairly successful as a stuntman on westerns in Hollywood when he got the news about his lymphoma." Too bad he hadn't been a humble stand-in, I thought. When mortality came a'calling, he could have just stepped out of the shot and sent in the male lead. A quiet settled over the table, which McKeever solved by going to the bar and bringing back a fresh round of drinks. Clementine sighed and sipped and picked up the story.

147

"It took him away very quickly," she said. "Toward the end, when he knew he had very little time left, he called me to him. We'd been living just a few miles apart, and grown used to spending evenings together. Now, all of a sudden, I was sitting at his deathbed. I didn't know what to say. I would start to reminisce about our childhood and our trips to the circus and how we were in awe of our parents way up there on the wire, and then I just shut down. It didn't matter to Josh. He had called me not only to say goodbye, but to ask a favor of me.

"For the first time, he told me about the treasure he believed was here on *Quietude*, about his conviction that he had come very close to finding the object of his explorations. He felt certain that he had pinpointed its location. To that end, he had drawn a second map, a very specific one, one without which, he said, the first map was virtually worthless. As he was finishing it, he received my letter. There was no question in his mind but that he must return home. But before gathering his comrades for their last all-for-one conference, he had crafted the perfect hiding place for his second map, a place in plain sight where no one would ever think to look. He had told only one of the No Strangers about the hiding place, and that only after they had returned to the States.

"Josh was aware of my sympathy for the people of Ukraine. He wanted me to come here, find the treasure and use it to send aid to that nation under siege. He told me how to contact the members of his old crew. He felt it imperative that they be let in on his plan. If they didn't want to come along, they were to hand over their sections of the Maracaibo map, as he called it, by way of giving me their permission to look for the treasure on my own. Well, not completely on my own. He said that he had confided to Dante, and to Dante alone, where to find the hiding place of his second map, the key to the first. But he hadn't told him how to employ it. That knowledge he had kept to himself. Moments before he left us, he explained the workings to me. I believe he was on the verge of telling me its location when, as they say, he breathed his last.

Chapter Thirty-One

Baseball fields are pretty much the same, even in the bigs. Here on *Quietude*, in what you might call the *littles*, where we have only two, Buck O'Neil Field and Paradisiac's Park, the only differences are how far back the outfield fences are. The mounds are the same height and one is no closer to home than the other. The bases are the same number of feet apart. My Poppy says in the bigs the umpires look like *undertakers*, whatever they might be. Here the umps wear big chest protectors and masks like catchers but underneath they just have on baggies and slippahs. Too hot to wear black.

I decided to cancel our hike to the leeward side in favor of trying to find my pocket watch. Soon, I thought, I should show my Poppy the big map. I don't know how to work it as a treasure map. Maybe it *isn't* a treasure map. But I do know that it's a map of *Quietude* and he's the king of this place so maybe he can figure it out. But my watch is mine and mine alone. He gave it to me forever and for always, not for such a little while, but for my whole life long. He tells me that when he presented it to me on my fourth birthday (this is another thing I don't remember), he said, "Wilder Kathleen, this watch will tell you the time for as long as coconuts fall, coyotes howl and the whales dive deep far out at sea." Well, that's what he says he said.

I thought I should find PW and see if he wanted to go on a pocket watch hunt. He's probably the best hunter on the island, though I don't guess he's ever gone looking for an antique timepiece. He kind of steers by the stars, even during the day. The sky tells him the time. I got lucky when the first place we looked for him was at No Hodaddies Allowed Beach where he was shredding with his little girl, Kalahari on his shoulders, just like he used to do with me. It made me a little sad to see and be so grown up now. But I do love Kalahari. She's almost old enough to be a River Otter. I can hardly wait. I'll be able to braid her hair in the dugout. Even since my friend, Heiata, taught me the art of *cordage*, girls and women all over the country come to me to do their hair. And if Kalahari makes the team, she can help us make up cheers. She has grown up speaking both American, through her mom, and the clicking language of PW's people. Maybe we could work some of those clicking sounds into the cheers. We'll be like the singers and musicians in Shake It Up, Baby who clack woodblocks together and clap their hands and snap their fingers instead of using instruments.

When he came in, all dripping and smiling with the sun shining off the seawater on his skin, I put on a little pantomime show so he would know what I wanted to do. I wasn't wearing my vest but I pretended to reach into its pocket and pull out my watch. Then I pretended to open it, look at it, get annoyed, wind it, tap it, hold it up to my ear, shake my head in frustration and stuff it back into the pretend pocket. PW was watching me like a movie in my Poppy's projection room.

"That's the wrong panto," said Izzy. "You're telling him that the watch doesn't work. Who cares whether it works or not. Lemme try," said Izzy. She reached out to me but I didn't know why. Impatiently, she pantomimed taking off a vest. I pretended to take off the imaginary vest and handed it to her. She pretended to put it on. She buttoned it up and tugged on the ends. "Pretty sharp," she said, sticking her hand in a pretend pocket and bringing it out empty, looking confused. She patted a lot of other pretend pockets. Where could it be? She got down on her hands and knees and dug a big hole in the beach, frantically flinging sand aside. No watch. She stood up and collapsed into my arms, sobbing uncontrollably.

"Now *that's* a panto," she whispered into my ear.

PW appeared to be deeply moved. He pointed inland, in the direction of the Grieving Window and our family cottage. It would take us about an hour to hike—or *trek*, as my Poppy says whenever he has to walk more than ten feet—over to the mountain. If PW had put the watch in my toy chest at our cottage, I would have seen it. He must mean the mountain. I began to wish I'd brought my horse.

On the way over, I fiddled with our batting order in my head and wondered where my watch had turned up. PW knows the island better than anyone, better than me even, but he got here first, three years before I first *wowed the crowd*, as my Poppy says. PW just naturally kicks around, it's his style. He spends about the same

150

amount of time away from his family as my Mumza does out in the great world but he does it all right here on *Quietude*. His wife and daughter are used to it and it's OK because he finds places no one else knows about to take them swimming and surfing and he makes picnics with food he finds along the way.

I must not have been paying attention, just following PW, with Izzy following me and when I looked up, we were back by the mock-up of the Naughtylass, right in front of the watering trough where our search had begun. He stopped beside the trough and reached into the soft quiver where he keeps his arrows. I'm so used to seeing it over his shoulder along with his bow—he even wears it when he surfs, one time I saw him shoot a fish and never even left his board—that I forget he has it with him. He hunts for game birds to feed his family and taught me how to fish with a bow and arrow in our rivers. We have a lot of rivers, it's very different where he comes from, there aren't any rivers there, but I guess they aren't sad because they don't know. I didn't see anything he would want to hunt here in the pirate compound though. He wouldn't shoot a horse, he's a gentler of horses, and all the pirates are his friends. I saw him shoot a snake one time but I didn't see any snakes just now. He taught me how to skin a snake and cook it in a fire, but I didn't like it much. I'd rather eat mangoes or crab claws or Queenie's cornbread.

But when he reached into the quiver, he didn't bring out an arrow but the good old not-a-flute. Every time I lose track of it, it comes back around, like an old friend when you need one most. PW used the end of the bamboozler to draw a rectangle in the dirt beside the watering trough. When he stood inside the rectangle, put his hands on his knees and stared to the west, I could tell he had drawn a pretend third base coaching box. Then his eyes darted suddenly upward, as though a River Otter had just clubbed a hard liner deep to right center. He began to pinwheel the not-a-flute the way he does to wave runners around. Izzy caught on before me. She said, "He wants us to circle the bases. C'mon, Cap, bust it down the line."

Well, there weren't really any bases, but she seemed very sure of herself. So I lit out and tore around where I thought the bases would have been if there were any and I hoped no pirates were watching. Izzy was right on my heels.

151

I pretend scored standing up but Izzy, looking to beat a strong throw from nobody, went barreling in old school-style with a head-first slide, her hand reaching out to brush an imaginary home plate and avoid an imaginary tag. She looked up at me and gave me her goofy redhead's grin, her face all dusty. She looked like she had scored a perfectly real winning run. Oh, to be seven again.

PW spread his arms, hands stretched out with palms facing down in a safe sign. For a second, he looked like one of our huge frigate birds with their humongous wingspans, but, because he'd opened his hand, the not-a-flute slipped from his grasp and fell into the watering trough, right where we had found it in the first place.

It was The Discovery of the Not-a-Flute, Take Two, as we say in the movie-making biz. It was my first take two. Of course, I'd only ever played in one scene in a movie, but I nailed it the first time around. One Take Wilder, that's what my director, Mister Buchanan, used to call me. I glanced over at Izzy.

"Would you like to....?" I said.

"Not me, Cap. I'm beginning to think the bamboozler is bad luck. You go right ahead." I reached into the trough, as I had done once before. When it broke the surface, the tadpoles—my Poppy calls them "wild commas"—scattered and I closed my fingers around the not-a-flute and pulled it out, dripping. PW raised his left leg, bent it and did a breaking a bat over your knee gesture, only it was me and not he holding the bat, aka the not-a-flute.

"Look in it, Cap, that's what he wants." PW was giving us a second chance, but a second chance to do what? He kept his eyes on me, running his fingertips through his greying beard thoughtfully. Izzy may have thought the bamboozler was bad luck, but she obviously wanted me to crack it. Her eyes were wide as she looked at me and then at the not-a-flute. Well, it couldn't hurt to look. Maybe it really was a magic wand, because stuff seems to be getting in there all by itself.

Chapter Thirty-Two

"Josh's funeral was the ideal setting for a reunion of the No Strangers to Danger. They could catch up and kick around old times even as they mourned. I was able to get in touch with them all, passing along my brother's request that each bring along their section of the Maracaibo map. The old esprit de corps kicked in and everyone showed up with his part of the map. Only Dante cared about the money it might represent. All the others had saved it out of sentiment. One of them said to me that, as a keepsake, it was a greater treasure than the one it was supposed to unlock. Some had come from foreign parts, perfectly willing to make the journey to pay last respects to Josh. Dante, as it happened, was living right down the road in San Pedro, getting by on doing some salvage diving. I took a moment alone with the members of the crew, explaining Josh's wishes regarding the map, the treasure, *Quietude*. I placed his proposition before each: that he could either join my expedition, his section of the map entitling him to a share in the treasure, or he could decline by handing over his portion, which would stand as his pledge to aid the people of Ukraine. It was all very hokey. Five members of the band solemnly placed his part of the old map in my hands. They were trying to be serious, but I thought I detected grins just under the surface. Not a one of them had ever really believed in the map in the first place. They believed in friendship, and in solidarity, and this was their way of honoring both.

I saved my meeting with Dante for last, explaining what Josh had confided to me. I had the map, I told him and knew how to operate the device which contained the key to the map, but I was also aware that only he knew of the device's whereabouts. He was adamant about holding onto his own piece of the map. When we began meeting at Barney's (his choice) to make plans for our departure, I asked him what he'd been up to since the old gang had disbanded. He was rather evasive, slippery even as he was braggadocio. He hinted at exploits in distant lands, tight spots he'd been lucky to escape from unscathed. He never said as much, but I gathered that he'd been working as a mercenary until his nerve failed. I don't think he minded being a killer for hire, but had grown tired of people trying to kill *him*. By this time, he was I think the term is 'burned out.'"

I had met him once, briefly, in Moscow, the day I lost my parents and Josh and Dante found a foursome of traveling companions. He was then as hale and hearty and ready to roughhouse as any of them, well-muscled, bright eyed, hopeful. In L.A. I was shocked by the contrast in both his appearance and his manner. He was haggard, unshaven, his hands shaking. At the funeral, he had worn what I took for a Salvation Army suit, but when we met at the bar, he was dressed in dirty camouflage fatigues. After two drinks, he grew increasingly bitter and belligerent, lashing out indiscriminately at officers he had served under, at the women—low down whores each and every one—who had taken him for a ride. After four drinks, none of the other patrons were safe from his abuse, both verbal and physical. But I knew I needed him to keep my promise to Josh.

I didn't think anyone would want to work with him in his condition. So after our first meeting, I took him to a stylist, had his hair and beard trimmed, and bought him an L.L. Bean safari outfit and a few other items of apparel. Eventually, he found a boatman at a marina in Santa Monica and they hammered out a schedule for rendezvousing on the island. I made him dry out for a few days before we left, not that it did much good, since he started ordering drinks the second we stepped on the plane, and, as you know, it's a very long flight. He had never agreed to Josh's plan to help the people of Ukraine, his intentions for the treasure were entirely self-serving and we quarreled about it constantly, his bitterness on full boil. He felt the treasure was his rightful inheritance. I countered by saying he was entitled to one sixth of it only, he claimed that since we were a search party of two, he was entitled to at least half.

"The only time he relaxed his guard was during the hour or so we spent with Bess. Maybe he recalled his earlier time in Daffadowndilly with the No Strangers. He modestly accepted her thanks for the good work they had all done. When Bess invited me into her kitchen to prepare what she called 'an island version of high tea,' Dante took the opportunity to look around the cottage, saying he wanted to make sure the work he and the boys had done was holding up. I'm sure that's when he removed the device from its arrangement.

"After saying our goodbyes, we began to walk down the path that leads, I believe, to your baseball field. I knew there was a game in progress because I could hear the cheers from way up in the hills. Dante pulled up his shirt to show me what looked like a dark wooden wand of some kind stuck under his belt, grinning. I asked him if that was the fabled hiding place and he nodded, demanding that I show him how to use it. Well, I was going to have to tell him at some point, but I decided, rather stubbornly, that this was my last chance for a negotiation. I told him that if he didn't agree to divide his share of the treasure, donating half to the cause that Joshua had espoused, I, the one with both the map and the knowledge of how to operate the wand which held the key to the map, would as soon go to my grave than partner up with him any further. He grew livid, called me a lot of really nasty names and threatened me with violence. His anger provoked my own and I responded in kind. The names I called him were only marginally less impolite than those he had thrown in my face. When he put his own face a few inches from mine and snarled, 'You've probably been fucking your big brother since you were twelve. That's why you two have always been so sweet on each other,' I slapped him as hard as I could. It stunned him. And while he was rocked back, shaking his head and trying to regain his balance, I obeyed the impulse to grab the wand out from under his belt and took off with it." Her listeners were all a little stunned ourselves. No one said a word. We just waited, and watched as the memory returned, fresh, clear, terrifying. "I had a few seconds head start, but I was on the edge of panic. We had been here for about three hours, I didn't know the terrain, apart from Bess, didn't know a living soul and I was unarmed. I'm a fast runner and in better condition than Dante was, but I knew the adrenaline rush provided by his need to answer the insult I had dealt him with the blow would allow him to run me to ground eventually. For a moment, I had both the map—which I had secured beneath the sweatband of my hat—and the wand, but I felt like I was running for my life.

"I decided to ditch the wand. If I were able to get away, I could go back for it and wait for his temper to cool. If he caught up with me, I would still have a bargaining chip. I was flashing by all sorts of spots but none seemed right. If I just tossed it into the underbrush, I might not be able to find it when I retraced my steps. I didn't dare stop to go through the procedure Josh had acquainted me with to open the wand and retrieve his second map. There was no time, I had to keep running. I was starting to tire when I came into a kind of compound, with a corral full of horses on my right and what looked like a watering trough for them on my left. On yet another impulse, I tossed the wand into the trough, hoping against hope that it was watertight.

"I might well have outdistanced Dante, had I not tripped in the middle of a meadow just past the compound. I struck my head on the ground and was a bit groggy when he came upon me. He kneeled down over me and pulled a pair of gardening shears out of a pocket of his cargo pants. I had seen them on the table of the porch of Bess's cottage as we were going in. He must have taken them as we were going out. I suppose a prosecutor would say that bespoke premeditation. He raised the shears over his head, his eyes rolled back in his head as though he were undergoing a seizure. Fortunately, I remembered a stunt man's fight scene move that Josh had taught me. Before Dante could bring the shears down, I grabbed his wrists, holding them in place while putting a leg between his legs for leverage and bucked my body, lifting with my leg to flip him over onto his back. He lost his grip on the shears. We both turned over and began to crawl toward them from opposite directions. We each made a grab for them, but I was an instant quicker. I had them in hand and started to get up, but he was on his feet by then and threw a punch that hit me in the throat and put me back down. Then he leaped on top of me, which turned out to be the biggest and last mistake of his life. I had managed to raise the shears to ward off attack just as he was leaping. If they had been a stunt man's knife, they would have collapsed inwardly and harmlessly upon impact. But they were tempered steel, a solid as can be and he was lunging onto them. A second or two later, it was evident that he would never attack anyone again. I rolled him off me and the next thing I can remember was standing under a waterfall, looking at you folks across the way, with no idea that three days had gone by."

"What became of your hat?" asked Jake, after we had done our best to digest this blood-curdling story. "The one with the Maracaibo map under the sweatband?"

"I have no idea," said Clementine. "It must have come off while I was running away from Dante."

"And you never made it back to the watering trough?"

"I guess I didn't. I don't think I could even find it now."

We had neither the map nor the key to the map. I had given Wilder back the not-a-flute which several of us now knew how to open in order to discover nothing whatsoever. Someone else had hit upon the trick of cracking it and now had the contents. We knew only that it wasn't Dante, whom we had buried with a plain marker. I could send a team of small boys out to scan the landscape for Clementine's hat, but even if it were found and the map was still under the sweatband it wouldn't tell us much, not without the key, which seemed to be roaming our island home in search of a keyhole.

Mister Smirnoff, who had listened quietly to Clementine's story, contemplatively stroking his Van Dyke, now spoke. "Miss Clementine," he said, "There is no reason why you would remember me as I was before our encounter at the Beanery of Barney. Until today, I did not recognize you, except for those recent conversations in California. But our paths crossed long before that. I was there that dreadful day in Moscow. I saw you but we did not meet. I did meet your brother, may he rest in peace. It was I, in fact, who introduced all the members of the No Strangers to Danger as I showed him around the cafés where they joined forces for the first time. I saw your parents fall to their deaths. It has taken twenty years for me to say please accept my condolences. They were both great artists. I am thinking now that they went only from the high wire to one even higher."

Chapter Thirty-Three

"You do it this time," I said to Izzy, making the breaking a bat motion over my knee. "You middle infielders are said to have good hands." She had been watching me closely when I'd opened it before, and learned the lesson well. She must also have been paying close attention when I'd read her a few chapters of the *1001 Tales of the Arabian Nights* during sleepovers in the bunkhouse of our cottage. I could tell when she said, "Behold! The ancient secret of the bamboozler lies within!" She opened the not-a-flute, turned it long ways and gave it a little wiggle. Into the palm of her hand dropped the golden chain of my pocket watch. She narrowed her eyes and nodded, as if to say *Now we're getting somewhere*. Maybe so, I thought, though I had no idea of where. PW set off to the east. We had no choice but to follow.

I wrapped the chain around my wrist two times and fastened it to itself so it would stay on. It made a pretty bracelet. As I walked, I felt my new bracelet and thought it might be trying to tell me something. My Poppy once explained to me about a thing called a *chain of evidence*, which means one thing leading to other things in a mystery story. But they need to be things you can touch. That's how they get to be evidence. I touched my bracelet and wondered if it might be a *watch-chain of evidence*. What would it lead me to except for maybe my watch? After it had gone missing, I had been led, twice, along with Mizz Izz, to the pirate's watering trough. I will always remember exactly how the water looked, rippling a little like Holy Toledo's muscles as he's trying to twitch a fly off his hide when I reached down to pick up the not-a-flute.

"Where do you suppose PW found my watch chain, Izz?"

"Maybe it fell into the grass and he thought it was a little snake?" she said, sort of embarrassed.

"But how could it have gotten into the grass?" I said. She looked around for a minute, avoiding my eyes.

"Oh, I remember now," said Izzy, as though the answer were a lazy fly ball that had just come down. "I took the chain off your watch to see if I could hook it onto the sundial. I thought it would be cool to have a *pocket sun dial* and maybe the chain would change it into one. But there was no whatayacallit *clasp* on the sundial. I tried making it go onto that *gnomon* thingie you told me about but it didn't fit, so I gave up."

Since I had no idea where we were going, I let PW lead the way. To my surprise, he walked straight to our family cottage. He knew he was welcome, my Mumza loves PW, so he didn't bother to knock, just barged right into my bunkhouse and went straight to my toy chest. Again, he reached into his quiver, but this time he pulled out the waterproof pouch I had been storing the six parts of the old map in. I had been keeping the pouch in my toy chest, so he must have taken it out and now was putting it back. He bowed to the chest, set the pouch on its lid and walked over to my bunkbed to lie down on the lower. Izzy had already claimed the upper. She loves bunk beds (as you know, she's only seven) and says they're better than horseback riding because you never get bucked off. What was PW up to now? Only one way to find out. When I opened the chest, the first thing I saw was a puzzle box. It was a puzzle my Mumza had had made out in the great world and brought me for my birthday. It's based on a blown up photograph of Futon's map of *Quietude*, the official map he made for my Poppy, with all the names of our rivers and mountains and villages and stuff. That's what the lid of the box looks like. There must be three hundred pieces to the puzzle. Even though I know where they are all supposed to go, I've still never finished it so far. But the last time I had opened the chest, the puzzle box was down near the bottom. This time it was right on top.

I took off the lid of the box, expecting to find a jumble of the little curvy-swervy pieces you're supposed to fit together but the pieces were all gone. In their place were the parts of the older map of *Quietude*, all fit together. At least, the first five parts were of the old map. The sixth was a drawing in yellow chalk, the same chalk used for PW's map, the one I call the *trail-blazer*. It looked like something I had seen before. But where? Not at the palace or our cottage. Not at

159

Bess's cozy home in Daffadowndilly. Then I knew.

It looked kinda like an old *steamer trunk* I think it's called that Queenie has in her tower. She keeps her stockings and other girly stuff like that in it. But hers is set on its end and has little drawers for those silly-frilly clothes I wouldn't even know how to put on. The one in the picture was longways with its lid open. Flowing over the sides were lots of small round things that had lines and stars coming off them so they would look all sparkly. Was one of them supposed to be my watch or what? The drawing was in the place where the caves were on the old map. Part six, which had been so dark, was now very sunny, almost as if my watch had come out from behind a cloud. When I lifted out the drawing, the real part six was right under it. What did this mean? Had he put it directly on top of part six as a clue or had it slid there when I lifted the box out of the toy chest? This puzzle box was growing more puzzling all the time. I put all the six original parts back in their pouch but I took the yellow drawing out and hid it in the not-a-flute. PW watched me and smiled.

Tomorrow is the first game of the first ever championship series for the Crown of *Quietude*. There was no time now to follow this new clue. But, as Izzy might say, the croc was ticking.

Chapter Thirty-Four

"It's good to have you back."

"It's good to be back. It's not every woman who has a hot waterfall named after her."

"It's not every woman who's as hot as your waterfall."

"Applesauce." Bonny-speak for flattery. She had always enjoyed what might be called visions of wonder-houses. The cottage was her first chance to put them into play. Built in two wings, you had to cross a narrow ascending bridge from either side to reach the master bedroom elevated over a plunge pool filled with golden carp.

Really, it bore little resemblance to a cottage. We only called it that because it sounds so damned homespun saying *the family cottage*. Sometimes we called it *our summer home*, a private joke seeing as how on *Quietude* it's pretty much always summer. Since we weren't bound by tradition, as were the good ladies of Daffadowndilly, Bonny had let her imagination roam free. She was about to add a pantry so she could start putting up guava and mango preserves to take to our neighbors. The east wing, initially intended to receive company— Bonny felt that my tree house palace might strike some visiting dignitaries (and her old friends and sisters when they came to call) as a bit too much of a bachelor pad—had become instead a clubhouse for the River Otters. At frenzied sleepovers, they played board games like Monopoly and card games like Crazy Eights and Go Fish. They invented baseball-related board games that reminded me of the old Strat-O-Matic, making up complicated rules I didn't understand. Their voices, when engaged in these pursuits, always sounded like they were throwing dice in a back alley in Constantinople. Wilder and her sidekick were designing Windward League baseball cards with pictures of the players and stats on the back for next year's Opening Day.

If you opened the trap door on the floor of the bedroom—as Wilder and her sidekick had taken to doing—it was a simple matter to drop fish food into the pond from high above it. So simple that a contest merely based on accuracy would hardly be a challenge to a young ballplayer. Even I had been able to it. So the game they played most often was to see whose dropped portion was gobbled the quickest by a carp, which really made it a game of chance rather than skill but no less fun for all of that.

The carp lived pretty well on their own, growing plump on a diet of water insects and their larvae and the zooplankton that lined the pond. But these beautiful red and golden fish were not averse to snacking on the snails and frogs the girls collected and bombarded them with from their high vantage. When I pointed out that it was rather mean toward the snails and frogs, Izzy responded with a muttered oath she must have picked up from the boys on the team. I felt sternness was called for. "Do you know what that means?" I said. Wilder leaned over and whispered in her shortstop's ear.

"It means" Izzy said, "You are the sovereign lord of all you survey and I your humble subject." She gave Wilder a thumbs-up and I had trouble keeping a straight face. Their contests made me miss the birthday parties of my boyhood, where we would play a game of trying to drop clothespins into the mouth of a milk bottle. I could not now explain to my daughter what either a clothespin or a milk bottle even was.

They were quite serious about their game, using a stopwatch to time the results. Thinking of the stopwatch made me wonder about Wilder's pocket watch. I'd gotten used to seeing her shirtless in an old man's vest with the watch-chain hooked to a button and the timepiece itself tucked into a pocket, a good look for a nine-year-old girl. I should get her a slouch-brim hat to go with the vest.

Surrounding the cottage were gardens of lavender and pikaki, hibiscus and plumeria, as well as a shaded patch where we grew the Tahitian gardenia called "tiare." Across the way, some months before baseball season commenced, Bonny had sewn a field of sunflowers, which she called "hosannah plants," so that all the River Otters could enjoy a steady supply of sunflower seeds to chew and spit in the dugout. As soon as I'd told our girl that was how they did it in the bigs, she would not let the matter go. She'd had better luck talking her mother into the sunflowers than she did asking me to grow bubble-gum.

162

"I think I've found a spot you can use for a wine cellar," I said. I told her about the caves and the water idling through them. "It might be difficult getting the bottles in and out, but Wilder can probably rig some kind of pulley-and-basket lash-up that will allow you to lower the bottles in and pull them back out without damaging a one." She seemed pleased. Bonny wasn't lavish with emotional displays, but you learned to read telltale expressions of happiness in her. A small smile might signal delight in a big surprise.

On *Quietude*, the only fireplace outside of Daffadowndilly was in the sitting room—which herself referred to as the "front parlor"—of the cottage's west wing. Deep, floor-to-ceiling and built of local creek rock, it was impractical, utterly uncalled for, unreasonable unto absurd, really. Surplus to requirements, as Jake might say. But Bonny adored a fireplace, and since mothers outrank kings, I didn't even bother to cast a vote. We suffer almost no cold nights. Generally, the temperature bottoms out around seventy-two degrees Fahrenheit. If you moved here from Minnesota or Manitoba or Minsk, you might begin to hanker for the thrill of your old town blizzards. But Bonny came of age in southern Florida, where the wise step from air-conditioned cars into air-conditioned condominiums. So her take on the matter was that if the thermometer dipped below seventy, it was *cold*, Mister. She mounted a gauge in every room of the cottage, including our bedroom and Wilder's downstairs sleeping loft and one outside next to each of the Dutch doors that allowed entrance.

You best believe she waited for those below seventy days like a kid for Christmas morning. She had determined that four a.m. was usually the—well, I can't say *frostiest* hour but the one when the heat and humidity hadn't quite gathered their forces—and that's when she got up and took her readings. It was more important than sleeping late. When she was off on White Ops expeditions, she left instructions with her students on *Quietude* to gather driftwood and create an enormous pile of it on the north side of the cottage. It looked rather like a snowdrift. *Snowdriftwood*, that's what it was. Wilder loved to carry in armloads of the firewood and help to set it ablaze. She and her mother each changed into flannel nightgowns and sat before the fire with their knees drawn up, staring into the flames and planning our futures. Futures planned by firelight, that's what we had.

Though the temperature this morning advised otherwise, I had granted her an exemption from the 72 degrees rule so we could lie in front of a fire on a day when it was already over eighty to welcome her home. After she'd had time to decompress, I thought it best to fill her in on the details of our current involvement in treasure hunting and involuntary manslaughter. Her first concern was, of course, for Wilder's safety, though we were united in our determination to keep her from learning about Dante's demise. Her championship series was about to commence. Let her life be about baseball and horses for now.

"So, to recapitulate: A woman named Clementine, late of southern California, came here with a map left to her by her brother, who along with his crew, was here nine years ago building the cottages of Daffadowndilly. In short order, she proceeded to kill the man who accompanied her, but she makes friends quickly and no one seems to miss the fellow. The map, now lost, points the way to a fabulous stash of treasure, left here at some time in the distant past by parties unknown. The alleged treasure, nature unknown, will be used, when found, to aid the people of Ukraine, though at the moment, none of us has the slightest idea of its whereabouts or what form it takes. Right so far?" It all sounded so gossamer, when she put it like that.

"Dead right. But I'm betting on there being a treasure."

"Why?"

"It's a good story. I'd like to see how it plays out." I told her about the not-a-flute and she agreed it was an intriguing artifact. I was thirty-eight when Bonny and I met, she twenty-three. Why she kept coming back to me for so many years before we became Wilder's parents was a persistent mystery. Now we were a family. But for two decades before we became one, she had always found me. It was especially tricky, because more often than not, we were both on the move, all over the globe, yet somehow she was able to plot (or intuit) a course that would intersect with my own. She had better sense than to throw in her lot with a poet, a man who practiced his craft in the margins of contemporary life, yet again and again, she would make her way to whatever godforsaken outpost I was calling home and sweet reunion would carry the day. Sometimes the reunions lasted for a fortnight, sometimes months, sometimes but a weekend. I was never ready for her departures, but I learned to expect her back. I've come to believe I was her safe harbor. She knew, of course, that I was a goner from the first. From the moment we had joined hands in the shallows of the Gulf of Mexico, other women might turn my head, but my heart never followed.

"Three days from today, we will make the long march to the leeward side for the River Otters' first road game. Care to join me?"

"I'd love to be your date, Sugarcane, but can we meet up at Paradisiac's Park? Your Little Coconut has invited me to ride over on Holy Toledo!, an honor I can hardly decline."

"I understand. Maybe I'll pick up a cute hitchhiker along the way."

"A definite The king is dead, long live the king moment there." I could never tell if her jealousy was real or more a way of making me feel wanted. I dared not even think about her being with other men in foreign lands where superior plumbing was the rule rather than a rarity. Not a one of those lands boasted either a hot waterfall or our daughter, however, so I felt pretty safe on that score.

"Well, today we can walk hand in hand down to Buck O'Neil Field." Thinking it over, I remembered the field was about a half hour's walk away, damned near a hike. "Or I can have Brigitte brought round and walk you to the car, which will allow me open and close your door for you, one of the few things I miss from the mainland."

"Will the king be throwing out the first ball?"

"Or the first drunk. Will you be dolling up?" Because she traveled the wide world, and required a variety of outfits, Bonny maintained a full wardrobe at the cottage. Whenever she took a trip, she brought back a gift for Wilder, a new dress or blouse or suit for herself and a packet of moist towelettes for me. Yes, it's true. My name is Ace High and I am addicted to moist towelettes.

"I'll surprise you."

It had proven an outstanding idea to build the cottage below the foot of the falls. Bonny herself had contributed an ingenious variation on in-home spas: Thanks to the help of an engineer and a few young finish carpenters, a warm stream was diverted through our sitting room, with a sliding mahogany panel that opened and closed at the pulling of ropes to cover the meandering water whenever it was not in use. Sometimes the three of us, as a sunrise ritual, would open the cover and congregate over coffee and smoothies to begin our day. The smoothies were made of mango and passion fruit and pineapple and lots of freshly squeezed lime juice. We would read aloud or just share whatever was on our minds. Then Wilder would head out to care for her livestock and I got to watch my beloved being perfectly content. We had moved from the hearth to this homemade waterway.

Bonny's job was so demanding that she tended to carry worry like a knife at her own back. It relaxed her halfway when she returned to the less stressful work in the classroom on *Quietude*, but she could only relax fully when reclining in warm water. On her rare days off, she woke up in our sleeping loft, introduced herself into the sitting room stream, luxuriated there for a time over coffee, then fixed a picnic basket and took it up to the falls where she could kick back for hours, utterly carefree. Whole days went by like that. Usually I would leave her alone with her thoughts (or her attempts to escape from thoughts) and sometimes I would make use of a pair of fine binoculars I kept handy and gaze at her from an ideally situated window of the cottage, just to remind myself of how lucky I was. Then I would take her a glass of Chardonnay and get on with my rounds. Bonny happened upon the binoculars one morning, and held them out to me along with my coffee. "Taken up bird watching, have we?" she said. "Tweedle-lee-dee-dee-dee, tweedle-lee-dee-dee. Tweet tweet, tweet tweet." I replied, quoting Bobby Day's immortal tune, "Rockin' Robin," (1957), which Wilder loved to pick out and play on the mighty Wurlitzer. Nothing more was ever said on the subject.

As the king, I did some minor adjudicating. Since we do not own land, boundary disputes—which, properly speaking, could therefore not exist—were tricky to settle to the satisfaction of both parties. It became a matter of compromise, communality and our barter-based version of favor for favor. It wasn't as though we were crowded, after all.

The strangest case brought before me thus far had been that of a heartsore young swain who petitioned for permission to challenge his romantic rival to a duel. Well, I love Raphael Sabatini as much as the next loafer-king, but it struck me as inadvisable. We have our share of rifles, mostly in the hills and the interior, in the hands of those who hunt wild boar and game birds. But handguns are not permitted. It was one of my earliest decrees, along with the banning of plastic materials brought on-shore. But it was well-known to all that the Palace Guard—a cadre of boys whose mothers and sisters make colorful uniforms for them in which to bivouac about my tree house on ceremonial occasions, marching around hup hup with knees up in imitation formations and maneuvers on the beach pretending to be defenders of the realm—are well supplied with cold steel: sabers, rapiers, cutlasses, foils, you name it. But all the blades are blunted, as are those in the "fencing academy" headed up by my old friend and former arch enemy, a one time star of the Venice boardwalk who styled himself Sarto!.

I decided to allow the duel—with blunted swords and no bloodshed. Fencing masks were worn and a winner declared when one of the combatants made a palpable hit upon the face or head of the other. He was then permitted to swat his foe three times across the backside, putting the matter to an end. The best part was watching the fair lass whose favor was being fought over jump up and down on the sideline clapping her hands and crying out in excitement as the boys lunged and parried, but then rushing in to console the loser and walking away with him into the sunset.

"Hey!" said the disgruntled victor. "That's not right! I won!"

"Love, war, etc." I said, but I could tell he wanted more, so I added, "Boy howdy and hey nonny no," making a sort of Pontifical gesture in the air before him. He was still a bit crestfallen, so I pinned an old French Medal of the Nation's Gratitude (circa 1945) I'd bummed off Sarto! onto the boy's chest and thus was honor satisfied.

I walked out each day and spent time with a handful of my fellow citizens, not hearing complaints so much as enjoying congenial conversations. In time, I became part confessor, part counselor, part straight man, part family member. Like anyone who finds himself in such a position, I soon learned how little wisdom I had to impart or sound advice to offer. Instead, I took my cue from Walter the Studious: I became a good listener. When people feel the need to pour their hearts out, it is so they can be sure they are not alone. You don't need to come back with much.

But these light responsibilities were *pomme frites* petite compared to the burdens Bonny shouldered. When she acted as the schoolmistress of *Quietude*, she had all the best and none of the most pernicious aspects of her avocation: students eager to learn at their books in a building not unlike a tropical barn, one raised by local hands. And not a single principal/superintendent/supervisor/board of education or state-mandated last minute curriculum alteration by way of botheration. She could attend to her work and the results were right in front of her in the bright eyes and quick minds of the children in her care.

But getting drawn back into the daily maelstrom of White Ops doings took a terrible toll on her—psychically as well as physically. The faster she trained new appointees to take over her old tasks, the faster they were sent into various trouble spots to build schools like emergency refugee camps. The emergency was permanent, only the settings changed. And her replacement as director of the outfit had yet to be named. She had promised us that the conference in Mozambique would be her last hurrah as head honcha. Thereafter, she would plant her feet in the sand of *Quietude* and return to simple school-marming. I wondered. She so loved to get out and around.

I remembered the moment when she had, at long last, announced her retirement. We were in the sleeping loft sipping nightcaps, when she said, out of nowhere, "All the administrative claptrap—" making *administrative* sound worse than *claptrap*—"the invoices, the bills of lading, the cargo manifests. I'm getting carpal tunnel from signing off on things. And I spend so much time in the air that my jet-lag is bending back on itself. My bones feel like they're all in different time zones. I end up grateful for the small arms fire in the trouble spots because I need the adrenaline rushes to stay awake."

"Well, darlin', retirement needn't curtail your travels. You can still take trips with Wilder Kathleen." She had been acquainting our daughter with the campuses of the world's great universities. So far, they'd been to Oxford and Cambridge, the Sorbonne, Harvard, Yale and Brown, Santa Barbara and Santa Cruz for the surfing. If I remembered rightly, next up would be British Columbia and Amsterdam. I suspect the last two made it onto the list because Bonny had always wanted to see those places. As for Wilder's father, he would rather she matriculate on *Quietude* where he could play catch with her. "And trying to keep pace with her mischief will provide the adrenaline rushes."

I paddled over to her, a distance of about two feet. "How about I make you a martini while you slip into your mystery attire and give the king a thrill?"

168

"With a twist, your majesty." My fiancée-for-life, bless her, does most everything with a twist.

We had repaired to the master bedroom, I had donned my fanciest caftan (it was infused with vertical lines of golden glitter) and my favorite fedora, a forest green, brushed velour number from the Schlock shop in San Francisco and was lying in a hammock about to take the first sip of my own martini when she emerged from her closet, a roomy enclosure she could have occupied full-time quite happily, in a dress that would make it problematical for other spectators to follow the progress of the contest, such a sacrifice would be required to tear their eyes off the starting pitcher's mother: The most delicate handmade needle lace in pale champagne, her shoulders and arms bare, the bodice nearly to her collarbone, attached by two slim silken straps to a golden ring around her neck, backless, full-length and form-fitting with slits to the hip on either side to show her legendary legs to their best advantage as she walked. Champagne, mind you. A dress that could toast its hostess. She looked like a mermaid who had emerged from the sea with a few scallops of foam clinging to her artfully. I think she was naked underneath the lace. But a gentleman cannot ask about such things. A gentleman must simply find out.

"Have you nothing to say?" she said.

"My faculty of speech has gone on sabbatical. My heart is strong, but my knees are weak. You are stunning."

"Well, since we are attending a ballgame, I thought a ball gown was in order."

"Then let us, dear lady, go have a ball." On the way out to Brigitte, I could not, for the life of me, figure out how to walk in front of and behind my daughter's mother at the same time, thus taking advantage of two spectacular views. But I was happy to settle for walking beside her and holding her hand.

Before firing up my ride, I turned to Wilder's Mumza, picked up her hand and held it to my lips. Bonny grinned her notch-out-of-an-apple grin, took off my hat and tousled my hair, though there was barely enough left to tousle.

"You know," she said, "I'd like to meet Joshua's sister and extend my sympathies. Her welcome to *Quietude* seems to have been a pretty

169

rough landing. I know you're partial to your unusual seating arrangement when attending games at Buck O'Neil Field."

"It's true. I enjoy an overview. It allows me to feel I'm watching the game in the third person, a lordly narrator in the manner of an eighteenth or nineteenth century novelist. And it makes it easier to tell how well Wilder is locating her pitches."

"In that case, the River Otters' starting pitcher's mother hereby gives you permission to leave her in the cheap seats while you run yourself up a palm tree. I'd like to be on the first base line, but the exact location isn't so important, just so I have a good view of our girl. And do you suppose you could arrange for Miss Clementine to be in the seat beside me?"

"Sure. I'm something of a mover and shaker in these parts, you know. She already agreed to be there. I'll just tell her she'll be in the VIP section. You two haven't met, have you?"

"No. And I'd appreciate it if you don't tell her that she'll be sitting next to the starting pitcher's mother, or that I'm the starting pitcher's father's girl. Okay?" I looked at her inquisitively but she pretended not to notice.

"All right. So long as you promise to tell me later what you're up to."

"Deal." She gave my hand a squeeze. I didn't mind waiting. For the moment, I was satisfied with knowing that my fiancée for life was once again doing something with a twist.

Chapter Thirty-Five

Game one of the first ever championship series for the Crown of *Quietude* was being played at Buck O'Neil Field. We had a slightly better won-loss record than the JJs (Jumping Jehoshaphats) so we get to be the home team, which means we have last ups. The turnout was even bigger and the fans making an even greater ruckus before first pitch than the crowd for our last game against the Goofballs. Singers, dancers, ukulele ladies and drummers were making it feel like a beach party on our ball field. The coconut man with his trusty machete was making that wonderful *ka-thunk* sound every few minutes. A boy had made a little shack with a sign at the top that said *Prawn Shop* and was trading jumbo shrimps for whatever anyone offered him. Mister McKeever had nine of the fine imported hot dogs with buns and mustard and ketchup delivered to both dugouts. My Poppy was up in the palm tree in his ritzy beach chair. It has a pair of binoculars in a sort of holster on the side so he can see me magnified, and a drink-holder so he can set down his thermos when he picks up the binoculars. My Mumza was sitting where I could see her on the first base line next to a lady I didn't recognize. It wasn't one of my Mumza's many sisters, I know them all well. An old friend, maybe? Queenie was on the third base line sitting in full lotus on her sedan chair with a cute boy holding a parasol over her. This time she didn't need to stay neutral, she could holler for the River Otters without giving offense to any of her fellow citizens and used-to-be subjects from Her Majesty's Grace.

The three small boys with the biggest lungs blew on conch shells to *proclaim* our taking the field. We ran out one at a time to our positions, each of us announced by his or her name and number. My number is eighteen, my lucky number because I was born on August 18. Poppy Tobago, who sings as well as she used to act in movies, did a sweet version of "Row Row Row Your Boat," our national anthem. My other Poppy, my dad the king, who used to be a ballplayer, did an okay job of throwing out the first pitch, considering that he did it from his beach chair. Even though he couldn't plant his feet to get his legs under him, he lofted one that sailed high over the backstop and made it all the way to me on the mound. Let's play ball, *Quietude*-Style.

I set down the first nine batters I faced in order, getting plenty of swings and misses, the only hard hit ball being a liner right at me. I threw my glove up in front of my face before I even knew what I was doing and lickety-split there was one down. Other than that, I was keeping the JJs off balance. I could tell by the looks on their faces when they walked away from the plate that no one in the Leeward League had ever seen a scroojie before. And my heater had continued to improve, maybe just because I am getting bigger and stronger and also learning how to pitch by pitching so often. I could paint the corners or miss just off them on purpose to keep the hitters guessing.

Izzy and Ella Rose and Jubilee and me had been working on our new cheer during batting practices. The boys on the team don't like making up cheers and refuse to perform them. They think it's as girly as Queenie's silly-frillies. I just thought it was fun, and it made me feel closer to my Poppy who used to be a poet before he became a sovereign lord. No one but the four of us had heard it yet. In the bottom of the first, we gathered in the home team on-deck circle, kicked up our legs and laid it on the crowd.

"Welcome all you near and dear/friends and family come to cheer/The Otters mean to make you proud/So raise your voices long and loud/We shall leave Jehoshaphats/with broken hearts and broken bats/Elsewhereville will stand so tall/When Zip-a-Dee-Do-Dah/Takes a fall." We won a big round of applause but our bats must have slept through it because we fared no better than our opponents. Their pitcher, a gangly fourteen-year-old dude named D'Artagnan, was a hard thrower but wild enough to make hitters nervous when they tried to dig in on him. You never knew where the next pitch might be headed and we don't have batting helmets. After four innings, we had three base knocks—an infield single beaten out by Ella Rose, a bloop into no man's land by Tobias and a line single by me that a throwing error by their left fielder turned into a double—though I was stranded at second—but we hadn't put up a run. I had kept the JJs off the board as well, thanks to some nifty

172

glove work by our defense. My Poppy says that Izzy and Jubilee from Tennessee pull off the double-play like a *pas de deux for turning two*, whatever that might mean. This time, they turned a real pretty pitcher's best friend in the top of the fourth on a hot smash up the middle after the only walk I had issued, keeping the bases empty and nothing but goose eggs on the board.

After I had fanned my seventh Jehoshaphat, I looked into the bleachers and tipped my cap to my Mumza. One row above her, I noticed how the sunlight was flashing off of someone's eye. He wasn't wearing sunglasses, so the light wasn't bouncing off a lens, but *off of his eye,* which didn't make any sense. Not unless it was a glass eye! That flash of light was telling me that Captain Primo was back! He had shown up for the first Championship game just like my Mumza had made it for the pennant clincher. He is famous for his glass eye because it has a tiny skull-and-crossbones painted on it. It might have been kind of undignified but I couldn't help myself. I waved at him. I waved and waved and waved until he held up his hand and made a special pirate sign at me, the sign for a hook. You hold up and bend the index finger of your left hand and move the thumb and index finger of your right hand over it. It was our old way of saying hello, or, as Mister Mckeever would say, high-dee-ho. For a pirate, a hook is what you would put on your wrist if you lost a hand to a shark or in a sword fight. But now, here, at Buck O'Neil Field, in the bottom of the fifth inning of a scoreless tie in game one of the Championship series for the Crown of *Quietude*, it also meant a second thing—go to the deuce, aka (as Izzy would say) my twelve-to-sixer. In other words, my curve ball, known wherever baseball is played as a *hook*.

I took his advice, thinking maybe I'd better go easy on the scroojie. I'd been through their order twice, meaning all the Jehoshaphats had seen it at least once. Now they'd be looking for it, thinking *She's not going to run that thing by me again, no matter what it's called* and before they knew it, my twelve-to-sixer would buckle their knees. When I went into the dugout for the bottom of the fifth, I noticed that no one was talking to me, or even looking at me. It was confusing. Usually the boys make smart alecky remarks to razz me and the girls make encouraging ones to buck me up. They had never all been quiet before. But when I looked out at the scoreboard where small boys hang the numbers that show how many runs each side has put up, I saw nothing but zeroes. I knew that since our first three hits, we'd gotten one more when Elijah bounced a seeing eye grounder through the left side, but we still hadn't given PW a chance to use the not-a-flute to wave a runner around third. Had any JJs gotten as far as second? I had issued that one base on balls but the runner was erased thanks to Izzy and Jubilee's grace around second base. Then I knew why I was getting the silent treatment.

There's a thing in baseball I've never seen written down, only spoken aloud, so I'm not sure whether it's spelled *no-no* or *know-know*. The second way might be true because everybody *knows* what's going on before the pitcher (me) figures it out and that's why my teammates were clamming up. So they wouldn't jinx it. But I think the first way is the right way because the other team has *no* base hits. Not a single, double, three-bagger or round tripper. No matter how many times my Poppy and I try to explain to my Mumza what a no-hitter is, she just doesn't get it. "But they *hit* the ball!" she says every time. "So how can it be a no-hitter?" She's very stubborn but me too so I just have to keep trying.

Oddly enough it didn't make me nervous to realize I was throwing a no-hitter. If I'd been throwing a *perfect game*, that would have made me nervous. A perfect game is when the pitcher allows no baserunners whatsoever, either by hit, walk or error. They are very rare. But my Poppy and Mister McKeever both say that a regular no-hitter is what's called *a dime a dozen*. I know what a dozen is but I'm not so sure about a dime. But what they mean is a pitcher can throw one just by getting lucky. A perfect game, on the other hand, means good stuff plus great control. I couldn't throw a perfect game because I had already walked that one dude, so I could just settle down and worry about the Otters putting some crooked numbers on the board. In the Championship, we play two out of three, so game one was really important. We definitely didn't want to travel to the leeward side already down by a game in the series.

By the top of the seventh, I still hadn't given up a hit. But we were also still locked in a scoreless tie. If my aching arm could coax three more outs, we would have our last ups. If we couldn't score, we'd go to extras and I'd have to pull myself and put in one of my teammates to pitch.

174

The leadoff hitter was the only girl on the JJs, which made me want to be her friend, but I could show no mercy. By this time, my heater was not so hot anymore. But I still needed it to set up my breaking stuff. I could tell that the girl's hands were shaking by the way her bat was shaking. She was scared of making a mistake. I thought she would swing at anything just to get it over with and go back to the bench to be with her teammates. I put a not-so-fastball right under her hands and she swung awkwardly, hitting it off the handle into the dirt. Then I put another one a half a foot off the outside corner and she swung again, hitting it off the end of the bat, squibbing it foul outside of first. She was in an 0-2 hole, but she'd hit the ball two times and now she didn't look quite so frightened.

Before she could get too confident, I poured in a scroojie right down the middle. Because my heater had cooled off, the scroojie was moving toward her at about the same speed she had just seen twice. So naturally she thought it was a fastball which would not break but beg to be walloped for extra bases. And it was going to cross the heart of the plate, right where she could hit it! That was what she must have thought, anyway, until, just as it was about to reach the plate and she was starting her swing, the scroojie swerved suddenly inward, freezing her as it nicked the inside corner. Sorry, sister. One down.

D'Artagnan, their tall starting pitcher, was up next. The JJs had used four pitchers while I was trying to go the distance, so he probably wasn't as tired as me. He stepped in and swung his bat back and forth in a way that was supposed to look menacing. But it reminded me of Izzy and made me giggle. D'Artagnan thought I was giggling at him, which seemed first to confuse and then to anger him. Both of my parents have told me that, as a pitcher, I can turn *male pride* to my advantage. This seemed to be a good time to give it a try. I remembered a pitch that most hurlers call an *eephus* pitch. The Negro League immortal, Satchel Paige, called it his *nothin'* pitch because it had nothin' on it. Instead of trying to burn it past the batter, or to fool him with a dipsy-doodle, you throw it high in the air toward home, almost like you were trying to teach someone how to catch pop-ups. I showed it to Izzy once when no one else was watching. I told her it was an eephus and she said, aka the *lollipop-up*. You gotta love that girl. D'Artagnan, full of anger and confusion, wanted to teach me a lesson and he really let it rip. But you have to wait for an eephus pitch to come down, and even then it's hard to time it right. He got his bat on it, but could do no more than hit a can of corn out to Walter in center. The used-to-be king gathered it in. Two down.

Even more than I wanted not to give up a hit, I wanted to keep anyone from going deep. The Otters didn't want to be playing catch up in the bottom of the seventh. Home runs don't happen often in our games. We are kids between the ages of seven and sixteen. Only the older boys have the power to hit one out. It used to be done by driving one into the gap so it could roll forever, or just hitting it over the outfielders' heads if they were playing shallow. But now we've put up fences for the Championship. No matter how deep our fielders played, if one went over the wall, it would be one long elephant ride to the leeward side.

In the bigs, they have what are called *foul poles,* which tell the umpires whether a ball is fair or not, a long goner or just a let's-do-it-over. On *Quietude,* we don't have concrete to sink a pole into. So we transplanted palm trees to do the same job. The JJs' catcher, a chunky right-handed dude whom I had struck out all three times I'd faced him so far, looked like he could hit one a country mile if he ever made contact. I wanted to throw my first pitch just off the inside corner, hoping for a swing and miss. But it leaked out over the plate and he took a big rip, a little out in front, and hit it on a high arc down the left field line. I thought it might never come down, but when it did, it fell out of the sky and disappeared into the branches of the palm tree/slash foul pole. I guess it hit a coconut up in the tree, because that's what fell on the head of the left fielder, who had never given up on making the catch. Since he was standing to the left of the tree, in foul ground, and coconuts do not curve when they fall, the umps ruled it a foul ball. Strike one. The real ball was found by a kid in the stands who raced off to trade it for some shrimps.

I wanted to climb the ladder and get him to go fishing on a high one out of the zone, but knew I was running short of giddy-up. That long foul had been a very loud strike one. The left-fielder dude looked kind of wobbly, so the umps gave him a minute to recover from his coconut-on-coconut injury. None of our teams have extra players, so they couldn't put in a sub. He put his hands on his knees,

176

took a few deep breaths, then held his arm up to signal he was good to go. After he trotted back to his position, getting a polite round of applause from the crowd, I broke off a beauty of a twelve-to-sixer that started at the catcher's ribcage and ended up at his shoe tops. He swung over it and stirred up nothing but a breeze. Strike two.

I took off my cap, wiped my forehead, leaned in and pretended to look for a sign. Zachariah, as a kind of joke, put down the thumb and forefinger circle with the other three fingers sticking out, meaning OK, Cap, throw whatever you think best. I had struck this dude out once with a fastball, once with a curve and once with a scroojie, so he wouldn't have any idea of what to look for. I nodded at Zach, went into my windup, reached back for one last heck-a-doozy heater and challenged him to a game of what's called *country hardball*. I couldn't have thrown another to save my horse's life, that's how whipped my right arm was by this time. To his credit, the catcher dude got his bat on it, but only enough to lift a high pop-up into foul ground outside of first. Ella Rose drifted over, keeping one eye on the ball and the other on the low railing in front of the bleachers. The wind was messing with the ball, so she had no time to line it up. At the last second, she extended her glove into the seats and caught the foul just as it was about to fall into my Mumza's lap. The crowd erupted and then erupted again as Ella Rose gave the ball to my mother, just as though she knew I wanted her to.

Bottom of the seventh. I had my no-hitter, but it wouldn't count unless we could secure the win by walking it off now. I was due up fourth, but hoped the game would be history by then. I was as scared as the poor girl on the JJs. They were going with their fifth pitcher of the game. If we went deep into extras, their whole team might have a chance to pitch. The heart of the order was due up before me: Jaxxx, Alakai and Walter. We all wanted Jaxxx to work a free pass so we would have the winning run on base. We've grown so used to his walking that Tobias, who is French, calls our third baseman the *boulevardier*, which is probably a good joke, if you speak more French than me. Jaxxx did everything in his power to make it happen, fouling off everything the new dude on the mound had to offer. But on the tenth pitch of the at-bat, he waved at and missed one in the dirt. Alakai came to the plate, looking to end the thing with just one

177

swing. He is our best pure power hitter and probably thought it was his responsibility. But he was overmatched by a fastball, a humdinger of a curve and another fastball. He slammed his bat on the ground in disgust and trudged back to the dugout, leaving it up to our center fielder.

Walter, who used to be one of my baby-sitters, is a keen student of the game. He works the count, works on making contact, going with the pitch, taking it the other way when he shouldn't try to pull it. He prides himself on putting the ball in play. In other words, he is not a big masher. So it was a bit of a surprise when, after calmly working the count to 2-0, he uncoiled on a fastball right down the pipe and drove it over the fence in left-center. *Way* over. It was a no-doubter. Neither the left-fielder or their center-fielder even moved. Both looked up, shook their heads and began walking slowly in. Never has there been a team captain so happy to be stranded in the on-deck circle.

We didn't just walk it off. We danced it off, whirled it off and twirled it off. We cartwheeled and shrieked and screamed blue murder. We were all talking at once, with Izzy talking the fastest while she did handsprings out of the dugout and all the way onto the field. PW danced a Bushman dance in the coaching box and waved the not-a-flute. We did the new cheer again and this time even the boys joined in. The crowd was rushing onto the field to celebrate with the players. I remembered to walk over to the JJs dugout and tell their captain it had been a good game and that we would see him on the leeward side in three days. We all know how much it hurts to lose a close one. I sat down next to the girl whom I'd struck out and introduced myself. I told her she did a good job getting the bat on the ball and was going to be a fine player. She had been crying, but now she smiled a small smile so that she was crying and smiling at the same time. She said her name was Gwendolyn and I told her it was good to meet her.

My Mumza came down and introduced me to her new friend, Clementine, and they made a big fuss. Queenie was helped off her sedan chair, shook my hand and said *Those old Jehoshaphats never had a chance, girl.* Mister McKeever said that Buck O'Neil himself would have been proud of me. My Poppy, down from his palm tree (which he sometimes calls the *crow's nest*, whatever that might be)

178

congratulated me on the no-no, unless it was a know-know, gave me a big hug and told me he couldn't find his eyeglasses. He often loses them at the games because he has to take them off to use his binoculars. I told him to keep doing king things and I went to check his chair. His glasses weren't in the binocular holster or the drink holder. But there is a pocket on the back of the chair. When I patted it, I could feel something in there. I reached in and found two things. The first was a pair of eyeglasses. The second thing was what is called a *coin*. My Mumza has taken me to a lot of different countries to check out schools she thinks I might like to go to when I'm older. At the airports and the schools they have *vending machines* you can get strange kinds of food and funny drinks out of if you put in one of these coins. I've seen many coins from these different countries but I knew this one wasn't from any of them. The way I knew it was that I had seen it right here on *Quietude*, even though we don't use money. It was familiar to me because its *likeness* (that means something that looks just like something else) was carved in wood above the swinging doors to the saloon where my Poppy issues his decrees. It was a doubloon. Not a drawing or a carving, but a real honest to goodness gold doubloon.

Chapter Thirty-Six

Some days, there are corners that only music can go around. I was leaning against the mighty Wurlitzer picking out songs I hoped might provide inspiration: "Down the River of Golden Dreams" by the Boswell Sisters, the Mighty Diamonds version of "Sneakin Sally Thru the Alley," and "Take Me Down to the Water" by the Sacramento band, Proxy Moon.

Whenever I don't want to talk about something, McKeever was the ideal person not to talk to. Sometimes, when feeling more expansive, I bounce other things off him, things I am ready to share, and either he listens attentively or just spaces out, it's hard to tell. We are better at spiraling sideways, riffing off nothing in particular to unclutter our minds by laughing and drinking and girl-watching until our optic nerves were worn to a happy frazzle. An endearing thing about *Quietude*: You never hear nervous or dishonest laughter. There is laughter as plentiful as our creeks, but it's the laughter of those who understand not only the trials, troubles, tribulations and travails of others, but their gratitude as well, their eccentricities, their goofs. I ruled over a country whose citizenry, though composed of people from all over the world, found the same things funny. It seemed to me the laughter of those who have abandoned bitterness, having come to the conclusion that, as they say in the old movies, bitterness is a sucker's game. We are good at getting on. And, as the old hippies would say, getting down.

"Do you think any other species of animals have sexual fantasies?" he asked.

"Hard to say. How could you tell?" We pondered this imponderable for a moment, listening to Leroy Carr doing "How Long Has that Evening Train Been Gone." McKeever loved all train songs. "It may be unanswerable," I said, "but that doesn't mean it isn't a good question. We should put it on the questionnaire."

"What questionnaire?"

"The one we administer to applicants for citizenship."

"There's a questionnaire?"

"There could be. We just have to make it up."

"I'll get right on it." Jake strode up, having rushed over from the Idyll Dipper to join the strategy session. He looked freshly shaved and fully awake, how I do not know. He pumped in a quarter and followed McKeever's selection with Dire Straights's "Angel of Mercy," which segued into my own, "Die Rockin'" by Whiskey Meyers out of Palestine, Texas. My old friend, Peter Bralver, a brilliant poet, mathematician, amateur physicist, Talmudic scholar and eco-warrior, wandered up wearing a t-shirt that read "Boogie Till Your Buddha Nature Passes Out on the Bathroom Floor" and a pair of worn brown corduroy trousers. About five-eight and a bit tubby, you might mistake him for a meek, bespectacled intellectual if you hadn't known him as a fierce defender of whales and dolphins who had gone to sea with Greenpeace in his middle years to stand up to the harpoons of whalers violating international law. I had known him since high school in the San Fernando Valley.

"What's shakin', Pete?" He toked on one of his ever present hand rolled cigarettes, usually half-packed with reefer or infused with drops of hash oil, and exhaled like a pasha at his hookah.

"Good morrow, old friend," he said. "I woke up and made a pot of chrysanthemum tea and took it outside to enjoy the early morning light. I saw a bird with a white throat flashing by—I think it was a swift—and it seemed like an omen of some kind. So I followed it for a while and realized I was on the path to you palace. I lost sight of the swift but I remembered a song on your jukebox I could play in its honor. Mister Buchanan, could I bum a quarter off you?" Jake was probably the only person in the country with pocket change. He dug out a two-bit piece and handed it over. Peter dropped it in the slot and pushed two buttons, rewarding us with a violin solo that was tantalizingly familiar. Sort of a hippie-gypsy kind of deal. It took me back. I looked at McKeever. "1969?" I said. He nodded.

"About then, yeah," he said. Then the lyric came up. "White bird/in a golden cage." I turned to Cassidy again. He has trouble recalling the names of his ex-wives but is hell on sixties musical outfits. "What was that group called?"

"It's a Beautiful Day," he said. I looked around.

"Right. But the group?"

"That was the name of the group," he explained patiently.

"It must have been 1969," I said. "Pete, you get two more songs." He chose John Fogarty's spritely, hopeful "Don't You Wish It Was True" and Sandy Denny's heartbreakingly hopeful "Quiet Joys of Brotherhood," both characteristic of Peter, both reminding me of Clementine and her brother's hopes. Dante's life seemed to have screwed him into the ground, but even he would be a part of the effort to aid the struggle of Ukraine if we could lay hands on the treasure. It was as though I, or we, the collective unconscious of *Quietude,* had brought together all the elements necessary for a classic chronicle of adventure and summoned them to our shores. I'd begun to feel like a character in a story Laurelai was reading aloud to my family. Or were we, like the No Strangers to Danger in their blind obedience to Joshua's whims, merely indenturing ourselves to fanciful notions? Are the semi-tangible toys we call ideas, with their incomprehensible instructional manuals, in our minds for no reason? At least the not-a-flute was real. I remembered the way PW used it to conduct runners around third base. Maybe what Wilder's sidekick called the "bamboozler," practically the only wholly tangible element we had to go by, was piping us all toward an end known only to itself. "Do you have any thoughts, or even crackpot theories, as to where this treasure might be hidden on our island?" I asked Peter.

"If you start at the point where I am standing," he said, "and set out in any direction, you will find treasure in abundance. Material wealth in the form of earthly bounty will surround you. But if you mean wherewithal, in the worldly sense, I wouldn't have the slightest."

It wasn't really a meeting, more like our island version of old men who gather each morning in a favorite coffee shop, kicking over the old days as the new ones grow few. I enjoyed the company of these gentlemen, but none had any fresh insights on treasure hunting. Neither had the songs provided a sudden satori moment, as I had hoped. Maybe I would catch sight of a white bird and it would lead me to the loot. We had Clementine herself in our presence, but apart from awakening McKeever from his long hibernation, it hadn't done

182

us, or her for that matter, a bit of good. One of the small boys had found her buckskin hat, but it was as empty as my head. The only head in all the land whose contents might have contained a solution belonged to the dead man in the meadow. Jake, the youngest among us and the one with the most at stake—i.e., he would have to return a sizable advance if the story didn't pan out—was, for once, bereft of useful suggestions. He drifted back to the Idyll Dipper, Peter to his hut to solve quadratic equations or translate Han Dynasty poetry, leaving McKeever and I to brood in companionable silence.

We repaired to the library, where he accepted a vodka-tonic. Well, "accepted" may be misleading. Since he knew that Wilder's Mumza had rendered the royal cupboard bare, if you didn't count foodstuffs, he had packed in an enormous flask of Grey Goose. I, as the host, contributed tonic, limes and ice, thanks to my trusty generator, and we talked about Wilder's first Championship game. It was a good thing that he had taken her under his wing. Good for them both. He needed to get out and about a bit more and she benefitted greatly by his coaching.

"A no-hitter!" said her father. "And she's only nine! Maybe one day she'll be the first girl ever to pitch in the bigs."

"She would need to leave *Quietude*,"

"An expansion team?"

"They'd have to expand the meaning of the word 'expansion' first." he said.

"Well, she can play in the Windward League for another seven years," I said. "By that time, she'll be almost grown and probably more interested in marine biology. And may well have ascended to the throne." Desirous of lightening my friend's load on the strenuous, nearly tenth of a mile hike back to the Hibernaculum, I suggested another round. He saw the wisdom in this, and politely acquiesced. Rather, he pulled out the big flask—"flask" may also be misleading, the thing looked like a canteen in a movie where one is shaken to show how little water is left when so much trackless desert stretches before the hero—and gurgled some Grey Goose into two tall cocktail glasses. I splashed in tonic, a few cubes of ice and squeezes of fresh lime, the smell of which counts as a form of transportation, so reliably does it carry me away.

"I should get back to the cottage. Are you going to be able to make it to the game over on the leeward side tomorrow? I'm sure it would help to steady Wilder's nerves if her pitching guru was standing by."

"I think I have an old inner tube somewhere in my cave," he said. "Maybe I can catch a ride on an eastbound river."

"Or you could call shotgun and go over with me in Brigitte."

"Far freaking out, so to speak. I'll see if I can find my Koufax jersey. Hi-dee-ho."

I might be a king-sized bust as a private eye and/or treasure hunter, but I still knew how to be a family man. I took McKeever's blackthorn walking stick out from under the bar where I'd been hiding it from him and headed for our summer home. I didn't get very far. I had barely struck out, swishing the stick about like Tom Jones and making up silly dialogue aloud when I was embarrassed by my own daughter, who crossed my path quite suddenly on horseback, pulling on Holy Toledo!'s reins. Lost in my reveries, I wondered if she would call out, "Stand and deliver!" Instead, she said, "Hi, Poppy. Do you think we could go back to the palace for a minute? I need to talk with you, in secret. What I'm about to tell, you must not share with another living soul, except for Mumza, of course. There's a thing going on, a thing I've been—" She paused for a moment, "*investigating*." She looked at me to see if she was using the word correctly. I nodded my encouragement. "It might be nothing, nothing important that is, or it might be a whichamacallit, a *matter of grave consequence*. Whatever it is, I'm pretty sure it's a king thing."

Chapter Thirty-Seven

"Albatrosses on the pond, River Otters!" I yelled. You're supposed to say *ducks* on the pond, meaning there are runners on base so let's cash them in, but we don't have any ducks on *Quietude*. Or any cash, for that matter. But we ballplayers do love our clichés. "Let's bat around! Big inning! Everybody hits!" I clapped my hands and hollered for all I was worth from the top step of the dugout. PW whirled the not-a-flute over his head to give our baserunners the idea.

When we got close to Paradisiac's Park, plenty of people were lined up waiting to go in. Everyone was talking excitedly and holding their kids on their shoulders. Holy Toledo! could tell it was a special occasion. I knew because he started *prancing*, taking high fancy steps and Tickety-Boo slowed down and lifted her front feet way up one at a time and held them in the air for a second before setting them back down. It was like both of them knew this was a moment that called for what is called *pomp and circumstance,* whatever they might be. No matter where you take her, an elephant does make an impression.

It was a wonderful surprise when my Poppy and Mister McKeever pulled up in Brigitte. In the backseat, wearing fancy hats, were Bess and three other ladies of Daffadowndilly, all dressed up in their finery, with gloves and everything. I don't think they had ever left their village before since moving here from mother England except to all walk together down to the beach once a week in their old-fashioned *bathing costumes.* They waved their dainty wave at me, and I waved back my big team captain wave. Bess has been showing me how to wave like the Queen. You have to really tone it down.

I needed to remember that although we were in enemy territory, I was still the princess of the whole island, including the leeward side, and I was supposed to carry myself with oh what's that thing called? *Aplomb*, that's it! What a cool word, sort of like a plum and sort of like a bomb. My Poppy told me not to throw at any batters' heads and not to kick dirt on the umpire, as if I would ever do such things. I think he knows how important this game is and just wants to give me some fatherly advice. He's a good dad but he doesn't know anything about horses or elephants and my Mumza is pretty much in charge of my schooling so baseball is the main thing we share. He teaches me all the clichés so I'll be ready if I'm ever called up to the bigs.

I was plenty nervous when I had shared my big news with him. It took longer than I meant it to. We went up into his library and he gave me a bottle of sarsaparilla. It's what kids' drink in my favorite movie *Shane* so he keeps some for me at the Palace. I had brought along both maps in my saddlebag, PW's map, the one he made for me, and the other map that I don't know who made but I found the six parts in six different places thanks to PW's map. At first, I thought about going to where PW's yellow chalk drawing showed the chest was to see if I could find it, but then there was game number one and after that I found the doubloon. It was too big a secret to keep to myself. I hadn't even shown it to Izzy. I knew she would want to look where PW's drawing suggested we go and see if there were any more like it. If there were she would probably use the doubloons to make jewelry for the River Otters. But she is sort of a little sister to me and I didn't want her to get in trouble. Her parents are very strict. One time I walked her home when she was late from a game and we kept stopping to play catch, which only made her later, and her father, who was a farmer in Australia, said, in a real serious voice, "Isabella Kelly, you get in this house right this minute. You're going to get what's coming to you now, of that you may be certain." "*Isabella?*" I whispered. "My my," which was what I thought Bess would have said. Izzy's punishment wasn't so bad, she just had to go to bed without her supper, which is what her dad calls dinner. But it had been my fault, so now I wanted to be extra careful.

I spread the six parts of the second map out on the bar, putting the pieces together so my Poppy could see the story they were telling, a story that went from far out at sea to an island that must be this one long ago in old Polynesian times. He didn't say anything, just studied the map, looking from its left side to the right. I had put the original part six back in place and kept the yellow chalk drawing in my toy chest, where I thought it belonged, not being so grown-up and serious looking as all the original parts.

"Where did you find these, Wilder Kathleen?" What should I say? They were in my backpack with my study guides? The six places where PW had hidden them were our secret places. I shouldn't tell about those, because the secret was his as well as my own.

"I found them in my toy chest," I said, finally. Well, that was kind of true. They had turned up in my toy chest after I put them there. He looked at me for a long time but didn't say anything.

"There's something else, Poppy. Something that might make you glad that you lost your eyeglasses." I was very happy to change the subject. I was wearing my vest and reached into the pocket where I would keep my watch, if only I had it. Really, I was stalling for time, like when I'm not sure which pitch I want to throw next, so I walk around the mound and smooth out the dirt with my cleats. I was having what my Mumza calls a *crisis of conscience*. She has taught me to always tell the truth, and now I couldn't decide if I had told a fib or not. Is it a fib if you leave something out? In my mind, I went back over what I had said, and then I went ahead.

"You remember after the game, you asked me to look for them? Well, I did. I looked in your beach chair."

"I remember," he said.

"I found them in the back pocket of the chair. But that wasn't all I found." Out of my vest pocket, I pulled the doubloon. "I also found this."

"May I?" said my Poppy and took it from me. He weighed it on his palm, looked at both sides for a long time, flipped it into the air, caught it and said, "Would you mind if I held onto this for a while?"

"No, Poppy. Is it a lead, do you think?" When I found it in the chair pocket, the first thing I thought was that it was a special coin that would play songs without end on the Wurlitzer. Maybe that's what doubloons were for? But then I realized it was too big to fit into the slot on the jukebox. "Not like a lead off first if you're hoping to steal second. A detective kind of lead, like you told me about? Could it be one of those?" He looked at me and smiled.

"It might well be, Little Coconut. Not to overstate the case, but I daresay it might just be the lead of a lifetime. Whataya say we go see if your Mumza is making breakfast."

"Oh, Poppy, you know perfectly well she'll be waiting for *me* to make breakfast for *her*. She's a wonderful mom, but she should never be allowed in the kitchen."

Sad to say, the Otters not only didn't bat around, we might as well have pounded ourselves into the ground. Every time we got a runner on, we hit into a double-play or made a base-running blunder and ran ourselves into an out. I pitched okay, giving up only two runs on four hits over six innings before giving way to Ella Rose, but those two tallies were the only ones scored by either side. The series was tied at a game apiece. I felt bad, but I should have felt worse. Here I was the team captain of the River Otters in a deadlock for the championship and all I could think about was that I hadn't told the whole truth to my Poppy. I had given him the map and the doubloon, so what else was there? He and Mister McKeever and Mister Buchanan and Queenie would know what to do with these things. They were not part of a starting pitcher's job. Okay, there was the matter of the chalk drawing and the matter of my missing watch. The drawing was a present to me from PW so I thought it was okay for me to keep it to myself. And game three would be the decider of the Championship. Couldn't I worry about my watch during the off-season? My Mumza had told me it was what is called an *air loom*. Air is the invisible stuff that's everywhere between other stuff, for birds to fly around in and baseball players (and other people) to breathe And a loom is a machine for weaving cloth. So I guess an *air loom* is a machine for making clothes out of thin air? I don't know what that has to do with telling time, I should ask Bess. But I could tell that my Mumza meant it was important that I take good care of my watch. When I thought of Bess and my problem at the same time, it occurred to me that my watch might be, as the good ladies would say, *winding me up*. That's a joke, in case you didn't notice.

Chapter Thirty-Eight

On the way over to Paradisiac's Park, while McKeever did his best to explain the rules of baseball to the four elderly British women who had, to my delighted surprise, taken me up on my offer to chauffeur them to the leeward side in Brigitte's back seat, I had time to consider the matter of the elusive key to the formerly elusive map. We—the trackers of the treasure hunters—had been assuming that Dante had it concealed upon his person. He had made it easy to look for by becoming dead. But the carefully partitioned map my daughter had brought me, after being sequestered in six extremely secure locations by PW, was obviously the original—not a copy, not a forgery, not a cleverly tricked-out replica. The paper, or parchment, was old but still sturdy enough that I was able to handle it without fear of it crumbling.

If I was reading the black dots correctly, they stood for other islands in the Pacific to our west. The body of the map consisted of rivers and peaks drawn crudely in blue-black ink, waterways and mountains I could put names to, not surprisingly because we had named them ourselves. I could follow the few landmarks until the map's terminus at the Widow, in the vicinity of the caves where Creole and Jake had helped me into and out of the series of chambers.

It was not a map made for tourists. Or, rather, it looked to have been made for one particular visitor to these parts. One washed up here and hopeful of a return trip. I thought it conceived to help a sailor find this island amidst a number of others sprinkled into a vast continent of water. Rather, first to find the island, then to find something *on* the island once he had made his way back. There were none of the lines of longitude and latitude which would have made it so much more useful if you were trying to use it as a navigational tool. It must have been drawn in haste by someone who needed to get moving, someone fleeing from pursuit. An aid to memory which had never been put to use.

McKeever was holding forth on the finer points of the infield fly rule and the balk call (neither of which I've ever understood so well myself) and the good ladies were chattering agreeably, though I didn't suppose they would retain a particle of the info he was dispensing. After breakfasting at the cottage and before setting out in Brigitte, I had returned to the palace and done some research on the doubloon Wilder had left with me. I was convinced by the look and the feel of the thing that it was genuine and a contemporary of the map. It was like holding a miniature round time machine in my hand, a small golden Tardis.

On the return trip, the mood was, understandably, a bit more subdued. I asked Cassidy to move to the back seat, where, to make room, one of the ladies of Daffadowndilly perched on his lap, an adventure even greater, I expect, than going for a ride in an antique luxury car to the far-off leeward side of the island, Bess taking the passenger seat in front. Her eyes darted about, lighting up at each new sight that greeted them. I had to believe that a woman so observant and alert of mind would have kept a keen eye on the gents who were building her cottage: fed them to keep their energy up, supplied them with refreshment, followed their movements.

"I suppose the young lady, Clementine, shared her sad news with you," I said.

"Yes, her brother's passing was a shock to me, even though I'd not seen him for years. He was such a young man." Her eyes misted over and she looked down, trying to compose herself.

"So you remember him well?"

"Joshua? Oh, quite well. He was my favorite, I think. He worked twice as hard as the other lads, but was the only one to take the Sabbath off. Not as a religious observance, you understand, those boys were all happy heathens, or pagans, perhaps, or merely young men so full of beans they hadn't a thought to spare for the afterlife. No, it was because he loved to hike, and that's how he spent his Sundays. Tramping around, he called it."

"Did he have any favorite hikes? Spots he liked best?"

"I don't know of any favorite *places*," she said. "But there was one peculiarity about his jaunts that I did notice. He always set off on what a seafaring man would call a south-easterly course. Never north

190

or west. I used to tease him about it. 'I thought you Yanks were always supposed to Go west, young man.' He would say, 'Are you *Josh*ing me? And we would laugh and laugh. He was a fine lad."

The village of Daffadowndilly was not, needless to say, on the Maracaibo map, having been brought to life but nine years past, but my recollection of that map, given its abrupt lopping off of the entire leeward side of the island, insisted that a south-southeasterly course which commenced at the spot where Bess's cottage now stood, would lead, inevitably, to the caves below the southern slope of the Grieving Widow, the caves which, despite their relative insignificance as a topographical feature, nevertheless figured so prominently on the map. I had been quite recently in those caves, sliding down a wet channel over smooth stone. Now the caves began telescoping in my mind, receding and diminishing, as though forming a new neural pathway. I felt a distinct chill. Or maybe it was just the wind off the ocean. I speeded up a touch to increase the breeze blowing through Brigitte so that the ladies would need to hold onto their hats, their laughter growing downright giddy, even Bess rallying to join in the merriment. I might be on a case fraught with that old devil peril but there was no need for these good-hearted gardeners to know what one of their old boys had gotten up to with a pair of the ladies' own purloined shears. The old girls were having the time of their lives.

On the way back to Daffadowndilly, I swung past the faux *Naughtylass* and asked the Captain to meet me at the palace in an hour's time. I got there before him and did my best to brew a pot of tea for my guest. Preems, though he makes the best LSD on the island and can, not infrequently, be found at his opium pipe, stays away from strong drink the way I avoid tea. I counted myself lucky to find a box of the stuff in a cupboard. And it was bulk tea, so I couldn't just boil water and dip in a teabag. Black tea sounded about right for a pirate, now I just needed to find a teacup and a strainer. As the king, you'd think I would have serving girls for this sort of thing. Wilder would probably have known where to look, but I ended up settling for an old mug that might once have held shaving soap. I got even luckier and happened upon not a strainer but a thing I think is called a brewing spoon, which looked like a small, very pretty silver torture device. And here, bless me, was a lemon. I climbed up to the

191

library with the tea things and pulled down a handful of encyclopedias to add to the one I had been perusing earlier.

All was in readiness when a familiar voice called out "Ahoy!" from below. Calling out "Ahoy!" would seem an affectation coming from anyone whose regular greeting it hadn't been for the better part of a lifetime. But it's standard issue to the Captain, even as hi-dee-ho to McKeever.

As a hedge against BBNGs striking a reef, foundering, going bosoms up and thereby smashing our delicate bottle economy to bits, a number of gentlemen, mostly in the interior and in the mountains, built and operated backcountry stills, which is how our one successful export, *Quietude* Shine, had made its way into the world, and how Captain Primo came to find himself in southern California. When the first sample batches were ready, he had designed a label, found suitably piratical-looking bottles, kicked off and MC-ed the launch in Venice with a two-headed party held simultaneously on *Heather & Yawn* and at the tiki bar known as the Wiggle Room, above which I was bunking at the time. When the product proved to be a universal success, he stayed to oversee shipping and distribution and to tend bar at the club. When he was ready to make his way back to *Quietude*, the dancing girls, who found him an agreeable softie, prevailed upon him to stay. He'd been gone for nearly two years before returning recently to flash signs to Wilder from the not-so-grandstand at Buck O'Neil Field.

"Come on up, Preems. Let my rope ladder be your rigging," I called down. He knew where to find me and soon was settled in on a tall, high-backed stool with his favorite beverage steaming before him. He would have felt right at home in Daffadowndilly, I thought. Maybe the good ladies could book him as a guest lecturer one day. I, less civilized, settled for coffee doctored with Armagnac. As I had anticipated, he was instantly fascinated by the doubloon.

"What is it saying to you, Preems?"

"A lot, Mister High. Its name and time stamp and place of origin. On the front here, as you can see, is the date, 1778. The Latin inscription, *Hisp et Ind Carol III D.G.* can be translated to 'By the grace of God, Charles the third, King of the Indies and Beyond.' Charles is the bewigged cat portrayed hereon, looking like a sort of European George Washington. He was the king of Spain from 1759 until 1788. He was considered, in his day, to be an 'enlightened despot,' a term that would fit Mister Putin nicely as soon as you removed the word 'enlightened.' History looks pretty kindly on Charles, though he once lost Florida to England."

"A weird sort of soccer match, but go on."

"On the B side, we find a royal shield and more Latin, *Auspice deo in utero Felix*, meaning, roughly, 'Under God's will we shall happily prosper.'"

"Thanks. I was wondering who Felix was and what he was doing with a uterus. How do you suppose it might have come to be here?"

"I can only conjecture. Given the date, we can speculate that it was, at one time, on a ship of Alejandro Malaspina, a Spanish naval officer who undertook a circumnavigation of the globe from 1786 to 1788. His ships made stops in the Philippines, Australia, New Zealand and Tonga among points further west. But he wasn't scouring the world for the lost gold of the Aztecs or anything like that. On the contrary, he is now regarded as a Spanish counterpart to Captain Cook. His explorations were primarily scientific, specifically, botanical in nature."

"Leaving us to wonder both why he would be sailing with a chest of doubloons and in the following of what directive he might have covered the enormous distance from Tonga to the island we know as *Quietude*."

"There's nothing in the historical record to indicate he ever got this far east or even this far south. Of course, since this island was uncharted until quite recently, there could be no mention of it in his log, but I think it likelier that when he was looking for new plant specimens far to the west, he was marauded by—" Did a gleam come into his good eye as he said? "Pirates. Pirates or privateers under French or British protection who relieved him of the gold he was carrying just as you or I, were we out in the great world, would carry traveler's checks. Specie speaks even louder than currency and no specie with greater volume than gold. It would have been what you or I would call 'pocket money.' or 'operating capital."

"Very well. Since we cannot know how it came to be here, what can you say about its value in today's market?"

"I can speak to it with some authority, having only recently retired from dealing in some of the stuff myself. A standard sized chest would hold over 20,000 of these doubloons. More like 23,000 if you filled it to the brim. Which brings us to an interesting problem."

"How you would cart it out?"

"Well, actually, two interesting problems. The weight of the thing and the difficulty of hauling it out, as you say, being the first. It would weigh upwards of a thousand pounds. You say the treasure hunters are down to one. Two strong men wouldn't be the equal of such a task, especially if its underground. You would need either a rope and pulley and strong men hauling or beasts of burden providing the muscle. No, carrying the chest to a getaway boat is out of the question. Here's what I would do: Have a vessel nearby, ready to weigh anchor at a moment's notice, take canvas bags of doubloons one or two at a time with as many men as you can recruit passing them down the line. You say there's only one hunter still standing, and that a woman? Well, she and her late partner must have been planning to meet up with a boat, its crew members under orders to get the bags on board in a hurry, probably in the dead of night." That idea lined up with what I took to be Dante's original plan, the boatman bringing his vessel in on the leeward side, the three hunters loading it up under cover of darkness and slipping away. But by now, the scheduled time for the rendezvous having passed, would the boatman have cast off, fearing that something had gone awry?

"Which brings us to the second problem."

"Lay it on me."

"I'm on firmer ground here than in guessing about a possible history. I have some experience in moving such pieces. The 1778 value of a chest of gold doubloons would have been impressive, no doubt. But now, when each coin can be sold individually to collectors on the internet for about nine grand apiece, or to auction houses for amounts in that ballpark, the amount could be truly staggering, upwards of a hundred and eighty million dollars."

"A tidy sum."

"Yes. You could buy a town in Kansas, maybe even a house in northern California. But you would want to take your time. And you could afford to take your time, because there would be no need to look over your shoulder for the law. You wouldn't have to fence the doubloons because they'd be found money and there's no need to fence found money.

"If you were to move them in bulk, it could flood the market and the net value would decrease drastically. But as I understand it, Clementine wants to get the treasure, supposing it exists, to the defenders of Ukraine and let them decide how to translate it into armaments, bullets, first aid supplies, stuff like that, right?" I nodded. "Well, then, that would be the freedom fighter's call. Leaving us with one final problem—where is the stuff?"

"Where would you have hidden it, Preems, had you needed to stash such a haul in your heyday?"

"I've always preferred going five fathom deep with such valuables. Sunken treasure is so much easier to retrieve than buried treasure. Less strenuous."

"Granted. But we cannot drag the Pacific. It's an extremely large body of water."

"Right you are. A smaller body, perhaps. Small and local. That's where I would look."

It had been a long day. Back at our cottage, Wilder and her sidekick were crashed in her bunkhouse, not even bothering to bombard the carp. I couldn't think of a thing to say that would ease their depression over the tough loss on the leeward side. They had to learn for themselves to shake off disappointment and make ready for the climactic contest of this, their maiden season. Bonny had unsaddled Holy Toledo! for Wilder, put the stallion in his paddock, brushed him down and given him hay and water, ordinarily our daughter's job, but her Mumza knew full well how downhearted our girl would be and covered for her. Knowing she would want to wash off the evidence of her long ride, I went right to Bonny's Falls to have a word with her. I had hoped we could speak of her time with Clementine during the previous game, but my subjects on the leeward side, who rarely enjoy a sighting of their sovereign and people, especially little girls, kept bringing me small tributes and gifts—homegrown vegetables, baked goods, carvings, trinkets, articles of clothing, the only snow-globe I've ever seen on *Quietude*—and I had decided we should speak of Clementine privately.

I had enough sense to take her a glass of cold Chardonnay. She loves the contrast between the chilled wine and the warm water of the falls. She scoots a little ways up, so that the water is still striking her back but stays out of her glass, a technique she has perfected over our years here.

"Hey, Sugarcane," she said. "Thank you. Pretty cool to have a king for one's sommelier. I could get used to this."

"You and me both," I said. "But I come with an ulterior motive. I've been wondering why you wanted to sit next to Clementine at Buck O'Neil Field, and why you asked me to dummy up about your identity. You promised me you'd come clean and, under the circumstances, you can come clean twice at the same time." She took a sip and looked at me.

"Oh, I just thought she might open up and speak more freely around someone who, like herself, was new to *Quietude*."

"You passed yourself off as a tourist?" She nodded and grinned.

"And did she? Open up?"

"Yes. It occurred to me that since her arrival, she had spoken only to other folks with an interest in this treasure you're all going on about: You, Jake, Creole, McKeever, your émigré. I just thought she might loosen her girdle, as they used to say, around a woman with a treasureless agenda. She asked me if I was new to the island, and I said yes, I was visiting an old friend. How about her? She said she had been here about a week and couldn't, I quote, 'wait to get off this rock.'"

"Well, she's pretty driven by the desire to lay hands on the treasure and get the spoils to Ukraine. We all are. Those folks are under the gun."

"I know that's true. But I didn't get the impression her motivation was all that altruistic. She mostly spoke of how dismal she found our standard of living. She was eager to return to an upscale condo and a jacuzzi and a four-star restaurant." Were we talking about the same woman? I wondered. "Then, in the usual way of ladies when first they meet, I asked if she had any children or siblings. No kids, thank god, she said. I had a brother, but he recently passed away. Had they been close? I asked. Oh, when they were kids, she said, but not for years. I asked her if she worked and she told me that as a younger woman, she had been quite gainfully employed by an upper end escort service, got out early and used the money she saved to take acting classes."

"Acting classes, you say?"

196

"Yes, that's what she's doing now, acting. Mostly on television. A few film roles. Some stage work. She mentioned some things she'd been in. I pretended to have seen one of them. It was almost true. I slept through one of the movies she mentioned on a flight from Zurich to Zanzibar." I wondered why none of us had thought to ask her more about herself. Her reason for coming here, her *mission*, or so it seemed, had consumed all the members of her audience. Was that what we had been? An audience? With the exception of Mister Smirnoff, none of us could provide independent confirmation of anything she had told us. Contacting Dante would take a seance, and the rest of us, in our dealings with fawn woman, were rookies as surely as Wilder's sidekick.

"This is all quite fascinating, and I thank you for taking the time. But I still wonder about your initial impulse. Why did you want to get into her head in the first place?"

"Well, to begin with, McKeever is easy. He's been hiding out in that cave of his for so long he would have built up a decade's worth of fantasies to project upon her. And you're so insulated. Forgive me, Sugarcane, but you may have developed an immunity to skepticism here on your enchanted isle where no one is trying to put anything over on anyone else. Jake is more worldly, but he's onto a story, which tends to tunnel his vision. If whatever gaudy line of patter she's dishing helps him to sniff out the finish line and put the story on the spike, he'll buy into it. And the Russian gentleman—Smirnoff, you say?—well, according to what you've told me, he's had a sort of paternal crush on Miss Clementine since she was a child. All she would have to do to enlist his sympathies would be to parrot his own anti-Putin line and he would have no reason to doubt her. I just thought you needed fresh eyes."

"What about Creole?" Bonny and my secretary have been friends for many a year.

"Sugarcane, I know you think of Wilder's godmother as a savvy dame, but that may be partly because you love using expressions like 'savvy dame.' One thing you need to remember about her is that, savvy as she may be, the dominant note in her personality is sympathy. When she saw the state of mind the woman was in when you found her wandering around by the waterfall, the state of mind she was *acting* like she was in, and heard her story, which I suspect is

197

partly true and partly improvised, Creole would have signed on and never looked back."

"All right. But if you suspect Miss Clementine, just what is it you suspect her of?"

"Duplicity, deception, and deceit," she said. "Our dear country of *Quietude* may be little more than a series of garden paths, but I believe she is leading you all up one of her own devising. Whatever it is she claims to want, I would look to its diametrical opposite for the truth of the matter. Your Miss Clementine herself really *is* one world class savvy dame."

The principal difference between the cut of Bonny's intelligence and my own is that hers has a well-developed practical side. My own experiments in practicality consist entirely of making sure the ice-cube trays are filled. Could Bonny be right and the rest of us duplicity's dupes, up to and including my secretary? Had my vigilant posse turned into an adoring fan club? What had Mister Smirnoff said? That Clementine was passionate in her distrust of her partner in treasure hunting? He, the émigré, had waited for the man, i.e., Dante, to avail himself of the facilities at Barney's and spoken with the woman in the bar. But had he ever spoken one-on-one with the man? Not that we knew of. He had only Clementine's side of the story to go on.

Three elements were cozying up to one another in my mind: the Maracaibo map ending in the middle of the island by the small caves, my vision of those selfsame caves, like a prehistoric back to the womb fantasy, and Primo's theory that a small local body of water would be the ideal hiding place for treasure. Sunken rather than buried, he had said. And, really, who better to trust than an old pirate in such a matter?

Chapter Thirty-Nine

Sometimes in baseball we say that a game is win or go home. Since game three of the Championship Series was being held at Buck O'Neil Field, we would be at home even if we lost. But if we lost, there would be no lobster for the River Otters. We all want to go down in history as the first winners of the Crown of *Quietude*, but so do the JJs. We were playing in front of our hometown crowd, but plenty of fans from the leeward side had trooped around the island to root for their guys. My Poppy had come down from his palm tree and was sitting next to my Mumza along the first base line. It was good to see them holding hands and trying to stay calm. Queenie and Mister Buchanan were sitting close by my folks and a half-dozen of the good ladies of Daffadowndilly were grouped together under their parasols, rooting in their dainty way. Captain Primo and his crew of old sea dogs were waving cutlasses and polo mallets in the air, looking very sporty. I didn't see my Mumza's new friend Clementine, but I saw plenty of my old friends. PW, in the third base coaching box, took off his top hat, bent over, perched the hat on his bottom and walked around thus, always a big wow with the crowd.

From the first pitch, you could tell that neither team was about to give an inch. I was throwing the game of my life, even better than my no-hitter. I was rested and would never be readier. Mister McKeever, since the last game, had shown me how to do what's called dropping down and throwing *side-arm*. Izzy, the great aka-er calls it the *side-winder*. Instead of delivering the ball straight overhand or at a three quarters angle, you throw it with your arm kind of parallel to the ground. It's hard to control but it makes the batters real nervous, like the pitch is coming at them out of the bleachers or something. They jump back out of the way and then the ball crosses the plate. And even if you miss with it and it goes all what the Hawaiians call *buckaloose*, it's still useful because it makes the hitters even more nervous and they just want to get the at-bat over with.

There's another, even more unusual way of throwing a sidewinder, it's called *submarine*. The pitcher drops her arm down even lower, until her knuckles are almost scraping the dirt of the mound just before releasing the pitch. I had practiced throwing both of these ways against the trunk of the banyan tree and with the sidewinder I did pretty well, but with the submariner, I had been missing the whole tree a lot of the time, and it's a very big tree. But I really wanted to try it in a game at least one time so the Captain, himself an old submariner, could see it in action.

But the JJ's big guy, D'Artagnan, seemed to have grown even bigger and stronger since the previous game. He was rearing back and bringing serious heat. He didn't have much in the way of breaking pitches but his number one moved so well he could make it go up, down, in, out, so it was sort of like its own breaking ball. Neither team's base coaches had much to do.

Since the beginning of the season, we have gone from playing like little kids who couldn't tie the laces on their cleats to being pretty darned agile with bat and glove alike. Before our first game, my Poppy had told me I had to learn to *trust my stuff*. I didn't know what that meant when he said it, but I know now. I had stopped nibbling at the corners and could *graze* them with slow curves after setting up the hitter with a heater just above the letters. It's all about upsetting their timing.

We went to the seventh in a scoreless tie. My infielders were up on their toes. Jaxxx had applied a kind of oil called *brilliantine* to his dreads and they really did look brilliant in the sun. I caught a flash off them just as I was about to try to get a first pitch strike over on their leadoff hitter. I took a breath so deep it filled me up and made me feel wild and free and unbeatable, as though the air was made of what my Poppy's friend Peter Bralver calls *charged particles* (which Izzy, big surprise, thinks would be a good name for a baseball team, The Charged Particles). As I was going into my wind-up, the cyclone hit. My Poppy tells me that in the bigs over the years many games have been called on account of rain, snow, hail, and one time in the Texas League by something called *grass-hoppers*, but I do believe that the Windward League may be the first in which a game has ever been halted by a cyclone. It never would have stopped a game on the Leeward side because they don't have cyclones over there. But here

200

in Elsewhereville, we were going to miss out on our last ups. At the moment, it felt like no one would ever have any ups again. But I've been through these things before. This may be my first year as a starting pitcher, but I'm a veteran of cyclones. They blow themselves out pretty quickly, but you need to what's called *duck and cover* until the storm wears itself out and play can resume. The whole crowd ran inland within a minute. One second the bleachers were full of fans, the next they were empty. I saw Mister McKeever ushering the good ladies in the direction of the big cave where he lives. That's where people usually go when a cyclone strikes. As team captain, I needed to get the River Otters to a place of safety. The thing you want to watch out for is falling trees or getting whipped across the face by branches lashing like crazy in the wind. I thought Mister McKeever's cave would fill up quickly and then I remembered the small caves by the big waterfall at the foot of the Widow. They were just the right size for nine River Otters. And while we were there, I could check to see if PW's yellow chalk drawing was a real lead. A long time ago, I hid six jars of peanut butter I'm not supposed to have in one of those caves. And three jars of maraschino cherries a waitress named Moxie at the Doubloon traded me for doing her hair in braids. And one enormous jar of the big black gumdrops the pirates have been giving us. We could hold out for days! Well, for the rest of today anyway. The game would have to be rescheduled and picked up where we had left off.

"Follow me, Otters!" I called out and we ran like nine ballplayers all trying to beat out a close one at the same time, heading straight for the Grieving Widow.

201

Chapter Forty

I couldn't figure out how to haul a loveseat up a palm tree, so I was
with Bonny along the first base line. "Isn't this about where you sat
with Clementine?" I said. "Exactly the same," she said. "I don't think
she's here today." And wasn't I one lucky monarch not to have been
high up in my beach chair when a cyclone walloped the west coast of
Quietude? These thrilling meteorological events are entirely
unpredictable, but even as my subjects were taken by surprise, all
remained calm, acting with purpose rather than panic. I found
Bonny's hand in my hand. "Get to the cottage as fast as you can," I
said. "Wilder probably went to ground there, but I'm going to check
the palace just in case." She gave me a squeeze, slipped off her shoes
and dashed away like the high school track star she had been back in
Florida. A good thing the dress was slit up both sides, it allowed her
to take long strides. It may not speak well of me either as a father or a
king, but I couldn't help watching her for a second. While I was
doing so, PW blew by me, in a hurry to join his own family no doubt.
But rushing past, as though he were finishing the first leg of a relay
race and I about to begin the second, he slapped the not-a-flute into
my hand. I took off at what might be called a dead run if that phrase
could be taken to mean sprinting at the speed of the no longer living.

   I had begun to fear that a homing instinct could have sent Wilder
to the palace, by no means the safest place to ride out a cyclone.
After the thought entered my mind, I couldn't shake it. The palace
was all too close to our west coast and the upper stories, though
charming, were susceptible to being blown to hell and gone by high
winds. She would probably know better, but how is a man of sixty-
eight years to get into the mind of a nine-year-old girl? What if she
took it into her head to go up into the projection room and watch,
oh, I don't know, say *Hurricane* (1937), a fun way for a rough and
tumble tomboy to pass the time during a cyclone? The crowd had
dispersed like the tadpoles in the pirate's watering trough when you

202

reach a hand in. I hadn't seen Clementine during the game and now I saw no one at all. I hobbled for my royal residence, glad of the tailwind.

Ten minutes later, pitifully winded, I checked the three floors of the palace and found all rooms uninhabited. Surely Wilder had led her mates to the cottage to hunker down in her bunkhouse. She would want to make certain that the suddenly obstreperous weather hadn't spooked her horse. I was being a nervous Nellie daddy. I sat for a minute at the bar of the library to catch my breath and have a quick snort. I hadn't forgotten that my fiancée for life had left me on a liquor-free diet, but I remembered that long ago, Jake had brought me two airline vodka miniatures which I had thought to transfer to an ice-cube tray as part of what I called my "cyclone preparedness program." It was the one place my lady had neglected to look. Only then did I notice that I still had the not-a-flute in hand. Had PW slapped it into my palm just to lighten his load, or was there a reason? What the hell, I thought, and, cracking open the tray and sucking down a couple cubes of pure Grey Goose, I went through the moves to alakazam PW's conductor's baton, Izzy's bamboozler, Wilder's not-a-flute, Dante's wand and Joshua's inadvertent bequest to *Quietude*. Inside it, neatly rolled, was a small map about the size of a dinner napkin. Unrolling it on the bar, I finally understood why the Maracaibo map was so short on details and why it stopped before reaching our eastern shore. This smaller model was a *subterranean* map. It laid out, with meticulous exactitude, a series of chutes and passageways beneath the caves which had been haunting me of late. This was the key that Joshua hadn't lived to use and that Dante had died for. I tucked it back into the not-a-flute, stuck the stick itself down the front of my jeans and made ready to head east. I needed to follow in Joshua's footsteps.

The map of his authorship, shown to none of his acquaintances, should have been a reliable guide. I knew I was in the right place, but could not for the life of me see how to get from the floor of the cave into the subterranean chambers beneath it, drawn so clearly on the map. The underworld and the over remained doggedly divided.

Edging forward, I tripped but caught myself on my hands. No serious damage. Tripping, a downfall by definition, had almost been

Clementine's, unless Bonny was right and it had definitely been Dante's. I needed to be more careful. The stone floor was hard but cool and mossy and I decided to rest for a moment. Who knew? Maybe reinforcements would show up and help me to my feet. Well, maybe not. As I was pushing myself up and making ready to stand, my right index finger caught on something. Close examination revealed it to be a sort of ring, roughly the size of a fastened handcuff. Scraping with a fingernail and tapping with a pebble suggested it was metal rather than rock. The pebble tinged against it rather than tocked. Had I entered a dimension wherein the stone age and the iron age merged? It took me a while to sit up, but once I had, it took little more effort for me to lift my left leg so that I might plant my foot against the floor of the cave, the better to test my ailing back by pulling on the ring. Nothing doing. I rested for another minute, took a deep breath and tried again, this time with a twisting back and forth motion added to the pulling. I was rewarded with a small scraping sound. That was all the encouragement I needed to press on. Or pull on. Straining with all my might (which wasn't much) and giving myself breathers at one-minute intervals, I began to feel I might not be the man for the job. McKeever was bigger and Jake was younger. One more try and then I could go make sure that Wilder and her friends were safe and reassemble our rag-tag search party, the better to mount a second assault wave on the vault. But on my final try, I felt whatever I was pulling on begin to grudgingly relax its grip. Too late to stop now. To my amazement, another yank resulted in a circular section of stone resembling nothing so much as a man-hole cover calling it quits. I lifted it out and set it aside. Though my back would never forgive me, I had gained entrance to the big hidey-hole down into which only one No Stranger to Danger and the piratical parties who had left the treasure two hundred years ago had ever descended.

From there it was easy. It was almost pitch black but though I hadn't thought to bring a flashlight, I always have a Zippo lighter on my person, despite not having smoked since my merrily misspent youth. I love the clicking sound they make and I keep it filled with fluid because you never know when a lady might ask a gentleman for a light. Fire seemed like the ideal form of illumination for looking down into the bowels of the earth, or so it felt.

Directly beneath me was a chute of solid rock, on an angle no scarier than a kiddie park slide, carved by moving water over the course of millennia, no doubt, and fairly smooth. I slid down it like one my daughter's age, finding myself on a ledge from which another chute gave me a second ride. According to Joshua's map, there should be a second ledge and a third, much longer chute leading to level ground. And so there was. I touched down to the sound of moving water somewhere off to my left. Or was it an echo of the falls overhead? Only now did it occur to me that I hadn't thought to bring anything that would provide a means of getting back out. The chutes that had led me in had no handholds. I could call out but the area was not densely populated and no one knew I was here. The fire-bringer would soon run out of fluid and be reduced to a monarch left alone with his thoughts in the dark. Hmm.

Chapter Forty-One

"Let's play follow the leader!" I said. I wished PW were with me and my fellow Otters. He and I used to play hide and seek in these caves. But our third base coach was probably taking care of his family until the storm blew over. Even in the middle of the day, it was dark in here, but I knew my way around pretty well and Izzy, thanks to her mom, had a little flashlight in her backpack. Her mother knows how often Mizz Izz gets lost and tries to keep her prepared for any *eventuality,* a word that just means whatever might happen. In no time, I had found the treats I hid for an emergency and handed them around to my team. Then I remembered that this cave led to a couple of others. We couldn't play any more baseball today, so we might as well play something else. I put the jar of maraschino cherries in my uniform pants pocket. It wasn't until later that I learned how two of my teammates had followed my example. The farther we went, the darker it got. I told Izzy to hold onto my shirt so she wouldn't get lost. A good thing, too, because only the beam of her flashlight kept me from stepping right into a big hole. "Shine your torch down here, Izz," I said to my shortstop. A *torch* is what they call a flashlight in Australia. All the Otters gathered around the hole, as though we were taking a meeting on the mound.

"Where does it go?" said Izzy.

"To China. No, Taiwan," said Alakai, our right fielder who is a whizz at geography.

"To Hollywood," sighed Ella Rose, our first base *babe.*

"To the North Pole, probably," said Tobias, our French-Canadian left fielder.

"To the Kingdom of Middle Earth," said Walter, our well-read center fielder.

"To a café on the bottom of the sea," said Jubilee, our second baseman who is a romantic girl.

206

"Maybe it's a fishing hole," said Jaxxx, our third baseman. "We should throw a rock down there and listen for a splash."

"I think it's a shortcut," said Jaxxx, our third baseman, but he didn't say to where.

"Let's find out," I said and climbed down.

Chapter Forty-Two

I sat in the dark, entertained by my new Wurlitzer, the sound of moving water, faint but unmistakable. I couldn't tell from whence it emanated but it was excellent company. I don't suppose you could find a deeper darkness, not on the surface of the earth anyway. No light could penetrate this chamber, neither sunlight, nor moonlight, nor starlight. When next the sun rose, I would not be able to tell. It should have been unsettling, but I felt strangely at peace. After a while, I began to hallucinate. At least that's what I thought was happening. A light as faint as the sound of the water appeared at the edge of my vision, and moved steadily closer. Was this a subterranean version of a desert mirage, a vain hope of salvation offered up by one's deprived senses?

The light moved toward me, accompanied by small scraping sounds. Soon it was close enough that I had to turn my head to one side to keep from being blinded. Then it was lowered and set on the ground. When my eyes grew accustomed to illumination, I could make out the form of a woman sitting on a boulder and crossing her legs nonchalantly. McKeever was right. They were very long. Most of my attention, however, was fixed on the flare gun in her right hand. She was pointing it at my head from about eight feet away. I wasn't certain she could kill me with it, even at that distance, but I knew I didn't want to find out.

"If you plug me with that thing, you won't be able to alert your boatman," I said. "You'll be well and truly stuck here. You will have found your brother's treasure but how are you going to spend it?" She coolly pulled a second flare out from under the band of her shorts and held it up, smiling sweetly. "Oh." I said. Not my day for witty repartee. Whether or not she could spend her treasure, I needed a way to buy some time. It occurred to me that in this chamber where it was always late night, I might do well to turn into a talk show host.

"I hear tell you're an actress," I said.

"The woman in the bleachers at the game?" she said. I nodded.

"Serves me right for shooting my mouth off," she said. "I was getting island fever."

"I'm about twelve years behind on American popular culture," I said, "so you'll forgive me for not recognizing you."

"I was counting on it. But you might not have in any case. I'm not exactly on the A-list. Though I've had a pretty good run on what you might call the 'T&A list.' I've been bumped off early on in a lot of low-rent erotic thrillers, after flashing my tits first, of course." She shook her head. "In the last one, I was asked to show my tits *after* I'd been killed, on a slab in the morgue."

"And you accepted the role?"

"A girl's got to pay the rent." She smiled. "Besides, the coroner was kind of cute. But I'm thirty-five and work is starting to dry up. I should have married money when I was still in my twenties and could have buffed the showroom floor with my ass."

Ah, the good old days. We all have some, don't we? Those enticing hours that exert such a pull on one's memory. We slip into them without really trying, imagining our way backwards, vaseline on our recollections' lenses softening them until they are as soft as we would like to believe those days had been. What was it Buck O'Neil once wrote? "Yesterday comes so easy." How true, especially now, when tomorrows might not come at all. I found myself wondering how long it would take to get used to being dead. In my own good old days, McKeever would have shown up at the last minute, thrown Clementine over his shoulder and carried her off to a motel room right next to the ice machine. Not now, though, he would be hosting an open bar in a cave full of his fellow citizens. Oh, well.

"Pretty soon, they won't even ask me show my tits. They'll just show me the door."

"Maybe you can graduate to character parts," I said. She smiled again.

"Okay," she said. "This is me auditioning for the role of a brave, humanitarian sister of a fallen hero. Do I get the part?"

"Was Josh really your brother?"

"Of course he was my brother."

"And your parents' deaths?"

209

"Exactly as reported by your Mister Smirnoff. And, yes, I was there. I don't remember Smirnoff, but I was only twelve and busy looking up to my older brother. My girlfriends all had crushes on him when we were in school."

"How much of the story you told us was true?"

"A lot. Most of it, really. There was, however, a certain amount of what you might call 'role reversal' involved. Dante and Josh saw themselves as some sort of brothers-in-arms. Josh considered his request that Dante help me recover the treasure and get the money to the people of Ukraine as a sacred responsibility. Dante likewise. Josh called me to his bedside in the eleventh hour and told me the whole story. We hadn't spent any time together for years, barely even talked. But on his deathbed, he related the tale of his time on *Quietude*, and whispered the secret of his hiding place, explained to me how to use it. He would have told Dante, from whom he had withheld this crucial detail so that neither of them could do it by himself. It was part of their whole musketeer deal. One for all and all for who knows what the fuck. But now there wasn't time. Dante was on his way from somewhere in central Africa and out of contact. So Josh rewired his plan and set it up so that Dante and *I* would need each other. Josh trusted me because I was his only living relative. He trusted blood. In my view, blood is no more trustworthy than your average mugger. If we'd been closer, he would have known that his sacred mission meant nothing to me. If you start handing out money to everyone who is deserving of the stuff, pretty soon you're on cardboard instead of velvet."

"You figured out pretty quickly what we all wanted to hear. Classes in improv?"

"Sure, and years of on-the-job training. When you go into audition and you're playing a scene you read for the first time the night before in front of a director, a casting director, maybe a producer, maybe a few half-smashed old leches calling themselves executive producers, you get good at reading the room pretty quickly. It's a survival skill, one that came in handy when I found myself alone in this Tinker Toy country of yours. Remember, I wasn't supposed to meet any of you people. But when Dante and I tussled and he lost, I got scared. I knew how to signal the boatman—she waggled the barrel of the flare-gun—"but I had no idea of how long he was prepared to wait

210

offshore. That was Dante's part of the show. So I was totally on my own." Bonny had been so right. Clementine, with her highly honed survival skills, had simply gone off script as the situation dictated.

"Tell me how that tussle, as you call it, went down? Was it anything like the way you described it to us?"

"There were definite...similarities," she said, smiling to herself. It must have been professionally satisfying, I thought, to be not only playing the female lead in this drama, but to be directing and screenwriting as needed. "One of us did take the gardening shears off Bess's porch. Just not the one I gave credit to the last time the subject was raised. "

"Did you threaten him when he refused to hand over the not-a-flute?"

"Damn right I did. He had been a No Stranger to Danger and probably figured he could outrun me and then outsmart me. But it was Dante, not I, who tripped in the meadow. How was I to know he had ditched the damned stick? I don't understand why he was even fighting with me at that point. I guess his blood was up. The part where I said he leaped on me was pretty close to the truth. I only wanted the damned wand. It was really more of what they call manslaughter in some degree or other than cold-blooded... you know."

"That leaves the question of how this conversation will end."

"Well," she said, "you're not a *young* man. You could go any time." I was afraid she might start quoting actuarial tables and interrupted her.

"Are you going to give out now with one of those 'The first time you kill someone, it feels wrong but after that it's surprisingly easy' speeches?" I said. "You may not have thought this through. How are you going to explain my corpse to my family and friends?"

"There won't be any corpse," she said. Your body will be disposed of. If I yell long enough and loud enough, some of your countrymen will find me but of their king there will be not a trace." What could she mean by that? I wondered. There was a rather pretty symmetry to McKeever living in a cave and I dying in one, but the thought didn't bring much cheer. I really wanted to see how the Championship series played out. The lantern she had carried down was on the ground at her feet. Maybe I could level the playing field by making a dive for it and knocking it over, leaving us both in absolute darkness.

She raised the barrel and sighted along it, squinting. At that moment, the cavern turned into a most extraordinary playground, as though the slides that had permitted entry had summoned a squadron of children to use them. One minute it was just Clementine and I and the next the darkness contained my daughter and her whole baseball team, one of them shining a light in fawn woman's eyes. Clementine, barely taken aback, held the flare gun steady. The kids spread out, as though taking their positions for infield drill.

"Hello, Wilder," said Clementine. "Your father and I are playing a little game."

"How about you and the River Otters play a little game of catch," said my Little Coconut, unleashing I knew not what, some small red missile that caught Clementine right between the eyes. It was part of a fusillade made up of three jars, a brown one, larger than Wilder's, thrown by her sidekick, Izzy, and a huge black number contributed by a tall young fellow I recognized as my royal predecessor, Walter the Studious. Wilder's jar, as I was soon to learn, contained Maraschino cherries, Izzy's Skippy Super-Chunk Peanut Butter (banned by Wilder's mother) and Walter's, lent weight and substance by an enormous number of black gumdrops, had triple-teamed Clementine, putting her down and rendering Joshua's sister unconscious.

"You beaned her," I said to my daughter, surprised not by the accuracy of her throw but by the uptick in her velocity.

"Well, Poppy, you told me not to throw at any *batters'* heads. My Mumza said this Clementine person isn't really our friend. Besides, I think she was going to hurt you with that thing." She pointed to the flare-gun, now lying on the floor of the cavern. I picked it up and tucked it into my jeans, trying to look debonair, as though pistols being pointed at me from point blank range were a daily occurrence in the king biz. Jake and Creole clambered down into the cavern, each bearing flashlights, a little late to the party but it was always good to see them.

"Hiya, Boss," said my secretary. "Sorry to be tardy to the rescue. My sweetie and I had to batten down the hatches at the Dipper."

212

Last came the Captain, hopping down nimbly from the third ledge and unclipping a narrow gauge rope from the back of his belt, letting it fall to the stone floor. "Hey, kids," he said. "I was afraid none of you folks would come prepared with an exit strategy." He pointed to his rope. "That thing is like a deep-sea diver's safety line," he said. It's solidly staked to the ground at the foot of the first cave. All you need to do is pull yourselves hand over hand up to the entrance."

"What about her?" I said, pointing at Clementine. Preems grinned his most piratical grin.

"I've got a big bundle of jerky and a jug of water topside," he said. "Enough to sustain life for a few days. After you've all cleared out of here, I'll bring them down and set them by her. Though the jug's not really necessary. There's a goodly supply of fresh water nearby. Let's let her stew for a bit while you decide how you want to deal with her. I know that you are opposed to imprisonment, Mister High, as am I, but it hardly counts as such since she came down here of her own free will, not to mention with murder in her heart."

"Right you are, Preems. What did you mean about fresh water nearby?" The Captain took one of those big police issue flashlights out of his belt and waved it off to our left. I followed him over and found myself beside a stone channel invisible until he shone his flash upon it. Here was the source of the sound of moving water I had heard and wondered about. It was like a natural canal, the pearlescent murmuring of its contents making its way... where? The Captain led me over and played his light down upon the canal. At this point, it was no more than two feet deep and just beginning to gain momentum and surge slowly southwest. First came a dazzling reflection off the surface, then, as the beam cut deeper, I thought I was seeing a school of cousins to Wilder's carp in the pond at our cottage. I leaned down and reached in, coming out with a handful of gold doubloons identical to the one which Wilder had found in my beach chair. They were piled up in an old chest which sat on the floor of the canal, taking up most of its width but leaving enough space on either side for the water to flow around it.

"It's heavy enough—not just with the weight of the booty, but the chest itself is made of iron—to sit comfortably on the bottom, here where the current is too weak to dislodge it. As I predicted, a small local body of water."

213

Suddenly I understood what Clementine had meant about the disposal of my earthly remains. I was to have gone into the river and floated downstream to my final repose somewhere in the vast Pacific. What a send-off that would have been. I would have been a far more royal personage in death than ever I had in life. But now I would get to see the end of the ballgame.

"But where is it coming from?" I asked my secretary.

"The falls," said Creole. "All the greater and lesser falls on the south side of the Grieving Widow."

"I thought they flowed into the Not a Care in the World," I said.

"On the north side of the mountain, they do," she patiently explained. "But on this side, it would appear that the water pools up, seeps down through the caves and becomes the headwater of an underground river, a river that I suspect flows beneath the remainder of the island."

"Where do you suppose it emerges and meets the sea?" I said.

"I have no idea. We should hold a contest for would-be-explorers. It'll be the *Quietude* version of finding the source of the Nile." *An underground river?* I thought, as blown away as a footprint in the sand. It was as though we had discovered the subconscious of *Quietude*. Well, the credit really should go to Joshua. In his tramping around, he had found this cavern, unknown to any citizen of the land he was passing through. His sister's distress letter must have come on the heels of his discovery. I turned to the Captain.

"How do you reckon whoever hid the treasure here in the first place managed it?" This sort of thing was right in his wheelhouse.

"I expect that their original intention was to hide the chest in one of those little caves up top. But they must have felt it could be too easily stumbled upon. Then one of their number must have heard, or sensed, water and put an ear to the ground. A few blows with a pick-axe later would have created an entrance through which the chest could be lowered on a rope."

"Okay. Let's say you're right and that's how it got in here," said Jake. "My question is: How are we to get it out?" I looked at my daughter.

"It would help if you had an elephant," I said.

214

Wilder, ever the team captain, had insisted that all eight of her teammates pull themselves to safety before she gave a thought to her own. Then she explained that her prerogative as a princess dictated that the rest of our cavern companions quit the joint before she could allow herself to exit. Command must come naturally to my daughter, because all complied. Soon it was down to just the two of us and Izzy's flashlight, which Wilder handed to me.

"Poppy," she said. "I believe we have all been players in PW's movie ever since this adventure began. I'm going to pay him the compliment of leaving this cave the way I know he would." Before I could raise either hand or voice to object, she raced to the underground waterway's bank and jumped in. "See you round the next bend in the river, Poppy!" she called out exuberantly. And then she was gone.

Every day was a day at the races for my daughter, she was both horse and rider. But how on earth was I going to tell her mother about this? was my first thought when I arrived back at the cottage after my dust-up with Clementine in the cavern. It was obvious that I hadn't been shot, so trying to elicit pity would availeth me naught. Even in paradise, mothers worry. Where is our girl? she would say and I would reply Oh, she went for a swim, neglecting to add that the swim was in a river which happened to be underground and whose mouth was no one knew where. Maybe I would tell her, over a martini, adding the twist of the river at the last possible minute. Or maybe I wouldn't. Mothers want to know *everything*. But, really, are any of us entitled to know everything? Our daughter was a surfer, a fly-fisherman, a horsewoman and a hero of sport. She could take care of herself. So brave and so conscientious was our girl, I thought she would always come true. I will admit to a mild case of nerves, which expressed itself in a sudden impulse to throw back a cocktail or two. I was saved by the princess herself, who beat me by an eyelash to the bunkhouse where I'd gone in the hope of finding her.

Chapter Forty-Three

Continuation of game three of the first ever Championship Series for the Crown of *Quietude*, top of the seventh inning, Buck O'Neil Field.

My Poppy always calls me a rough and tumble tomboy (whatever that might be) and it was pretty darn rough and tumble all right on that ride out of the cavern. Now I know how a real river otter must feel. I didn't know where it would go, but I knew it was what PW would do and he is my greatest hero, along with my Mumza, natch. All rivers go to the ocean, but would an underground river go *under* the ocean? I had all kinds of crazy thoughts like that as I was being swept along. Would it go into my dreams? I wondered, using my hands like tillers on a boat to stay in the middle of the current. Would it carry me to the Southern Cross? Imagine how happy I was when I came up in the lagoon and PW himself was drifting nearby on his board, almost like he was waiting there for me. I climbed on in front of him and he paddled us to shore. I made it to our cottage just in time to meet the king as he was walking through the Dutch door into my bunkhouse. He tried to be cool, but I could tell he wanted to pick me up and give me a hug. He settled for laying a low-five hand slap on my palm and saying "Welcome home, Little Coconut." He should know better than to worry about me, but parents can't help being like that.

In baseball, you could go to extra innings and keep playing forever, a ballgame without end, a game that would last your whole life and then you could leave it to your daughter if you had one. *Bequeath*, that's the word. But I wanted to get this one over with and go feed my horse and eat some lobster with my fellow Otters. But first we had to record three more outs and to put something on the board. My arm was telling me to get it done, it was one sore arm and the rest of me was tired too after all my recent adventures. I told myself I didn't have to strike everyone out, just let my fielders do their jobs and we would soon be eating those good kabobs.

I wanted to throw first pitch strikes, but the JJs leadoff hitter was ready for me. He smashed a wicked liner up the middle which Izzy was able to knock down but couldn't make a play on. Next up was our old friend Gwendolyn, the girl who had been so upset when she struck out in the first game of the series. Now she looked more determined than scared. But I fooled her with a scroojie, at which she took what's called an *excuse me swing,* looping a little blooper right over the mound. I tried to back-peddle for it, Izzy and Jubilee called each other off and it fell between all three of us. Two on and nobody out.

In baseball you know that not every call will go your way. But three in a row, all on borderline pitches and every one called a ball? With runners on base, I didn't want the batter to square one up and put us down by two or more, so I'd been trying to work the corners, but me and ump didn't see eye to eye on where the corners were. The ump was an old friend of mine but the dirt I would never kick on him wouldn't have been as dirty as the look I gave him as I toed the rubber and tried to steady my nerves. Zachariah came out from behind the plate and Izzy walked over from short for a little *tête-a-tête.* Tête-a-tête is French for a meeting on the mound.

"Maybe you can pick off all three runners," said Izzy. "Start with the dude on third. If you nab him, they won't be expecting you to do it again. So you whirl and pick off the dude on second. They'll be so freaked out, the dude on first will probably just wander off and you can nail him easy. This way, you don't have to worry about throwing a wild pitch and letting in the first run of the game. Put *that* thought right out of your mind." I guess she was trying to be comforting. Zach tilted his catcher's mask back and offered me a more practical piece of advice. "If it's hit on the ground," he said. "Let's try to make the play at the plate." Then they both trotted back to their positions. We had no outs, the bases were juiced and big D'Artagnan was stepping in. I could have used another cyclone right about then. In the underground river, I had trusted the current, just as PW has taught me to. Now I needed to trust my stuff, as my Poppy has advised me since I was old enough to throw at the trunk of the banyan tree.

Zach is the best in the backstop biz at knocking down pitches in the dirt but even so, I decided to lay off my twelve-to-sixer. If I got a swing and miss but the ball skipped past him a run would come across and I felt certain in my heart that the final score of this game was going to be one to nothing. I wanted us to be one and not to be nothing. I got a first pitch strike with a heater on the outside corner at the knees. Then I threw a scroojie that D'Artagnan thought was in his wheelhouse until it dove in over the inside corner under his hands. He nicked it foul down onto his ankle and hopped around in pain for a minute. When he stepped back in, I knew he would be swinging at the next pitch. He's the JJ's captain and would not want to go down on strikes when he had a chance to be the hero. So I had to put it where he couldn't drive the ball into the gap or over the wall. We needed to keep it on the infield if we were to prevail. He had seen my eephus pitch once already and would have figured out how to time it. I didn't want to throw two scroojies in a row, he would be wise to that, too. It had to be numero uno, the *Wilder High hard one*, as Mister McKeever calls it. And it had to be low in the zone, where the chances were good he would hit it on the ground. I so wanted my next pitch to be my last, best pitch of the season.

I burned it in low on the outer half. D'Artagnan tried to take it the other way, into right. My infielders were playing in, hoping to cut off a run should the ball be hit to them. Zach is a formidable figure when it comes to blocking the plate. The ball, a soft liner, flew into Jubilee's glove, one. She stepped on second before the runner could get his foot back on the bag, two. Then she fired the ball home. After the out at the keystone sack, the force was off, so her throw had to be on the money and Zach had to apply the tag before the runner coming down from third could touch home. Jubilee from Tennessee threw it straight and true and Zach came up out of his crouch, took two steps toward third and stood there like the sheriff in a western movie. The runner put his hands up and surrendered as our catcher tagged him gently with a tap of the ball on his chest. Three. Later my Poppy told me it was the first triple play in the history of Polynesia.

Bottom of the Seventh: The JJ's had looked a little stunned after the way the top of the inning had ended. But with every pitch, it was a brand-new ballgame because there was still nothing but goose eggs on the board. Wouldn't you know, I was leading off. I decided to hit lefty for the extra step out of the batter's box it would give me going down the line. Baseball is sometimes called *a game of inches* and I was prepared to battle for each and every one. As it turned out, I didn't need that advantage because I hung in long enough to work a walk. A twelve pitch at-bat ended with me standing on first. I took a short lead, mindful of being picked off and wasting an opportunity. I'm not as fast as Ella Rose, but I can motor quicker than most of the boys on the Otters. Ella, when she gets on, dances back and forth to distract the pitcher. My own style is quieter. Let him forget I'm there. That's my philosophy of base running. But D'Artagnan seemed to think I was a threat. He kept throwing over to keep me close. The Otters took to razzing him unmercifully from the dugout. Finally he whipped in a fastball that nearly took Tobias' head off. Their catcher was able to knock it down and keep it in front of him but it went a few feet up the third base line. Here was my chance to get into scoring position. I took off like Holy Toledo! when I touch his ribs with my heels. Their catcher pounced on the ball and fired it to the second baseman covering and I pulled up short, finding myself caught in a rundown, aka, a pickle. I darted back toward first, the second baseman walking toward me with the ball and tossing it to the first baseman who was coming toward me from his position. The shortstop was backing up the second baseman, so there was nowhere for me to go. I was well and truly trapped. My only hope was that one of them would make a bad throw. I feinted back and forth, trying to trick them into making a foolish move, but they were closing in relentlessly. Out of the corner of my eye, I saw PW in the third base coaching box, doing a thing I had seen him do once before. When I saw it, I knew what he wanted *me* to do! Before I had time to change my mind, I dashed at the second baseman who took a toss from the first baseman and was making ready to tag me out. I leaped straight up into the air like a long-legged antelope called a *springbok* that PW had just been imitating. They have that name because they *spring* into the air when they want to see far over the plain where big cats might be coming for them. The only cats coming for me were infielders. Little Gwendolyn, the second baseman, looked quite surprised when I dove over her head and rolled just as I had at the foot of the banyan tree for my dad, landing a foot short of the base and reaching out to touch it before she could touch me with the ball. The way the springbok leaps into the air is called *pronking*. We could leave the

219

jumping to the Jehoshaphats. It took a River Otter to pronk those old JJs good and proper. PW took off his top hat and bowed to me, that's how he says *way to go*.

D'Artagnan, a bit out of sorts about way things were going on the bases, turned his attention back to the plate. Tobias didn't have to get a hit, but he wanted to move me over to third, even if it meant making an out. He made good by grounding one to the right side. If he had hit it to short or third, I would have been frozen at second, but shooting it to the other way allowed me to advance. With only one out, I was ninety feet from glory. Alakai came up, scowling with the desire to do some serious damage. With only one out, there were so many ways to score a run from third: a base hit, a sacrifice fly, an error, a passed ball or wild pitch. And I didn't have to break for the plate unless I was pretty sure I could make it. But Izzy was on deck, so this was our best chance to keep the game from going into extra innings. None of us wanted that. Crazy things happen in extras. Alakai must have been thinking the same thing. He wasn't about to get cheated. Three times did D'Artagnan unleash the pitch he calls his *thunderbolt*, and three times Alakai swung with all his might. But all three times he was under the thunder and forced to make the long walk back into the dugout.

My sidekick strolled to the plate, twirling her bat. Unruffled, undaunted and unafraid. She had no idea that she was the weakest hitter in the Windward League and that she was totally overmatched. She only knew that her teammates loved her and there's no better feeling than that. But I knew how let down she would be if she thought that she had let the Otters down. A feeling came over me, like I was myself and also a drawing PW had made of me in magic chalk. For a moment I felt I could do no wrong. I had been walked on twelve pitches, I had been caught in a rundown and pronked my way out of it. I had made it all the way to third base. What else could I do? I thought of something Bess had said to me a few days ago in Daffadowndilly. *Here on Quietude, I don't think it's possible to steal anything.* Then I thought, *maybe it's time to test that theory.* As a starting pitcher myself, I know we moundsmen get used to glancing over at runners on first but not so much at those on third. I took one step off the bag. D'Artagnan stared in at his catcher. I took another baby step down the line and stayed there. He blew the first pitch by Izzy who was just starting her swing when the ball whomped into the catcher's mitt. I took one more step. He was so confident of mowing down our dear shortstop that instead of pitching from the stretch, he went into his full wind-up. It was just like our game against the Goofballs when their runner had been struck in the stomach by a line drive off his teammate's bat and said *oof*. But with Izzy at the plate, I had no fear of oofing. Then I remembered the way Izzy had sped around the pretend bases as PW waved the not-a-flute at the watering trough and how she had slid on her belly to touch a pretend home plate. Even if I had little faith in her ability to hit the ball, she could still be my inspiration. So when D'Artagnan reached the top of his motion, I took off, pickin' 'em up and puttin' 'em down like never before. The pitch was up around the letters for strike two, Izzy swinging through, her swing sending her backwards and out of my way. The catcher caught it high in the zone while I was sliding head first and trailing the fingertips of my left hand across the inside corner of the plate. I had stolen it cleanly and not even after my river ride had being safe at home ever felt so good.

We were not nothing! We were one! We were one and the Jehoshaphats were none and all god's children got fun, as the Captain would say. Little kids ran onto the field, rushing to the River Otters and asking us to autograph stuff. I signed baseballs and pieces of paper and one little girl gave me a crayon and asked me to write my name on her arm. She said she would never wash it again. I remembered to congratulate D'Artagnan and he said "This isn't over," like a bad guy in a movie, but then he shook my hand and said, "Good game, Dude." I remembered to what's called *commiserate* with little Gwendolyn and tell her she has plenty of good years left.

"Slick move, Cap. But, ya know, I would have clobbered that big dude's next pitch halfway to Sumatra."

"I don't doubt it for a minute, Mizz Izz. But that can wait until Opening Day of next season. I got the idea to steal home from the way you did it at the watering trough. You showed me the way, Mizz Izz. I copied your slide."

"Happy to help, Cap. Now it's time to celebrate with crustaceans. My mom was so sure we would win she sent me with a bib so I wouldn't drip butter on my uniform when I'm eating lobster. But I don't know what I did with the bib. Maybe it's in your ball bag. Oh, there's something I should give you before I forget. The other day, when you and me and Walter laid that mean lady low with our on-the-money throws down in that cavern, I remembered something. I ran straight home and looked in my sock drawer and guess what I found?" She reached down into one of her bloused-at-the-knees River Otters sox, pulled out my pocket watch and handed it to me, grinning her goofy redhead's grin.

"How did my pocket watch get into your sock, Izz?" I said.

"Well, what I remembered was that afternoon when I was by the watering trough the first time, my stomach said it was time to go home for lunch. So I raced home and had some tomato soup and I didn't want to drop your pocket watch in my soup, so I went into my room and tucked it away in my sock drawer. And then I guess I forgot about it. As you know, the good ladies gave us two pairs each. I must have been wearing the other pair since then. But when my mom was doing the laundry this morning, I pulled on my sox, the first pair, and I felt something which I thought was a candy bar and I just kind of scooted it up the side to save for later. Then when we were pulling off the triple-play, I felt it again and figured out what it was and what it *wasn't* was a candy bar. Pretty good detective work, eh?"

We had captured the Crown of *Quietude* and I had my watch back. Not a bad day's work.

The Palaver

After the fact detective work is a lot easier than the part when you have to go out and agitate the gravel. You can do it in a saloon, for one thing, surrounded by beautiful barmaids eager to hear how it had all gone down.

Wilder was invited to the palaver even though it was held in the Doubloon and she was only nine. The king made her a fake ID. You could tell it was fake by the big letters on it that read FAKE ID and the royal seal, a rubber-stamped image of a girl climbing a palm tree. The girl was based on Wilder herself which practically made it a photo ID, as well as being the only ID in the country. No one here carried ID, any more than anyone carried car keys. We all knew who we were. Many of us didn't even bother with pockets, but if you're going to have pockets, best they be uncluttered. No ID, no car keys, no receipts. Maybe a small seashell you found that morning on the beach and meant to put upon a shelf in your hut. The captain of the River Otters sauntered in wearing one of my fedoras and her vest, swinging her pocket watch on its chain.

"Well, Boss, what do you intend to do with Miss Clementine?" said Creole. I think she was a trifle abashed at having fallen for the woman's act in the first place. It was a uniquely Quietudian dilemma. Since we have no code of law, written or otherwise, it follows that we have no capital punishment or any kind of prison. We could plonk her down in a rowboat and set her adrift, crew-of-the-Bounty-and-Captain-Bligh-style. But that would be tantamount to a death sentence. Her betrayal of her brother's wishes and principles was, in the final analysis, a family matter and no business of ours. But her subtraction of her brother's old brother-in-arms from existence with a pair of gardening shears was an insurmountable sticking point, as it were. What to do? Dante had confessed to the émigré that he had neither wife nor family, so at least we were spared the need to notify anyone. I felt that, as the sovereign, I should be the one to settle the matter, but I could see no way for justice to prevail. After an hour's worth of senseless discussion, having come to no satisfactory conclusion, one of those lights I knew so well ramped up in Jake's eyes. Immediately, he flung down an idea like an unbeatable hand. I saw a flaw or two in it, but I had to admit it had a lot of merit. We kicked it around for a few minutes, tweaking and turning it this way and that, finishing just in time for the arrival of our guest of honor.

Wilder had been so right when she said we'd all been acting in a movie under PW's direction as the adventure of the treasure had unfolded. The world had been his third base coaching box, and he waved us around hot corners we could not see until all had scored and none were left stranded. Our Bushman conductor was now settled into a chair sipping on a bottle of Mexican beer, only the second time I've seen him take a drink in all our years together. Wilder was standing on the bar, acting as his interpreter. After a few preliminary questions and answers, he too vaulted up onto the bar, entering into a colloquy with Wilder composed of him talking a little with his voice, but mostly with his hands and his whole body, including dance moves and pantomimes, lending their back-and-forth a sort of old west vaudeville air. After a passage of movements and sounds, he would pause, take a sip on the beer and wait while she offered a rough translation. PW proved a prince of the histrionic racket as he acted out the narrative. He turned into a one-man repertory company, throwing in the calls of birds and their swooping movements when he wanted us to have a panoramic view, included the whinnying of horses, the swerving of fish, the posture of a coyote, spot-on imitations of various people, including the king, who came off as a rather confused sort of person, a doofus. Oh, well. You could immediately make out the characters he was introducing when he became Dante, Clementine, Wilder and Izzy. In his rendering, Izzy was even more confused than the king, small comfort to his majesty. He did everything but break into a buck and wing to tell his story. He became a tree, a stream, a waterfall, a cave. The hardwood bar became his longboard as he surfed when surfing was called for. I could all but feel the wave beneath him as he walked the nose. Out of his loincloth, he drew the not-a-flute and gestured with it eloquently. Here is what his audience came away with.

224

He had followed the stranger and the pretty lady to see where they were going. He had the sense that they were on a hunt. But for what? His people are hunters, so it was a natural curiosity. He tailed them to Daffadowndilly and when they left the village, he continued to tail them at a discreet distance. He knew them for strangers because he didn't know them as neighbors and friends. He saw the man toss the not-a-flute into the watering trough and figured he was hiding it from the woman. Well, this was a fun game, he thought, and decided to complicate the game and trick the strangers by taking it out of the trough. He taught himself to open the device and removed its contents, then put it back in the trough, an even trickier trick. He thought that finding it empty would make the strangers laugh. After the man and the woman had chased each other around for a while, with PW staying close by, he found the woman's hat on the ground. Inside the hat, he found the six sections of what we had taken to calling the Maracaibo map. The game had become a kind of puzzle and he wanted to be the one to solve it. Afterwards, he learned that the hunt had been more complicated than he thought at the beginning. It turned out the woman had been hunting the man. Then he saw Wilder and Izzy pulling the not-a-flute out of the trough. Wilder is one of his closest friends, so he wanted her and her little redheaded friend to be a part of the puzzle-game. When Wilder put the not-a-flute into her ball bag, he knew she was now playing the game too. He created a puzzle within a puzzle by hiding the six parts of the first puzzle he had found in the woman's fallen hat in six places that only Wilder would know about. He hid the parts when he knew she would be busy playing in a ballgame. That was why the River Otters had had to make do without a third base coach that day.

When he attended the movie party at the palace and gave Wilder back the not-a-flute, he knew that she would had hand it to her father, the king, and that he would show it to Jake, who was very good at games. But PW also knew that even if they cracked it, it would be empty because he was the man who had emptied it. So far, he had not shown its contents to anyone, thinking it would give either Wilder and Izzy or her father and Jake an advantage that neither had earned. He wanted the game to be fair. He drew up a map of the six hiding places, put it in the not-a-flute and gave it to Wilder and Izzy who now knew how to open it.

If memory served, she had rushed over this part of the affair in her account of it to me, saying only that she had found the map in her toy chest. I couldn't bring myself to fault her for this omission, however. We all need a private life. She may have been trying to protect PW, and he may have wanted them to think his and not the Maracaibo map was the original contents of the thing. In any case, while the two of them were off following his map, he went and checked out the caves on the south side of the Grieving Widow, led there by the actual contents of the not-a-flute, Joshua's own map. In the course of his travels he saw the woman we came to know as Clementine who also seemed to be searching for something. It seemed to him that she had not only been hunting for the man, but for something the man had been hunting too. He knew that when Wilder put the six parts of the Maracaibo map together, she also would want to look in the area of the caves for the last piece of the puzzle. He began to worry about her. What could be in the caves that everyone was so exercised about? Once he knew that we had brought Clementine in out of the warm, he set out on his own exploration. Joshua's map, the one we call the key, was very specific. It sent PW into the caves and underground into the cavern where the treasure chest was cached. To his way of thinking, the big stash of gold doubloons would not be of any great value, but he was perfectly capable of recognizing how valuable it was to the strangers, since one had killed the other in order to lay hands on it. We knew he had been there because he nicked a souvenir which turned up later. He pantomimed the doubloon by flipping an imaginary coin into the air, catching with his right hand slapping it onto the back of the left, grinning hugely.

Somehow, through forms of persuasion none of us were able to ascertain—at this point in the tale telling, his gestures began to be fraught with ambiguity, in so far as ambiguity can be attributed to a gesture, or perhaps his interpreter began to play fast and loose with his telling, hard to say—he was able to alert Wilder and her sidekick to the significance of the small caves, backing it up by placing the proof of his own visit there into the rear pocket of my beach chair at Buck O'Neil Field. He knew she would show it to me, along with the Maracaibo map, bringing me into the game. Finally, he brought me all the way in by slapping the not-a-flute, now holding Joshua's map to the subterranean treasure chamber, into my hand as we were dashing away from the cyclone.

During his performance, I recalled the dream I'd had a few nights before, wherein I'd followed PW all over the island without his taking notice of me. I wondered now if the spots he'd stopped at were the very ones drawn on the map he'd made for Wilder. As he was stashing the separate sections, was I dreaming of him doing so? Had I developed an aboriginal capacity for inhabiting two dimensions at once? A silly idea, probably, but in my dealings with my Bushman friend, anything seemed possible. In his old life, you battled the elements but loved where you lived and still found ways to laugh. A successful hunt, a little water, a little shade, and in the cool of the evening, you shared stories with your friends. His new life was much the same.

Chapter Forty-Four

Bonny and I were lying on the big bed in our elevated room at the cottage, she still wet from her waterfall and looking perfectly relaxed.

"So tell me, Sugarcane, what was the plan that Jake proposed for dealing with Miss Clementine? We don't have any dungeons and you can't clap her in irons. What does he mean to do with—what is it McKeever calls her?—Fawn Woman?"

"It's a solution only Jake could have hit upon. Since we have opted out of the crime and punishment business but didn't want to let her go scot free, he offered to alter the angle of the article he was already writing, alter it into a film script which the two of them, he and Clementine, would co-author. He feels the movie—working title *Treasure Island???*—" I drew the three question marks in the air— "would benefit immensely from one of its actual participants playing the role of herself, thus reviving her flagging career and making up for losing out on the aforementioned treasure." Bonny looked puzzled, and somewhat put out.

"I fail to see how making the woman into the star of a major motion picture qualifies as retributive justice, or even a step toward rehabilitation." She leveled a hard look at me.

"Wait. Jake, as you know, is a very canny fellow. He thought it through, thought it through instantaneously when the idea first struck him. He believes that once the true-life backstory, including the No Strangers to Danger angle and Josh's vow to aid Ukraine, have been bruited about in the press, the film will be a guaranteed smash. The talkshows will go crazy over it before it has opened. Jake is so well connected in the industry that he is confident of finding deep pockets producers and pulling down huge take home pay for the two of them both as screenwriters and actors." I paused, teasingly.

"Same question," said Bonny, who may have begun to realize she was being set up.

"One of the things that will be trumpeted about prior to the movie's release will be the announcement that both Jake and Clementine will be donating every cent of their salaries to the Ukrainian effort to kick Vladimir Putin and his dogs out of their homeland."

"So she will miss out on both the treasure and any financial gain from the film? Is Dante a character in the movie?"

"No. The story will be Dante-less. So she will not be implicated in his murder, which would serve no purpose in any case, since charges could not be filed. Joshua's part will be a star turn played by Jake himself. But Dante will not appear. Not in the movie, anyway."

"What do you mean?"

"Just this. Even as the movie is in production, Jake will be crafting a memoir telling the whole story, murder (or manslaughter in some degree or other) included. But he will put it in a drawer."

"To hold over her head?"

"Exactly. He has exacted a promise from Clementine that, for the rest of her working life, half of every penny she makes from this day forward be donated to Ukraine, until they have declared victory over the invaders and to help them rebuild their country afterwards. Should the political situation there stabilize, she is to establish a scholarship out of her own pocket but in her brother's name, the funds going to deserving Ukrainian students in the US."

"Can he make it stick?"

"Jake knows lots of show-biz lawyers," I said. "Hell, he knows *agent's* lawyers." Bonny smiled her approval.

"Well, that's better," she allowed. "Even more money than Joshua and Dante hoped for will be headed where they intended. And we can honor their memories. When Wilder is a little older, we can tell her the whole story." She took a sip of the martini I had made for her, with a twist. "Will the émigré appear in the movie?"

"His character will. But the émigré will not be played by the émigré. Jake is thinking of casting Brian Cox. Mister Smirnoff will be busy elsewhere."

"A not entirely unhappy ending," declared my fiancée for life. "Let me bartend for you this once, your maj."

She brought me a Grey Goose martini, icy cold, straight up and with two pimento olives on a toothpick that looked strangely familiar, even as had Clementine to the émigré.

"Hey! That's the toothpick from my Swiss Army knife! I've been looking for that thing all over the place. Where did you find it?"

"In the little jar of toothpicks in your kitchen cupboard, where else?" What a detective.

Afterword, Part One

The vicar showed up! At last! The good ladies of Daffadowndilly were all in what I believe is called a *tizzy* when he wandered up the path to their village after so many years, the slowest nomad of them all. The reason it had taken him so long to respond to their invitation is that he had gotten out of the vicar biz and was embarrassed to tell them. The ladies said it didn't matter what he wasn't out in the great world, here in our world of *Quietude* they would think of him as the vicar of their village. He is the first and only man ever to live in Daffadowndilly. As a used-to-be vicar, he already knew a lot about brewing tea and he's getting pretty good at chopping wood and lending a hand in the garden. He and Bess are planning to marry. I'm too old to be a flower girl, so I suggested that PW and Okie Dokie's daughter, Kalahari, take the job and she is *so* excited.

And do you remember the creek I mentioned earlier, the one chosen for our first ever creek naming contest, the one I said was kind of *dawdly*? Well, I won that contest with the name Lazybones Creek. Aka, the Slowpoke, Izzy told me to say.

I put PW's yellow chalk drawing of the chest and its sparkly coins on the wall of my bunkhouse over my toy chest. So far, no one has noticed. He chose kindness in the telling of our story in the Doubloon, omitting any mention of my watch-chain so as not to rat me out to my dad. He did speak in gestures of the drawing but I kind of skipped over that part.

I would have been let down now that baseball season was over, but I was so excited about showing the Captain Tickety-Boo's submarine trick that I forgot to be sad. On our walk down to the beach, he said he had decided that his remuda was too crowded in their corral, and that his old cutthroats would never get around to building proper stables. They could drink grog, whatever that might be, while in the saddle, they could play pirate polo until the sun went down, and he thought they would make good horse *thieves*, but, he

231

said, no man wants to wield a hammer with a hangover. I think hangovers are headaches you get from playing too much pirate polo. He thanked me for looking after the horses, but said he was thinking of setting them free. He would keep his chestnut mare, Blow the Man Down, so we could ride into the hills and down the beach together sometimes but let the others go their own way. He asked if I would like to be there when he turned the remuda loose. It would only happen once in the history of our country, and afterwards, he said, they would find their way into the hills and learn where water could be found and eventually there would be foals and a whole new kind of horse, a *Quietude* kind, made from the mating of the different breeds, would come into being. He said that since his crew had broken their mounts, those horses might not be entirely wild, not at first anyway. Then he said something I will never forget. The foals, he said, would have no memory of their parents being broken, but bred into them would be the kindness I had shown their *progenitors* when I tamed them by talking to them and grooming them and feeding them fresh fruit every day. That was the difference, he said, between being broken and being tamed. So as they ran free, they would be something more than wild horses. They would be Wilder horses too.

Meanwhile, I know the way to the underground river. And I want to go again.

Afterword, Part Two

Ten Things You Never Hear Anyone Say on *Quietude:*

1. "I can't catch a break."
2. "The game is rigged. It's all politics."
3. "You're such a fucking asshole."
4. "You're such a crazy bitch."
5. "So I'm all like totally like whatever.
6. "I'll need to see your license and registration."
7. "You don't know Jack shit."
8. "Have a nice day."
9. "Your call is very important to us."
10. "What?"

Folks here say, "I beg your pardon?" rather than "What?" when they
fear they have not heard you correctly. Being here in the first place is
about the biggest break anyone can imagine. We somehow manage to
get along without politics and the word "like" is never misused. It
must be something in the air. Since every day is a nice day (and, in
fact, each deserves a far snazzier qualifier than "nice"), it's
unnecessary to instruct your fellows to have one. If we'd had a central
casting, I would have enlisted a character actor to play the part of a
gentleman named Jack Shit, so that I could introduce him to others
by saying, "Do you know Jack Shit, by any chance?" As for those
unfortunate epithets by which men and women so often refer to one
another in the great world, I suppose one might have blackened the
air of *Quietude* out of my hearing, but so far as I knew, civility
between the genders was the order of the day. And since we have
banned cell phones (which, in the absence of cell phone towers, was
unnecessary in any case), we are happily left with the calls of birds
being very important to us. Item six is, I assume, self-explanatory.
What you frequently *do* hear are the ruminations of poets, painters
both amateur and of international reputation, photographers, a

retired novelist or two, a few sculptors, a few professors emeritus, a Nobel Prize winning chemist, a theoretical physicist, a constellation's worth of astronomers, a lot of marine biologists, a great many musicians, seamstresses, wood workers, carpenters, surfboard shapers and wave riders, builders of houses and boats, engineers, old reprobates, young barmaids and, of course, a plenitude of hammock and/or barstool philosophers. I had recently overheard one of the latter say to his companion in the Doubloon, "Are god's small pleasures, do you think, larger or smaller than our own?" and made a mental note to put it on the questionnaire. In a curious turn of linguistic events, the word "squilching," or sometimes its variant, "squenching," came, in time, to be part of the patois of *Quietude* pidgin. Its original meaning fell away, as is so often the case, and the new meaning, spun many times off the original, ended up as something like: To drive one gladly delirious, as in "It was squilching me [or squenching me] half out of my coconut every time she crossed her legs." Don't you just love the way language evolves?

Our national obsession with contests continues: We were wrong to think we had baptized all our rivers. The underground railroad of water that Joshua had discovered gave us a new opportunity. In due course, a big beach party/river naming was eventually won by Peter Bralver's entry: The Laughing in Its Sleep River. When Mister Smirnoff asked me why *Quietude* didn't have a flag, I thought Why not? But what? Our standard should reflect our priorities (i.e., taking it easy and taking joy in the wonders of nature). So we decided to hold a contest to find the most perfectly faded pair of girls' cut-off jeans and running them up a pole. How did we arrive at the winner? you might well ask. How brief the cut-offs were, how faded, how nearly worn all the way through, how fringy their fringe, all of these elements were considered. But a counsel of elders held that no reasonable judgement could be reached unless a woman were actually *wearing* the entries. Thus, a parade of beach babes, each with her partisans hollering their approval, etc, and the winning entry raised aloft in praise of our young nation. Long may it (or they) wave.

"I guess you can't judge a woman by her tummy," said McKeever. He looked as though the fates had played a cruel trick on him.
    "A hard lesson to learn so late in life."

234

"Oh, well. She probably would have balked at the idea of moving into a cave anyway." I related Clementine's tale of her career in motion pictures.

"Does showing your tits count as community service?" he said. Definitely not a candidate for the questionnaire.

"Why do you ask?"

"I thought she could get time off for bad behavior." We were leaning against the mighty Wurlitzer in the cool of the evening. My faith in the box had been renewed when it occurred to me that Proxy Moon's song "Take Me Down to the Water" could be considered a lead to the underground waterway, and The Boswell Sister's "Down the River of Golden Dreams" a better map to that which we sought than any we had in hand. Why, the Wurlitzer had been practically shouting the solution into my ear, had I only the smarts to hear.

"There's a train leaving nightly called when all is said and done," A line from Warren Zevon's "Keep Me in Your Heart" had been recurring in my dreams for the past few nights. I selected the song now and wondered how you can say goodbye to yourself. You can say goodbye to anyone or anything else, silently or aloud. You can try, anyway. You can try to say goodbye to your nearest and dearest, to places you love, to all flowing water, to the night sky and its many appointments as you make ready to join the earth. But I wanted *me* to know it would be OK were I to go away. I felt I should begin putting my affairs in order, as they say, but I had no clear idea of what my affairs were. I could divide up my worldly estate quite evenly by leaving my Rawlings glove to Wilder (who had already commandeered it any case) and my Swiss Army knife to her mother. We don't have a proper cemetery. Not enough folks have passed away during our dozen years as a nation to make it necessary. We do have graves here and there, mostly in spots chosen by the departed beforehand. And we have honored the requests of three of our countrymen who asked to be buried at sea. Maybe I could follow in my daughter's footsteps and be carried away by the underground river, coming to rest in our lagoon. What a sendoff that would be. I'd be a more regal figure in death than I'd ever been in life. Oh, what the hell, I thought. If the train leaves nightly, I could always wait around for the next one. Or even the one after that. The longer I thought about it, the truer it seemed that Mister Zevon's line, by providing such an open-ended timetable, was the One I Could Press for More Options, the very thing that Wilder had wanted for herself. My Little Coconut and her merry band had gone to a lot of trouble to save the life of the king, after all. I should give her a medal, or at least give her back the doubloon she had handed to me. Come to think of it, I had a book of Casey Stengel quotes I had never shown her somewhere around the palace. Hell, I hadn't even told her about Vin Scully. That was reason enough to keep cranking over for a while.

In due course, the boatman had been signaled—he had been patiently bobbing about in a little lay-by out of the rough surf, awaiting his payday. I let Wilder fire off the flare-gun. Being a loyal friend, she gave the second shot to her sidekick.

Mister Smirnoff wasn't a *Quietude* kind of guy. He was a bit of a hustler, lived by his wits. There was nothing wrong in that. But to be a hustler means you need to keep finding new hustles. And on *Quietude* there are none to be found. If he was looking for an angle, he would find only curves. If, however, he were tending bar at BBNGs, he would be surrounded not only by gorgeous island girls but gents with plenty of recreational cash more or less begging to be separated from some of it. I'd been considering making him a job offer. But I felt he would be more comfortable if it came with a quid pro quo. Favor for favor, as they say out in the great world from whence he had come.

"Mister Smirnoff, it's been a pleasure having you among us. Perhaps you will return one day." I had said to the émigré.

"Majesty, your country is closest I have found to words from prayer, 'on earth as it is in heaven.' I would like to show my appreciation. "

"I'm happy to hear it. In the days ahead, you will have a chance to perform a service to the crown—" I felt foolish saying it but I've learned it's expected of a king to sound like one every now and then, "and to the people of *Quietude.*"

"If it will help to unseat the ridiculous one, I will do anything you ask of me," he said. "I would like one day to return to my homeland, but not while this puffed up popinjay is head of state. If you mix together a bit of Stalin, a bit of Rasputin and a portion of Catherine the Great's horse, you end up with the pretender Putin. I love my

236

country and I love my countrymen, but I think this weakness for strongmen is gigantic flaw in national character."

"Well," said Jake, "It will be hard for him to put a good face on withdrawing his troops from Ukraine. If it should come to that, he will be ripe for a fall. Hell, he might die of embarrassment. He won't rate a tomb. He'll barely rate a roadside restroom named after him. The Vladimir Putin Memorial Lavatory."

I had gone off the apples-for-chickens trade with Kauai. I couldn't think of a way to ship and keep the apples fresh enough for it to work. We needed to go with a commodity that wasn't perishable. The answer was obvious: *Quietude* Shine, our celebrated home-grown white lightning. It was really more of an *off-white* lightning: smooth, tantalizing on the palette, it went down easy and didn't rile up the blood. Kind of a single malt rum. And made nowhere else on earth. Currently, we maintained only one distributorship, formerly run by Captain Primo out of BBNGs in Venice, California. But if our people on the mainland sent us a goodly number of the custom bottles he had designed, we could fill them here and ship the stuff directly to Kauai, timing its arrival to coincide with the Hawaiian's opportunity to toast getting rid of the damned chickens. I would need to get the old boys with their stills in the hills to cooking double overtime.

I put it to Mister Smirnoff that he represent *Quietude* in the transporting of the treasure to Ukraine, after separating out two modest pieces of the action, one for the boatman and another for himself. Thereafter, I suggested, he could do well to take over as barman at BBNGs. I felt confident that the dancers at the club would find him every bit as lovable as the barmaids at the Doubloon. And Jake could keep his promise to represent *Quietude* on Kauai, with my secretary by his side.

After two days on jerky and water, Clementine had emerged, if not a changed woman, certainly a chastened one. The Captain had relented and taken her a bucket to eliminate in and a small lantern, fearing that absolute darkness might drive her mad. Jake had no trouble convincing her to fall in with his plan. If the movie did well (and, really, how could a movie with three question marks in the title not prove to be boffo at the box?), she could parlay it into the second act of her career. After her emergence, she began to express remorse for bringing about Dante's end. It may have been genuine or maybe she was only getting into character for playing herself? Who could say?

After due consideration, Jake was convinced that the removal of Dante from the screenplay, though necessary in order to hold a Damoclean sword over Clementine's head, left the prospective movie wanting for suspense and dramatic tension, a problem he solved rather neatly by putting his head together with that of the émigré to slide an expanded (and altogether fictionalized, but, as we know, the phrase Based on a True Story over opening credits is a sort of cinematic spandex, stretchy as all get out) version of the story of the gorgeous unclothed escort, the iPhone and President of Russia into the script. Doing so would doom any effort to release the film in Mister Smirnoff's homeland, but the good gentleman himself claimed to know a guy who could get a copy into the Kremlin, a splendid joke.

Bonny has finally retired, but remains adamant—playfully so, but unbending still, in the matter of our never marrying. I don't know why she refuses to make an honest monarch out of me, maybe she just likes the phrase fiancée-for-life, or doesn't like the word wife. But no woman of woman born has ever been a better mother or a truer heart's companion. I know that I have done one thing right in this life: Chosen to start a country on an island with hot waterfalls. Every glimpse of her at her ease restores my equanimity. And, of course, I will never tire of watching our daughter, the princess and starting pitcher and my personal day after yesterday. For me, she will always be the answer to that old question which is its own questionnaire: What happens next?

Acknowledgements

My thanks and gratitude to Charles Collum for his ingenuity in not-a-flute design, to Laurelai Barton Nguyen for her unflagging enthusiasm and pertinent insights, and to Paula Suárez and Joey Glaser, without whose help this book, like its predecessors, would never have found its way between covers. I owe either a thoroughbred or a Ford Bronco to my daughter, Wilder Kathleen the Rage of Paris Larrain, who guided me toward the breeds of horses that make up Captain Primo's remuda. My thanks as well to Bonny Jean Russell Larrain, who encouraged me to continue when the book lay in ruins and I was tempted to quit on it. My illustrator/cover artist, Katherine Willmore, is a national treasure whose birthday should be declared an international holiday. There will always be a spot for her under a palm tree on *Quietude*.

No disrespect was intended toward Carl Perkins, who (along with Howard "Curley" Griffin) wrote "Boppin' the blues" and released it as a single on Sun Records in May of 1956. His version is the cats, but I'm even crazier about Rickey's (released in 1957) with his good friend James Burton, unmistakably, on guitar.

Praise for Michael Larrain's Previous Works

The Life of a Private Eye

Michael Larrain's noir murder mysteries (which he calls "noirvelettes"), which are set in southern California, have all the elements of a classic detective story plus some contemporary twists and turns as well. The Life of a Private Eye is brilliant. I like the mix of dream and reality, and sometimes I don't know which is which. I don't think it matters. It's very wise, very witty, very sexy and a must read. Praise be to Larrain for creating a cast of colorful and seductive characters, beginning with Jade Bellinger, that could compete any day with the cops and criminals of L.A. Confidential. Fans of old Hollywood films and aficionados of the fiction of Raymond Chandler will surely enjoy Larrain's romp in and out of swimming pools, bars, underground tunnels, tree houses, and a spectacular nursing home for aging, once glamourous stars and starlets. Larrain's private eye and narrator is as clever as Philip Marlowe and as admirable as Sam Spade. The noir mystery lives on!

Jonah Raskin, author of *Beat Blues*, San Francisco, 1955, a novel.

"I don't know how to speak about what I'm feeling when I read these poems, because the mystery created by Michael Larrain cannot be spoken of but by him. Reading Larrain's collection of detective poems, a genre he alone invented, you feel as if poetry itself is trying to take a selfie with you. And that's the greatest honor you'll have in this life. Or as if Good, as defined and extolled by Apollinaire—who also invented the word surrealism—transmuted to poetry on the spot and Larrain was there to take it down, a Raymond Chandler in Bardo. Yes, Readers, let yourselves into these detective poems and detect yourselves, as a weft of invisible evening gowns made of an Unknown substance, whether this substance is poetry, the one you would always secretly kill for, or just plain murder. The gates are open, the gatekeepers are gone, but not for long, so take your chances now."

Julian Semilian, author of *A Spy in Amnesia.*

Movies on the Sails

"First of all, don't be put off by my saying that *Movies on the Sails* is a revolutionary novel. It is not dreary, polemical, or resentful. It is not a "downer," a "bummer," or a "drag". It is, in fact, the least angry revolutionary novel ever written, and marvelous fun to read. It is not only a splendid catalog of many of the things in this world to love, it is also a treatise on how to love them. Others have commented upon the book's wit, dash, verve, and humor—all in abundance, it's true— but I prefer to celebrate its intelligence and idealism, ever present on these pages, quiet, cool, and intoxicating, like a banana daiquiri on the lips of a saint. If I recall, Jack Kerouac's introduction to Corso's 'Gasoline' said "open this book as you would a box of crazy toys...". Similarly, I would say open *Movies on the Sails* as you would a box of perfume sent to you by your Quebecois niece. So: hey walk right in, sit right down, daddy let your mind roll on."

Steve Wasserman, author of *Wild Goose Pagoda*

"This book is an enormous heart that changes form in mid-air —at one moment, a detective novel in the deepest groove of the genre; at the next, a Jules Verne adventure that suddenly surfaces, whale-style, just where least expected; and then the next, a baseball team serenading a jazz orchestra on tour through a tropics that just won't quit. It runs the gamut of the emotions, and always wins."

Cole Swensen, author of *Art in Time*

"One of the most natural imaginations writing, Larrain puts together brilliant language forms with a sexually charged picaresque theatre of light-hearted mind."

Jack Hirschman, author of *Endless Threshold*

An absolutely delightful romp into a better world. Five Stars.
"Let us journey off to the beautiful south seas island of Quietude.
(How I wish that it really existed). Peopled by citizens from around
the world who long for a simpler place and time; so they move to
such a place, and they create it themselves. A "revolving monarchy"
with "kings for a year." Currency is replaced by an informal barter
system. A 1948 Land Rover is the only vehicle, so you walk
everywhere. But there's also a murder mystery afoot; one that ends
differently than anything you've ever read. Above all, this Larrain
fellow can flat out write. He has a true gift - both for the language
and for story telling. While part of a series, *Fair Winds & a Happy
Landfall* stands on its own. It may be the best novel by Larrain yet.
Only a very few novels have ever made me sad that they came to an
end. This is one."

Amazon Reader Review, May 3, 2021.

**An Enthralling Adventure, Imaginatively and Poetically Told.
Five Stars.** "We were captivated within the first few paragraphs, not
only due to the explosive revelation therein, but also because of the
author's profoundly gratifying word craft/writing style. ("We"
because two of us read it aloud to each other.) The story flows at a
thoroughly engaging pace, through unpredictable twists and turns,
vivid descriptions of place, and a motley cast of well-developed,
unforgettable characters. author's self-revelations and introspective
musings create an intimacy often reserved for one's closest
companions, and made us feel like his most trusted confidants. We
loved the deepening philosophical introspection and poetry woven
seamlessly into the rapidly developing narrative. This is a grand
adventure, beautifully told - and offers a superb escape while
sheltering in place."

Amazon Reader Review, Sept 14, 2020.

"If you're going on a cruise or expect to be marooned on a tropical island, take Michael Larrain's *Fair Winds and Happy Landfall* along with the suntan lotion and goggles. The novel kept me entertained for a couple of weeks; I read a bit each morning along with coffee and a scone and had the feeling that I was on an island paradise with a cast of characters who seemed as real as my neighbors in Ocean Beach, San Francisco. Larrain is a great storyteller and his voice is enticing. The language is as playful as a pod of dolphins and as erotic as a school of mermaids. If this book doesn't make you happy and feel fair minded you better sign into a hospital and ask the nurse for the strongest pills she's got. Or better yet go back to page one and read Larrain all over again."

Jonah Raskin, author of *Beat Blues*, San Francisco, 1955, a novel.

Books by Michael Larrain

Poetry: *The Promises Kept in Sleep, Just One Drink for the Diamond Cutter, For One Moment There Was No Queen, How It All Came True, Falling Back to Sleep.*

Novels: *South of the North Star, Movies on the Sails, As the Case May Be, Fair Winds & a Happy Landfall, See You Someday Else, Like a Song Without a Sax Break.*

Children's Storybooks: *The Girl With the Loom in Her Room, Heaven & Earth, Homer the Hobo & Ulysses the Goat, Wilder & Wilder Still.*

Noirvelettes: *The Life a Private Eye*, Volumes I and II.

Memoir: *And for Each Other*, Volumes I and II.

Audio CD: *Lipstick: A Catalogue for Continuous Undressing.*

Made in the USA
Columbia, SC
24 February 2024

31964743R00133